Words Uns

This is a fantastic read. The storyline is gripping, well-told and perfectly paced. The main characters, unsurprisingly, are lovely as ever. Anna and Lily have always had this charming appeal, and *Words Unsaid* really spotlights it. They drive this story and its difficult subject matter home in ways that lesser characters would fail. This is a top-notch story and I highly recommend it. If you haven't read the other four books in the series, I'd suggest that you do. They are all too good to miss.

-*The Lesbian Book Blog*

The Lucky Ones

This is a story about love, and not just romantic love. It is about the love of family, friends, and yes, even a love of a community. This is also a tale of hope. For me, this is a feel good story, one that made me feel happy at the end. It is well-written, with a vibrant setting, well-developed characters, both main and secondary, and a story that left me with that feeling of hope.

-B. Harmon, *NetGalley*

A Proper Cuppa Tea

A Proper Cuppa Tea is a smart and sexy romance featuring two professional women. While their relationship first stutters from the distractions of their lives, when they decide to pursue it, the romance develops in a realistic, charming, erotic, and organic manner. These characters are well rounded and fully depicted. They have careers and responsibilities as well as relationships with other people. The blended plotlines and complications are integral to the potential for Lark and Channing's future together.

MacGregor's newest romance is a marvelous, entertaining, captivating book as complex and full-bodied as that perfect cup of tea. Put the kettle on to boil, find a cozy chair, and settle in to enjoy *A Proper Cuppa Tea*.

-Lambda Literary Review

The author did a remarkable job of bringing all of the characters to life for me. I was able to form a vivid image of each delightful character in my mind and I felt as though I could hear the witty banter between Channing and Lark. There wasn't a lag in the storyline or any unnecessary drama and I am very pleased to admit that the author made me fall in love with the charming English landscape. This story entertained me from the first word and I can't tell you how many times I had to suppress my laughter while I kept sneaking a read when I was at work. I adore British humor and I tend to fall in love (quite deeply, I must say) with quirky and sarcastic British characters who have a wicked sense of humor. If you love books with picturesque landscapes, feisty women, meddling and well-meaning friends coupled with countless cups of delicious tea, then this story is definitely for you!

-The Lesbian Review

Moment of Weakness

Moment of Weakness… is a romance that doesn't follow the usual track of a les-fic romance. The author's use of time in this story keeps the pages turning as the reader learns bit by bit how Zann and Marleigh met, what happened to Zann in Afghanistan, and who they are. I loved the story and the way I learned about Zann and Marleigh's relationship–not in a straight timeline, but moving backward and forward in time. KG MacGregor's characters are well developed and have flaws. I love that. I loved the romance. I highly recommend this book to KG MacGregor fans.

-The Lesbian Review

MacGregor has written a story that lulls the reader into thinking it will continue along a certain trajectory, then—wham!—we're thrust in another direction with a startling revelation we never saw coming. Every scene skillfully moves this tale along, adding to the tension. From desperation to longing, anger to disappointment, unconditional love to fear, all those moods and emotions and more are well portrayed. The superb writing, characters, and well-timed plot twists are skillfully done to make for an entertaining and revelatory story. *Moment of Weakness* explores the often unexamined tragic aspects of war, the power of true love, and gives the reader a thrill ride that lingers long after the last page has been turned.

-Lambda Literary Review

The Touch of a Woman

What makes this an interesting read beyond the standard plotline are unusual back-histories. The characters are well drawn, complex women, who will resonate with many. And their tender attraction is a reminder that real life isn't always about the grand passion, but a gentle falling.

-Lesbian Reading Room

Anyone But You

More than a sizzling romance, a well researched and well written eco-thriller... I loved the way the story was written: fast-paced, with great punch lines, a tidy, well thought-out and thought-provoking plot, at times witty, at times dramatic. Dating the archenemy added zest to the romance and both heroines were very believable and easy to like.

-Curve Magazine

KG MACGREGOR

Other Bella Books by KG MacGregor

Anyone But You
Etched in Shadows
The House on Sandstone
Just This Once
Life After Love
The Lucky Ones
Malicious Pursuit
Moment of Weakness
Mulligan
Out of Love
Photographs of Claudia
Playing with Fuego
A Proper Cuppa Tea
Rhapsody
Sea Legs
Secrets So Deep
Sumter Point
T-Minus Two
The Touch of a Woman
Trial by Fury
Undercover Tales
West of Nowhere
Worth Every Step

Shaken Series
Without Warning
Aftershock
Small Packages
Mother Load
Words Unsaid

Bringing ME Dreams

KG MACGREGOR

BELLA BOOKS
2022

Bella Books, Inc.
P.O. Box 10543
Tallahassee, FL 32302

Printed in the United States of America on acid-free paper.

First Edition - 2022

Editor: Katherine V. Forrest
Cover Designer: Kayla Mancuso

ISBN: 978-1-64247-406-0

PUBLISHER'S NOTE

Author's Note and Dedication

When I was twelve years old and ready to start junior high, my father was stationed to three years of Marine Corps recruiting duty near Pittsburgh. Until then, I'd lived my whole life in the South—North Carolina and Kentucky—and I had the Southern drawl to prove it. I'm not sure there's any age when it's easier to integrate accents and traditions, but I found junior high especially stressful. The first time I said *y'all*, my classmates howled with laughter and mocked me without mercy. I never said it again. You see, across most of western Pennsylvania, second-person plural is *yinz*, short for "you ones" or "you'uns." The Southerner in me thought that sounded ridiculous, and I cringed inside every time I had to use it. Also every time I said *crick* instead of creek, or *gum bands* instead of rubber bands. However, I rather liked their name for obnoxious jerks: *jagoffs*.

This book is set in Pittsburgh, so in the interest of authenticity, I've written my characters as *yinzers*. If they move away, they'll have to drop that dialect or face humiliation—just as I did when I moved back to North Carolina.

Lastly, I have the special honor of dedicating this book to a remarkable woman, **JJ Crabb**. Her kindness and generosity are an inspiration, and I'm grateful that she supports not only my work but also the causes I hold dear. Thank you, JJ—*again*.

Content Note

This book deals with subject matter some readers might find disturbing. Both main characters have lost loved ones to suicide, one of which is graphically depicted in a well-marked flashback located in the second scene of Chapter Two. Skipping that scene should not impact the understanding of this book, as the story centers on the characters' paths to healing.

If you or someone you know has suicidal thoughts, help is available right away. **Call the National Suicide Prevention Hotline at 800-273-8255.**

For the moon never beams, without bringing me dreams
Of the beautiful Annabel Lee
And the stars never rise, but I feel the bright eyes
Of the beautiful Annabel Lee

-From "Annabel Lee"
Edgar Allan Poe, 1849

CHAPTER ONE

Within minutes of posting the tranquil image to the online forum, Keenan McEvoy had garnered a dozen "hearts" and several cheerful replies. She'd taken the photo only hours ago at Oakberry Court, a nursing home she visited once a month with her dog, Bennie, who was racking up points toward advanced certification as a therapy pet. In the photo, he was resting in the arms of an elderly resident whose face was cropped to preserve his privacy. She hoped the photo would comfort people on the forum.

"Didn't I tell you this would happen? Everyone says you're adorable."

The languid cockapoo—a cross between a cocker spaniel and a toy poodle—lifted his head from her lap and wiggled his docked tail, an instinctive show of affection whenever he heard her voice. Anyone's voice, actually.

A few nights a week, Keenan logged on to the forum just before bedtime to check in with her "friends" and offer words of consolation and encouragement. She had no special training in grief counseling, but she knew as well as anyone their unique despair. Theirs was a club no one wanted to join—survivors of a loved one's suicide.

She'd joined the online bereavement group almost two years ago after struggling to move on from Annabel's senseless death. The group, sponsored by a county mental health initiative, had always met in person at a community center in downtown Pittsburgh until Covid forced it to go virtual, which Keenan preferred. She liked the anonymity and was glad they'd chosen to keep it going even after in-person meetings returned.

Over time her participation had changed from needing comfort and support to helping provide it. Bennie was her main conduit for that, and her buffer too, always keeping her one degree removed from the suffering of others. Watching him work his magic with the elderly and people in distress helped lessen her guilt over not being able to help Annabel.

As the hearts continued to pile up for Bennie's photo, a chime announced the opening of a private chat window, a forum feature she rarely used.

HALF-A-SET: *Bennie is precious!!!! Nice to see such a cute face after a really tough day.*

She didn't recognize the screen name, but then not all forum members were active posters.

HALF-A-SET: *This is going to sound weird but I noticed the stamp on the blanket in the photo — Oakberry Court. Is that the nursing home in Bloomberg?*

The startling reference made Keenan mildly uneasy. Until that moment, she'd taken for granted her relative anonymity on the forum, where she posted as Wingèd Seraph, a reference to Edgar Allan Poe's heartsick poem, "Annabel Lee," which she'd recited often as a declaration of love for Annabel. It was unsettling that someone following her posts knew exactly where she'd been that afternoon. Suddenly all the care she'd taken for privacy was wiped out by a stupid laundry mark on a blanket. Before she could resolve her paranoia, a third note appeared.

HALF-A-SET: *Just curious is all. :-) My great-gran lived at OC for a while but she passed on about four years ago.*

Fine if the others in the group wanted to share their despair in person, but Keenan had no interest in moving beyond the virtual community. She didn't need a complement of anguished friends in her real life. Half-A-Set could be anyone at all—obnoxious, unstable, needy. Or some guy laying the groundwork to hit on her. Just because they'd suffered a similar loss didn't mean they ought to be actual friends.

HALF-A-SET: *Sorry, didn't mean to butt in. Just wanted to say thanks.*

Whoever this was seemed to be reading her wary thoughts, and now was backtracking over the intrusion. She could ignore it. Or she could lie and say it was a different Oakberry Court. Either way she'd feel guilty for brushing off someone who'd paid her an innocent compliment…someone who'd faced a tragic loss and joined the forum looking for support. There was nothing unseemly about the actual note, she conceded. What harm was there in a polite reply?

WINGÈD SERAPH: *That's the one. I've taken Bennie there a few times to visit the residents. They love him.*

Surely she could say that much. It wasn't particularly revealing, since she'd already described to the forum how Bennie had eased her back into the world of the living.

HALF-A-SET: *That's got to be the sweetest dog I've ever seen. So laid back. He's on Xanax, right? LOL*

WINGÈD SERAPH: *Not a skittish bone in his body.*

Indeed, nothing rattled Bennie. While some small breeds were high-strung, loyal to only one human, he was eleven pounds of lively affection with everyone he met. His scruffy coat was mostly apricot with white markings on his face, chest and feet. His ears were more poodle than spaniel—not as long or floppy—while his wide, webbed feet proved his water dog ancestry.

HALF-A-SET: *Gorgeous little face.*

WINGÈD SERAPH: *He knows he's cute. Here's it from everyone.*

She immediately shuddered at her grammar mistake. Half-A-Set would think her an idiot.

WINGÈD SERAPH: **Hears**

HALF-A-SET: *No worries. I sometimes do that two. LOL*

The small infusions of humor were admittedly disarming, and Keenan relaxed a bit over her decision to reply. With a click, she collapsed their chat window into a corner of her screen and ticked through the forum tabs to check Half-A-Set's profile, which held only the basic information required of all members: female, thirty-four years old, lost her brother to suicide. That didn't mean any of it was true. She'd joined the forum three months ago, but her first public post had come only this morning, shortly after five a.m.

Hi to everyone. Sorry I've been lurking so long without posting anything. I can't tell you how much your stories have meant to me these last few weeks. I lost my twin brother to suicide almost a year ago. A boxed set, they called us. After 33 birthdays together, today's my first one without him. I'm not sure I'll ever feel whole again, but you give me hope this will eventually get easier. Thanks for putting yourselves out there to support each other. I'm living proof it really helps.

Keenan tipped her head back to swallow the lump in her throat, which mercifully didn't happen as often as it used to. Her work with Bennie routinely brought her into heartbreaking situations that required a firm grip on her emotions—end of life, sick or traumatized children. Now sitting alone late at night, she had no reason to maintain the brave facade.

Half-A-Set was a twin, which explained her tragic screen name. In her poignant post, she came off as emotionally mature and intellectually capable of expressing herself. Those traits, plus the fact that she'd just turned thirty-four—only three years older than Keenan—further eased her qualms about replying to a private chat.

WINGÈD SERAPH: *I saw your post from this morning. I'm glad Bennie gave you something to smile about today. He's good at that.*

HALF-A-SET: *I knew it was going to be a tough day. Gabe and I always had a huge party with family and friends but I didn't want to put them through it this year. Now everybody's going to feel like crap when they remember. Can't win either way.*

Keenan knew the downside of putting up a strong front so people wouldn't worry—they assumed she was fine even when she wasn't. Outwardly, she pretended not to mark special dates such as Annabel's birthday, which was next weekend. The last thing she wanted to do was draw them deeper into her grief.

WINGÈD SERAPH: *People don't realize how much we worry over their feelings instead of our own. You're right — in some situations there's no way to win.*

HALF-A-SET: *Exactly. I've been dreading this day for weeks.*

WINGÈD SERAPH: *FWIW, it got easier for me after the first year. Not easy, just easier. Seems like there's something extra painful about the first Christmas without somebody, the first birthday, etc. After a while though it helps to look back on it and realize you made it through a whole year.*

HALF-A-SET: *Makes sense. How long has it been for you?*

Two years, three months...eleven days. Keenan wasn't obsessive about that figure but she'd calculated it yesterday when Annabel got a solicitation in the mail for a credit card. Even dying wasn't enough to get removed from a marketing list.

WINGÈD SERAPH: *A little over two years. It was my partner Annabel.*

When a couple of minutes ticked by with no reply, Keenan began to bristle at the implication. Had the mention of having a female partner given Half-A-Set pause?

"What do you make of that, Bennie? The least she could have done before inviting me to a private chat was read my profile. Maybe I should have spelled out *dyke* with a neon font."

He licked her hand before rolling onto his back and twisting into a shape that shouldn't have been possible. Boneless Bennie.

WINGÈD SERAPH: *You still there?*

HALF-A-SET: *Sorry, that kind of blew me away.*

"Yeah, no shit." Secure and confident in who she was, she'd long ago stopped trying to accommodate people's bigotry just to get along. That didn't make it any less annoying.

HALF-A-SET: *It's hard to wrap my head around how far I have to go. First year, second year. Even a week feels like forever when all I hear is how I've got to move on. When you lose a twin, it's like a piece of you has been ripped out. Everything you've learned how to do, you have to learn it again on your own. Talk, walk, breathe. Even when*

Gabe wasn't physically beside me, he was always there. Like I could literally feel him. Probably sounds weird to most people. I'm sure losing your partner is just as hard…probably feels like your other half too.

Keenan released a shameful sigh. "Bennie, your mom can be a real shithead sometimes. You know that?"

Not only had she wallowed in her petty sense of slight, she'd been flippant over the special grief Half-A-Set was dealing with today. Losing a twin would ruin birthdays forever.

WINGÈD SERAPH: *Nobody gets to tell you how much pain you're allowed to feel or when it's time to move on. Everybody's different. All I know is I couldn't have made it this far without Bennie. He was the best thing that happened to me after Annabel died. Not saying pets can replace people, but he keeps me focused on the good stuff. We all have to figure out what works for us.*

Obviously Half-A-Set still faced an uphill climb, especially for the rest of her first year. There were no shortcuts when it came to processing grief.

WINGÈD SERAPH: *I'll be really honest with you, okay? When I first joined the forum I felt like I was trapped in hell. Some people wailed every day because they hurt so much. Others would chime in, saying things to comfort them. I read every single post. Stories like yours broke my heart, but they made me realize that how I felt was perfectly normal. Then after a few months I noticed something really cool — most people have a turning point. You see it when they jump in to support the new members who are trying to cope. Maybe it's because they've started to heal — or maybe like me they realize it just feels better when you help. These days I check in to post something about Bennie to make people smile — people who had a tough day like you did. I feel like I'm paying back all the help I got when I needed it most.*

HALF-A-SET: *So you think in another year or so I might be the one helping somebody else get through this?*

WINGÈD SERAPH: *I hope so. The pain never goes away but someday you can get to a place where you feel like, okay it doesn't hurt as bad as it used to, I survived. Now maybe I can help somebody else.*

Admittedly, she was painting a rosier picture than reality suggested, but she had a strong hunch Half-A-Set would find a way to heal. Given her muted presence on the forum so far, she wasn't there for the drama. She was there to learn how to live with her loss—and she would.

HALF-A-SET: *Thanks for the vote of confidence. I really appreciate you taking the time to chat, especially tonight. I wasn't sure if people on the forum even used this chat thing but I figured it was there, I'd give it a try. Your words give me something to think about. My friends all say it'll get easier but it means more coming from somebody who's actually gone through it.*

WINGÈD SERAPH: *Glad we could help. I'll add your name to Bennie's fan club.*

HALF-A-SET: *LOL. It's Gianna, btw. If you're ever downtown, maybe we could grab a coffee or something.*

Now that she was over her initial reluctance to engage, Keenan wasn't as spooked by the idea of meeting in person. Besides, she'd been back in Pittsburgh for almost three years and her old friends weren't exactly beating a path to her door. She'd been gone too long for that.

WINGÈD SERAPH: *I'm Keenan. Huge coffee fan.*

Gianna answered with the number to her cell phone, which Keenan pasted into her contacts before sending her own.

HALF-A-SET: *Great, text me sometime. I live downtown and I'm usually free most days after six. And weekends.*

WINGÈD SERAPH: *OK. Meanwhile Bennie sends his love, says to tell you happy birthday. Seriously, he said that word for word.*

HALF-A-SET: *:-)*

Gianna. Pretty name, maybe Italian since her brother's name was Gabe. Obviously outgoing.

She signed off the forum and nudged Bennie from her lap. "Way to go, Romeo. You just picked up another girlfriend. How many is that, a hundred and six?"

* * *

Gianna Del Vecchio closed her laptop and choked back a wave of tears, her umpteenth of the day. In another hour and thirty-five minutes, her first birthday without Gabe would be over. It was helpful to hear Keenan say how important it was to get the "firsts" behind her. Only one more to face—the anniversary of his death just five weeks away.

Left to her own devices, she'd have languished at home all evening in misery, looking through photos and videos of Gabe when they were kids. Instead, best friend Jazmine Sadowski had whisked her off after work to happy hour with a handful of their lesbian friends.

Briefly, she'd even considered Jaz's offer—"*I promise, just as a friend*"—to sleep over so she wouldn't have to be alone. But there was always a risk Jaz would push for more, and Gianna was determined not to open that door ever again. No more sleepovers with Jaz, even if it meant being alone in her heartache.

Her brother's death had left her with more than grief. Suicide added a sickening layer of guilt, the unshakable feeling that she could have stopped it if only she'd paid more attention to Gabe's emotional state. If anyone should have known he was a danger to himself, it was his twin. Her relentless sorrow had led her online to the forum in search of comfort and forgiveness. Perhaps she'd found that path from the woman who called herself Wingèd Seraph...Keenan.

Her birthday continued to tick by as she washed her face and laid out her outfit for the next morning. A new text message lit up her phone: *COULDN'T RESIST SAYING IT ONE MORE TIME — HAPPY B-DAY GIRLFRIEND!!!!!!!!*

Gianna dialed Jaz's number as she fell into bed. "I was just thinking about you. That was a really good idea you had, getting the girls together for happy hour. Just what I needed."

"Of course it was. Nobody knows you like I do, Gianna."

That much was true. Given their off-and-on stints as a couple across twenty years, Jaz had once been considered part of her family. But after she tried to buy cocaine from an undercover police officer three years ago—her second drug arrest—those days were gone and they weren't coming back.

"I take it you didn't hear from your folks," Jaz said.

"Believe it or not, Dad actually came by the apartment and slid a card under my door. Weird that he couldn't just walk down the hall to my office and give it to me in person. Signed both their names, of course." It was a sore spot that her mother had withdrawn from everyone since Gabe's death, skipping everything except weekly confession at her church. Her dad meanwhile carried on as usual, pretending he didn't think of Gabe at all. "And Stefan left me a voice mail."

"That was big of him." It was no secret that Jaz didn't care for her boss, Stefan, who happened also to be Gianna's cousin. "He busted me for cutting out early today, even when I told him it was so I could catch you before you left the office. Why does he have to be such a dick? He knew it was your birthday."

All three of them worked for TriState Healthcare Supplies, a midsized distribution company owned and run by Gianna's family. Gianna was on the executive track in customer relations, while Stefan held Gabe's old job managing the warehouse. Jaz oversaw distribution, making sure orders were complete and went out on time. Gianna had cashed in all her family favors to keep Jaz on after the arrest, since employment was a term of her probation. Without a job, she'd have gone to jail.

Gianna felt compelled to stick up for Stefan, who, because he was family, had inherited a job supervising over forty warehouse staff despite a total lack of managerial experience. "Stefan has to be careful not to show favoritism because of you and me. And he's probably anxious about the wedding too, so cut him some slack."

"If you ask me, Paige is the one who ought to be anxious, marrying a guy so full of himself. Anyway, I was thinking next year we ought to do your birthday bash a week early. You deserve your own day where you don't have to think about Gabe."

"It's funny you say that. I was just chatting online with somebody from that suicide survivors forum I joined. Her name's Keenan. We might meet up for coffee sometime. Anyway, she said holidays are easier once you get the first year behind you. So maybe next year's birthday won't be so hard."

There was no mistaking the hesitation that followed as Jaz digested her mention of meeting someone. Since they'd broken up three years ago, Gianna had only herself to blame for not making it clear that she intended to date other women. Covid had thrown a two-year wrench into her plans, and the long stretch without dating probably fueled Jaz's hopes they'd get back together. Now that restrictions had eased, she needed to put herself out there—even if it was just coffee with a woman from the grief forum. Jaz needed to see that she was moving on.

CHAPTER TWO

Keenan felt like a beekeeper wearing the oversized face shield that made room for her loupe, the magnifying goggles and headlamp she wore while she worked. Though she and all the dental clinic staff had been vaccinated against Covid, the physical safety protocols were an inescapable part of the job now.

Peering over the goggles, she checked the X-ray of the second premolar and clucked her tongue. Pediatric cavities were a frustrating fact of life. Addressing her dental assistant, she said, "Cassidy, let's make a note to recheck number twenty in six months. I think Michael's had enough drilling for one day. Right, kiddo?" She snapped off her polymer gloves and dropped them in the trash.

The nine-year-old murmured a prayer of thanks, his words still slurred by the last vestiges of lidocaine she'd used to deaden his mouth while she drilled into one of his primary molars. "I wish Mom would let me get a dog. I love Bennie so much."

"Everyone loves Bennie," Keenan said as she lifted the pup from his lap. "That's what makes him so good at his job."

Bennie's sweet temperament and insatiable love of petting made him the ideal lap companion for anxious dental patients, especially kids. She'd been bringing him to work ever since he passed his CGC, the American Kennel Club's Canine Good Citizen test. It was delightful to hear from so many parents that their kids looked forward to coming so they could hold him.

Michael eagerly accepted his new toothbrush, which was etched with *Westwood Family Dentistry* and the names, *Bruce McEvoy, DDS & Keenan McEvoy, DDS.*

"Don't forget to throw away your old one when you get home." She nudged Bennie down the hall toward her office, where he had a bed on the floor by her desk. After a quick report to Michael's mother in the waiting room, Keenan encountered her own mom in the hallway.

Connie McEvoy, whose glasses sat low on her KN95 mask to prevent them from fogging, managed the business side of the practice and sometimes filled in when they were short a dental assistant. Keenan had inherited what she considered her mom's best features: the same golden blond hair and deep-set blue eyes behind high cheekbones. She hoped to look even half as good as her mom when she reached her fifties.

"Brady wants you to call him, hon. Says it's urgent."

"Did he say what it was about?"

Her mom's voice lowered. "Something to do with a couple of kids. Go on if you need to. I'll tell your dad to finish up with Mr. Hasner."

Over the past two years, Officer Brady Carlisle of the Pittsburgh Bureau of Police had become Keenan's closest friend—and the nearest thing her parents would ever have to a son-in-law. He'd been first on the scene when Annabel died, treating her with such compassion and following up personally to see how she was doing. Four months later he sealed their friendship forever when he showed up at her door with eight-week-old Bennie, rescued along with dozens of others from a puppy mill near Sheraden Park. These days she repaid Brady's kindness by bringing Bennie to a police scene when someone needed comfort.

Keenan closed her office door for privacy. "Hey, Brady. Mom said you called."

"Any chance you and Bennie could give us a hand? It's a domestic on Acklen Street off Boggs. The mom went to the hospital. Now we've got two little boys, one's five, one's seven. Found them hiding upstairs in a closet. There's a social worker on the way, but she's on another case all the way over in Homewood. I thought it'd be nice if you could bring Bennie over…maybe hang out with us while we get their statements."

"Text me the house number." Boggs Avenue ran through Mt. Washington, the hilly neighborhood where she'd lived with Annabel. She'd always liked it for its stunning view of the city's skyline.

After a short ride against rush hour traffic, she parked behind a police cruiser in front of a brick house that might have looked welcoming with only a small amount of attention. Instead, paint peeled from the shutters and the small yard was overgrown with weeds. The most prominent eyesore was a ragged upholstered couch that had been left to the elements on the front lawn. A pair of small faces appeared briefly beneath a crooked window shade upstairs but then vanished.

"Come on, Bennie-Boy. Time for you to be sweet." She slipped him a treat before clipping on his leash, and stuffed a few more into her pants pocket so the kids could dole them out. As soon as Bennie's feet hit the ground, he tugged her toward the house like a man on a mission.

"Keenan, come on up!" Brady yelled from the porch, spiffy as usual in his fitted uniform, all black with short sleeves. The body armor underneath his shirt enhanced his already buff chest. He waved her in and disappeared back inside.

"There's your papa, Bennie. Handsome, isn't he? Not like you though. Nobody's as handsome as my—"

A woman's garbled voice suddenly exploded from the external speakers on the police cruiser, a dispatch to officers in the field.

Keenan stopped abruptly, shaken by a visceral memory. For a split second, it was *that day* again, with the maddening cacophony of emergency vehicles. She sank to the arm of the weathered couch and cradled Bennie to her chest. "That's my boy, Bennie...such a good boy...Mama's boy."

He responded with licks to her chin before resting his paws and head on her shoulder as though giving her a comforting hug.

If Brady knew she still had these sickening flashbacks, he'd never call her to a scene again. Those scratchy transmissions remained a stubborn trigger. Luckily she held in her arms the antidote for almost everything.

Two years, three months, twelve days earlier

After hanging his white lab coat on a coat rack alongside his daughter's, Bruce McEvoy squeezed behind the desk for a look at their proposed itinerary on the computer screen. "Your mom missed her calling. She should have been a travel agent."

"Hush, Bruce," her mother snapped. "This is complicated. We change planes in Miami, arrive in Santo Domingo at seven local time. They pick us up and it's a two-hour bus ride to the hotel in Vuelta Larga. Clinic starts the next morning at seven."

Keenan appreciated her mother's attention to detail, especially when they traveled abroad. All she and Annabel ever had to worry about was showing up on time at the airport. "How many of us are going?"

Her mom peered through the reading glasses on the tip of her nose. "The list says eighteen. Five dentists—that's you two and three instructors from Pitt. Three hygienists and three dental assistants, including me. The rest are dental students, probably second year. Any idea what this so-called clinic looks like, Bruce?"

"Jorge says the locals call it a pharmacy," he replied, his skepticism obvious. "That doesn't necessarily mean we'll have supplies."

Keenan scoffed. "Especially since half our stuff usually goes missing before we ever get there."

In some parts of the world, it was harder to find dental equipment than skilled volunteers to use it. Sterilization and hygiene meant something altogether different in rural clinics where even electricity and running water weren't a given.

Her parents were regular volunteers at rural pop-up clinics in the US, where she and Annabel had sometimes joined them. On occasion, they signed up for sponsored trips to impoverished areas such as this one on the northwestern coast of Ecuador, a region subject to earthquakes. This would be Keenan's third clinic abroad.

"Dad, did you remember to ask them about Annabel? We'd be crazy not to take her if she's willing to go. How many times do we get somewhere and wish we had a nurse? Plus she speaks a little Spanish."

"Jorge said he'd love to have her but it's too late to add her to the official roster, so she probably won't get any recertification credits."

"That doesn't matter. I just want to get her out of here for a while, get her mind on something else." Leaving Annabel alone right now didn't seem like a good idea given her recent state of depression. If she didn't go, Keenan probably wouldn't go either.

"I'm sure there will be plenty for her to do," her mom said. "She wants to come, right?"

"Her therapist thought it was a great idea. We were talking last night about that time we did the clinic in South Africa. She always says it was the most gratifying experience of her whole professional life."

Annabel had always suffered bouts of mild depression, usually triggered by stress. A family rift over the past year had seen it worsen dramatically. They'd hoped the move from their home in Columbus, Ohio, to Pittsburgh, where Keenan had grown up, would help break the cycle. A new home and job, new friends, and a closer relationship with the McEvoys, who loved her like family. It was slow progress, but progress nonetheless.

Keenan rose. "I should get on home. She'll have dinner waiting. I'll call you later and let you know if she says yes."

As strange as it sounded, a grueling week at a makeshift dental clinic in Ecuador was exactly what they both needed right now. In Annabel's philosophical musings the night before, she'd noted that her mother's recent death, heartbreaking as it was, had at least brought a semblance of closure to her anguish. There was nothing left to brood about, she said, nothing to gain from self-recrimination. She could put the past to bed once and for all. It was the first real sign she was ready to start moving on from the emotional trauma of the past year. Further proof had come later when she'd awakened Keenan around two o'clock to make love, something they'd done infrequently since the turmoil began. Finally, a glimmer of hope they were turning the corner.

Snaking her way through the neighborhood, she imagined a refreshingly upbeat conversation about Ecuador. It would be like South Africa, she'd say, where even their exhaustion had felt good.

Kids making the most of the waning daylight paused their street soccer game to let her pass. Their boxy rental house in Mt. Washington sat on a narrow, sloping lot, its front yard halved by a concrete driveway barely long enough for a single car. Annabel's Kia was parked at the curb beneath a streetlight that was just coming to life.

Keenan entered a utility room through the side door and climbed the steep stairs to the main floor. Most nights she got a whiff of dinner the moment she stepped inside, but tonight the kitchen was dark. "Annabel?"

A quick check of their bedroom and living room turned up nothing, as did a scan of the backyard from the kitchen window. Ordinarily they took a walk together before sitting down to dinner, a suggestion by Annabel's therapist to empty their minds of their daily conflicts so they could focus their evenings on nurturing one another. Perhaps Annabel had gone on her own when Keenan failed to show up at the usual time.

A note lay on the kitchen table beside Annabel's cell phone. Odd that she'd go off without—

My darling Keenan — What did I do to deserve being loved by someone as wonderful as you? You're the only person in my life who never once let me down and I love you for that. Honey I'm so SORRY for all I've put you through this past year. I know it wasn't fair, you did so much to try to help me fix this mess of my life and look at me — I'm broken to pieces anyway. You cannot blame yourself for anything!!

"Annabel!" Heart racing, legs shaking, she continued reading in mounting terror.

I need one last thing from you, my love. Call 911 — and WAIT for them to come. This can't be fixed, it's too late. My Sweet Keenan. Please PLEASE just sit down and wait for them. I don't want you to remember me this way. I'm so sorry to hurt you. It's a selfish thing to do but I just can't take this pain anymore. Be happy for me that I'm free and know that I love you FOREVER. ~ Your Annabel

"No...Annabel, no. God please *no!*"

Tossing the note aside, she raced back down the hall to their bedroom and flung open the bathroom door, bracing for a terrible sight but finding the room empty. One after another she opened closets, giving each a cursory check.

Only two hours ago, Annabel said she was still at work. She couldn't have been home for long. Not long enough to—

"Annabel, answer me! Where are you?"

Her frantic search took her into the backyard toward a small metal shed that housed yard tools and old paint. The padlock was missing.

"No no no...Annabel! *Annabel!*"

She yanked both handles, only to find they'd been bound together from within. Using all her strength, she bent one of the rusty doors, barely a sliver but enough. Annabel lay curled on her side, a fleece blanket tucked beneath her chin as though she'd gone down for a nap. A crimson river soaked the plywood floor. The air smelled of old pennies.

CHAPTER THREE

The westward panorama from Gianna's third-floor corner office was riveting at twilight as planes lined up on approach to Pittsburgh International Airport, their landing lights as bright as Venus in the mid-September sky. Her south-facing window afforded a more pedestrian view, a sprawling warehouse shut down for the day, with delivery trucks backed into their respective bays, ready to be loaded for the next day's run. Both buildings belonged to TriState, the company her great-grandfather had founded in 1950. They supplied disposables to hospitals and clinics, everything from bandages to intubation kits.

Gianna had earned her large office with years of service that began in high school, a part-time job pulling orders in the warehouse. Now with a bachelor's degree from Pitt in supply chain management, she'd worked her way up through the warehouse to VP of customer relations, a title reflecting her status in the family business. Her actual job was less sweeping— she managed TriState's customer accounts in West Virginia and southern Ohio and Pennsylvania—but she was called on often to help deal with problems wherever they arose.

One of those problems was sloppy work in the warehouse. On her speakerphone, she gently cajoled her cousin to pay closer attention to his crew. "Here's what I think, Stefan. Whoever's pulling these orders isn't taking the time to match the barcodes. They're just grabbing stuff out of the closest box and throwing it in a bin."

"I'll look into it, Gianna."

Personnel matters in the warehouse weren't normally her responsibility, but this order issue was rippling through the entire company. "I know your brain's fried with the wedding and all," she went on, "but I've gotten complaints from three customers who received generic disposables at top-shelf prices. This can't keep happening."

"And I promise I'll look into it. First thing tomorrow." From his dismissive tone, he was already home, his mind no longer on work.

"It's a simple fix. Just make sure all the inventory goes through the software. If you like I can come over to the warehouse tomorrow morning and—"

"Gianna..."

"Yeah, sorry." She slumped against her chair back and sighed. Not all her frustration was his fault. Mostly she blamed her father and Uncle Jack for putting him in charge of the warehouse before he was ready. Like Gianna and Gabe, Stefan had worked part-time pulling orders before going off to college, but after earning his business degree from Penn State he'd gone to work as a tennis instructor at a private club in the Poconos. After Gabe died, Uncle Jack had lured Stefan back to TriState with the promise of a high-ranking position that paid three times what he made teaching topspin. "Sorry if it sounds like I'm on your case, Stefan. I'm just trying to put these fires out. When the customers aren't happy, the buck stops at my desk."

"Better you than me, cuz."

"I'm sure we'll get it worked out." She wanted to end on a friendly note. "In the meantime...you're getting married in three days, dude. Enjoy your last days of freedom."

He snorted. "I've been hearing that a lot. While I have you on the phone..."

She smiled, wondering what favor he'd ask. Keeping up with the paperwork while he was on his honeymoon?

"It's about Jaz. She went off on Rudy this afternoon for taking a few minutes after lunch to grab a smoke."

"That's silly considering all the late nights he works getting orders ready to go out. His car's still down there at the warehouse. Everybody else left two hours ago."

"I don't know anything about that. But it's my job to deal with shit like that, not Jaz's. She acts like *she's* the boss. When I call her out, she gives me a bunch of lip, and it's like she knows I'm not going to do anything about it."

She didn't want to interfere with Stefan's authority, but Jaz's probation status complicated things. "You're the boss over there, Stefan. So be the boss."

"I know but she's your...friend." He squeaked it out as though he had doubts that's all she was. "I feel like she's daring me to do something. She knows I won't fire her."

"Jaz is my friend but that's not a license to do whatever she wants. You can always suspend her a couple of days without pay. She'll get the message."

"I wanted to do something like that but I figured she'd go crying to you. And if you stood up for her...that's all my authority right out the window."

Stefan's credibility with long-time staff was already tenuous, since he was only twenty-nine and still learning on the job. He wouldn't succeed without their support.

"You don't need my permission to dole out consequences, Stef. Just keep your cool and make sure whatever you do is fair, whether it's Jaz or someone else. This is business. Give her a warning first, but then you follow through. I'll back you all the way."

"Good to know. I don't suppose you'd give her a call and..."

"It really needs to come from you. But I'll give her a heads-up so she knows I've got your back, not hers." Gianna dreaded that conversation, given the giant chip on Jaz's shoulder. She'd get defensive and blame everyone but herself, but she had to learn that Gianna wasn't going to step in and save her from herself.

Hearing the whir of a vacuum cleaner in the distance, Gianna noted the time—seven fifteen. It was rare for her to stay this late but she'd needed to put this warehouse glitch to bed. Seeing her father's office light still on across the hall, she was about to pop in and say good night, but then Uncle Jack's angry voice spilled into the hallway. "That's bullshit, Paul. Nobody knows how this company runs better than the warehouse manager. Those were your exact words back when you made Gabe next in line. Now it's *my* son's job. You can't go back and say warehouse manager's not enough experience. I should remind you that Stefan dropped everything and came back when Gabe left. We owe him a future."

"Stefan definitely has a future here, Jack." Her father's voice was cajoling. "But he hasn't even been here a year. That's no comparison to Gabe. Gabe had sales experience too. Hell, he knew half the buyers on a first-name basis."

Gianna stopped in the hallway to eavesdrop, surprised to hear her dad mention Gabe. Their bits of conversation were jumbled at first until she realized they were talking about who would be TriState's next CEO.

"Look, Paul, I supported Gabe back then too but here we are. Stefan gains more experience every day, and I'm helping him build relationships with clients and the money guys. He'll be ready when it's time, I promise."

Her father groaned. "The point is he isn't ready *now*. That's what we're signing here, Jack. Gianna's our only viable option unless we name somebody outside the family."

Shaking with fury, Gianna braced herself against the wall. She'd managed the warehouse for three years right out of college before training Gabe to take it over. After his death, she'd been sent back down for six months to train Stefan. That Stefan would now leapfrog her to become CEO was outrageous.

"A family man needs a future, Paul. You of all people know that. We have to consider what's best for the company in the long run. I've got no problem with Gianna, but not everybody is as open-minded about the gay thing. The banks, for instance. And that Jazmine Sadowski…she's nothing but—"

Before Uncle Jack could finish his shocking assessment, Gianna's phone chirped loudly to announce a text message.

In an instant, Jack was in the hallway facing her. He still wore his golf shirt from an afternoon spent on the links while everyone else was working. "Gianna…"

She shouldered past him to confront her father, who stood by his desk, one hand in his pocket and the other holding a glass of scotch. With his five-o'clock shadow and loosened tie, he looked haggard.

"So it was always meant to be Gabe, not me. Is that right, Dad? Even though I've worked my ass off here since I was sixteen. Gabe took six years off to go play guitar with his friends."

"Nothing was decided for certain, Gianna. It's just a form we have to fill out for the banks before they'll sign off on a loan."

She whirled on her uncle, who at least had the decency to look embarrassed. It would be so easy to launch into a laundry list of Stefan's shortcomings but she wasn't going to tear him down to build herself up.

"I apologize, Gianna. I didn't mean to—"

"To what, Uncle Jack? Admit you've been lying all this time about loving me for who I am? Really glad to hear you don't have a problem with the *gay thing*. Got any more knives you want to stick in my back?" She shifted her icy stare to her father. "Why are you talking about this now? Are you stepping down?"

"No, of course not. As far as I know, your uncle and I will be running the company for another six or eight years at least." He looked for confirmation from Uncle Jack, who nodded. "We're reorganizing our debt is all. The bank called this afternoon for an update on our succession plan. We haven't filed anything since your brother died."

She heaved a sigh, noting her conflicting emotions. Relief that the company wasn't undergoing an upheaval. Colossal disappointment that her father had chosen Gabe to succeed him, despite the fact that she'd worked harder than anyone and was better prepared to lead. A mammoth sense of betrayal that her uncle—and perhaps her father too—viewed her sexuality as an impediment to her running TriState, so much that they'd choose a fledgling over her.

"By all means, let me know how I can help bring Stefan up to speed when he steps into the CEO job," she said coldly. "I've only worked here all my life. Shame I didn't know about all the other boxes I needed to tick."

They pleaded for her understanding but she ignored them, storming out before she could tell them both to go fuck themselves.

* * *

HALF-A-SET: *Sorry I couldn't make it. All hell broke loose right when I was leaving work. I would have been terrible company.*

Keenan couldn't help feeling embarrassed about her impulsive invitation. What was she thinking, texting to meet the very next day for a walk with Bennie at Point State Park? Gianna probably thought she was desperate for friends.

WINGÈD SERAPH: *No problem. It was spur of the moment since I happened to be out with Bennie. I have a cop friend who called us to help out at a domestic violence scene in Mt. W. Bennie's really good with kids. Calmed them down, got them talking about what happened.*

HALF-A-SET: *It's so cool you do that. I could have used calming down today.*

WINGÈD SERAPH: *Something to do with Gabe?*

HALF-A-SET: *No.*

HALF-A-SET: *Actually yes. I found out my dad and uncle had picked Gabe to take over the company when they retired. Threw me for a loop. Now they want to pick my cousin Stefan. I'm a million times more qualified than either of them. Some days Stefan can't find his ass with both hands. I came so close to telling them all where to stick it.*

Bennie followed her across the room, yowling once as if commanding her to sit. She complied, settling with her laptop in her usual place on the sectional sofa. He found his usual spot too, forcing her to reach over him to the keyboard.

WINGÈD SERAPH: *Let me guess, because they're guys. Right?*

HALF-A-SET: *And straight. I came out when I was 15. Everybody was like, we love you, we support you. But apparently not enough to have me running the company. F them all.*

Keenan let out a hoot that caused Bennie to jump down and start barking. "Sorry, Bennie. I knew there was a reason I liked this woman."

She'd missed hanging out with queer women, having left behind a whole community of friends in Columbus, where she'd gone to college at Ohio State and where Annabel's family lived. Annabel had been too traumatized to make new friends in Pittsburgh, narrowing their life to work and home.

WINGÈD SERAPH: *I don't blame you. Annabel's sister said she voted against same-sex marriage in Maryland. Love you sis, but you shouldn't have rights. Made for an awkward turkey day.*

HALF-A-SET: *An awkward every day is more like it. And especially this weekend because Stefan is getting married. Huge Catholic wedding. At least I'm not in the actual wedding party so I can walk out when I want to. It's all a big circus.*

Keenan swelled with a sense of outrage that made her reach for Bennie. It was that same feeling—the righteous indignation—that had fueled her support for Annabel when she first began confronting her past. Maybe if they hadn't been so strident about seeing justice done...

HALF-A-SET: *Meeting a client early tomorrow in WV — I should get to bed but wanted to say thanks for texting. Definitely ask again.*

WINGÈD SERAPH: *You too. I can make it most days after 5:30. Let me know if you want Bennie and me to go kick some ass. Though we probably can't. LOL*

Her fingers hesitated over the keyboard as she contemplated her impulse to attach a photo, her with Bennie on the deck last April. It was presumptuous. And for a selfie, not half bad.

"Oh, what the hell...here goes."

As the seconds piled up without a reply, she convinced herself Gianna had logged off already.

"That's it, Bennie. Let's go to bed." He was three steps ahead of her when her laptop chimed with a reply.

HALF-A-SET: *:-)*

The reply had a photo attached as well. Straight dark hair, brown eyes, olive complexion. Wearing a starched white shirt with an open collar. From the lanyard hanging around her neck, it was a candid shot taken at a conference of some sort. Very attractive, especially since her smile revealed a lovely feature Keenan happened to adore—a gap between her front teeth.

CHAPTER FOUR

Gianna sincerely hoped Stefan and Paige's marriage lasted long enough to warrant the outlay for such an extravagant wedding at Phipps Conservatory and Botanical Gardens, arguably the most opulent venue in Pittsburgh. If she ever had a wedding, she'd want it under the stars too—but not with this much hoopla. Twenty-piece jazz band, ice sculpture, sit-down dinner for two hundred. Endless champagne.

Another drink would have been nice but she'd already polished off two flutes in under an hour. She couldn't risk getting drunk and spouting off about how ridiculous it was for Stefan to be next in line to lead the family company. She understood now why it was so important for him to hold a top-level position: he was marrying into an obviously wealthy family.

Beside her at a cloth-covered table on the periphery, Jaz tugged her black Spandex shift downward to smooth the wrinkles that had gathered around her waist. "Jesus, this dress. The longer I wear it, the smaller it gets."

"Leave it alone. It looks fine." If she were honest, she'd have said it looked great. Short and curvaceous, Jaz was an attractive woman who knew how to dress. But the last thing Gianna needed was to give Jaz a reason to think she was being led on.

Gianna also had worn black at the bride's request, a V-neck shift with a strand of pearls from her great-gran. Only the bridesmaids wore color—mango chiffon, Paige had called it—crimped gowns that likely were headed for thrift shops or landfills as early as tomorrow. Thrilled that she'd been left out of the wedding party, Gianna draped a shawl around her sleeveless arms against the night chill.

Catholic weddings were an elaborate farce, she'd decided, with ordinary men like Father Michael pretending theirs was the official voice of God. All the same, she begrudged the fact that he'd never grant her the wedding sacrament.

Her parents had left the reception early after pasting on the expected smiles for the family photos. No doubt the spectacle had been too much for her mother, a brutal reminder that her beloved son hadn't lived to marry. To be honest, Gianna didn't feel much like partying either, but she had to be there for Stefan.

"We should dance or something," Jaz said, interrupting her morose reflections.

"I was considering getting sloshed instead."

"Go for it. I'm driving, remember?"

It probably was rude of her to drink so casually in front of Jaz, whose probation terms prohibited alcohol. It was dangerous as well, since too much champagne might lower her inhibitions. She couldn't risk dropping her guard with Jaz, even for one night.

"Nah, I should get a club soda or something."

"Wait here, babe. I'll get it for you."

That right there! After their breakup she should have put a stop to Jaz calling her babe, sweetheart, girlfriend. No wonder Uncle Jack had worried she still was a liability. Gianna hadn't convinced her family and friends their relationship was over. Apparently she hadn't convinced Jaz either.

Jaz returned with drinks garnished with lime to simulate a cocktail. "I don't know how you can sit here and smile all night at these bastards after what they did to you. And their golden boy—*ha!* They have no idea how many times a week we have to save Stefan's sorry ass because he's done something ignorant. Look at him out there strutting like a rooster."

"Give him a break. It's his wedding, for chrissakes. He's allowed to dance. Besides, it's not his fault the warehouse landed in his lap when Gabe died."

"I know. It's just frustrating what he gets away with. Coming in late, leaving early. You and Gabe never pulled shit like that when you were in charge."

She shouldn't have told Jaz what she'd overheard, as it only gave her more ammunition with which to complain about Stefan. She'd always had issues with authority and her dislike for Stefan had been instant.

"Don't look now but Jack the Slack's coming this way. Like father, like son."

Cocktail in hand, Gianna's uncle was the epitome of suave. Trim and fit for sixty-two, he was especially handsome in his tuxedo, and tanned from days on the golf course schmoozing with clients. He swung a chair around and straddled it to face her. "So how's my favorite niece?"

"Your *only* niece," Jaz grumbled. There was no love lost between those two.

"You look nice tonight, Jaz. Maybe you could take a stroll around to all the tables so everyone has a chance to appreciate you in that lovely dress."

"Sure, Jack. I can do subtle."

The two of them traded fake smiles, evidence of their cool relationship. When she left, he said to Gianna, "Look, sweetheart…I'm really sorry for our little misunderstanding the other day."

"A misunderstanding. Is that what it was?"

"That's exactly what it was. You know how I feel about you. One of my biggest regrets in life is not having any daughters, but I've always had you. I love you like my own, right?" He tipped her chin upward, forcing her to look him in the eye. "I got carried away when I was talking to your dad, that's all. Standing up for my son. You know what a passionate guy I can be sometimes. I was just spouting off. I happen to think you're great."

"Not great enough to run the company though."

"I never said that," he replied firmly. "I can't help it, I want big things for Stefan. It's only natural to feel that way about my son. But I said to Paul—and I know you heard me say it—that I'd be okay if it were you."

"If it came to that. Those were the words you used, Uncle Jack…if it came to that. You thought I'd make a decent CEO if there were no other options."

"Now you're putting words in my mouth. What I meant was if your dad felt strongly that you were the best choice—and if our financial advisors agreed—then I'd support that decision. Just like I know he'd support it if they thought it should be Stefan. We all want what's best for the company."

Gianna wanted to believe her father would support her over Stefan, but his silence the other night had been disappointing to say the least. Throughout her life there had been moments she'd felt the sting of seeing Gabe favored simply because he was a boy. It honestly wouldn't surprise her at all if her father gave in to back Stefan.

"Come on, Gianna. Everybody here can tell you're mad at me, and I know for a fact it's making some people uncomfortable. That's not what tonight's about. My son just got married. People should be laughing, dancing. Forgive me, please. What do you say?"

It gave her no pleasure to punish him. What he didn't seem to grasp was that his words had impugned more than her business acumen. They'd wounded her personally.

"Fine, I forgive you for spouting off," she said, forcing a smile. "You should be celebrating today. Especially considering how much you and Paige's family are paying for all of this."

His grin this time seemed genuine, and he went one step further by offering his hand. "Dance with me, sweetheart. Let's put an end to all the gossip, show them what family's all about."

Reluctantly, she followed him to the cobblestone dance floor and stepped into his affectionate embrace. A wave of couples joined them as the band struck up "It Had to Be You."

"One thing, Uncle Jack…" She managed to hold her smile for the benefit of those who might be watching, but her unwavering voice left no room for doubt about her feelings. "All my life I've looked up to you…I felt like I had an extra dad. So the idea that you'd throw me under the bus for the 'gay thing,' as you call it…that hurt. I expected better from you."

His face fell. "Gianna, please."

"That's all I'm going to say about it for now. But it's a talk the three of us will have again sometime soon. I need to know where I stand with the company." With Gabe gone and her personal life floundering, all she had right now was TriState. If their plan was to shut her out, she needed a plan of her own.

He sighed and hugged her tightly. "Losing Gabe, honey…I know you took that harder than anyone. The last thing I want is to hurt you more."

The fight went out of her as she wallowed in his comfort. Only at that moment did she realize this was another of the firsts Keenan had described as a challenge she had to mark—a wedding to remind her that Gabe wouldn't be there if she ever got to celebrate hers.

* * *

"This is called having no life at all, Bennie. Who else stays home on a Saturday night to wash their dog, huh?"

If she had one gripe about Bennie, it was having to bathe him twice a week. Not his fault, really. Besides loving every single puddle he passed on his walk, he also picked up remnants from all the sticky-handed children who petted him, and all the floors he rolled on afterward. At least he enjoyed baths, especially when she fluffed him dry with a warm towel.

They'd spent their Saturday at the public library in South Hills volunteering with a program called Paws to Read. When they got home, she'd posted a cute photo to the forum hoping to draw a response from Gianna, whom she hadn't seen online since they traded photos three nights ago. A wedding this weekend, she'd said.

"I guess some people have better things to do, huh?" She filled a plastic cup with warm water and gently rinsed his soapy ears. "But not me, Bennie. All I have is a dirty dog, right?"

Following her own shower, she stepped out before the mirror and studied her body with no small measure of vanity. Annabel had always raved about her slim hips and strong shoulders, a physique sculpted from spending half her younger life on a swim team. Even now, her short, straight hair kept its chlorinated blond hue from twice-weekly visits to the pool with her mom. Overall, hers was admittedly an androgynous look, one she cultivated with a basic wardrobe and a cosmetic routine that consisted only of soap and moisturizer.

She missed being touched. Even her own hand sometimes failed to arouse. She ached for the intimacy of lovemaking, of being filled like a vessel to be poured back into someone else.

Would sex ever feel that way again? Or would it always have the taint of Annabel's penultimate betrayal, waking her in the night to make passionate love and then taking her own life the next day?

Bennie tiptoed in and stood against the cabinet on his hind legs. Amazingly, he seemed to know when she was stuck in her memories and always showed up to render comfort.

"Look at you, all clean and handsome. Who's my boy?"

She often wondered how Annabel would have responded to Bennie. He might have given her a sense of responsibility to keep on living…something Keenan had clearly failed to do.

* * *

Back at her table, Gianna removed her left shoe to check the condition of her throbbing toe. Uncle Jack had inadvertently spun her into the path of Paige's brother, a hefty guy with gargantuan feet. In an instant, her pinky toe was crushed beneath his heel.

The reception was starting to thin out, enough that her leaving wouldn't be conspicuous. Except now Jaz was across the way chatting with a cluster of bridesmaids.

Trish Cantor abruptly slid into the chair beside her. A diminutive but formidable woman in her early fifties, Trish was a longtime TriState employee in charge of accounts for the northern regions of Ohio and Pennsylvania. Though she technically was Trish's boss, Gianna had grown up under her tutelage and considered her a mentor. This time last year, Trish was celebrating her own marriage—the second for both—to a man she'd met through an online dating service. "How are you doing, kiddo?"

"I have a broken toe. You?"

Trish pushed out her lower lip, an exaggerated pout. "Poor baby."

"Your compassion touches me, Trish." Gianna noted her black wraparound dress and graying hair swept back to show off silver and onyx earrings. "You look nice, by the way."

"Thank you, my dear. I wondered if you were thinking about Gabe tonight."

"I think about him every night…but yeah, he leaves a pretty big hole at something like this." Her voice quivered, as it did most times she spoke of Gabe. It pleased her that Trish was remembering him tonight too. "I catch myself looking around for him. Then it hits me that he's gone and it's almost like hearing it again for the first time."

"Good thing I carry these, huh?" Trish offered her a tissue from a packet in her purse. "I heard what happened with Jack and Paul. Want to talk about it?"

Gianna groaned. She'd told only Jaz, which meant Trish likely had heard the story directly from her father. No telling what version he'd shared or how far the gossip had spread.

"I just buried the hatchet with Uncle Jack…for now, anyway. If I think about it too much it still makes me want to scream." A fresh stream of tears stung her eyes as she recalled the hurtful words she'd overheard. "It kills me they think I can't lead the company because I'm gay. I'm not going to change who I am. Not for TriState, not for anybody."

"Of course not…but you could do yourself a favor, Gianna." Her sentimental look changed to one Gianna recognized as All-business Trish, the one who'd taught her how to be tough in the office. "If you're willing to, that is. The problem is I'm not sure you are."

"What?" Surely she wasn't suggesting something underhanded. Trish had always been a straight shooter. She had to know Gianna wouldn't do anything to hurt her family or the company.

"My friend, you have one glaring weakness, and everyone seems to know it but you." She nodded across the room to the table of bridesmaids.

"Jaz? She's not my weakness. We've been broken up for three years, right after she got arrested."

"Like you broke up after that business in high school, and again five years later? That lasted what, a month? Most people think either you're already back together or it's just a matter of time before you will be. You're still propping her up."

"How am I doing that? She doesn't report to me anymore—and it's going to stay that way." Gianna had held firm on Jaz's repeated requests for a transfer to the office, a coveted position as an administrative assistant—preferably *hers*. Jaz's brash personality wasn't suited to their corporate culture. "She's doing great right now, Trish. Not a single backslide since rehab. Do I love her? Of course, and I'm proud of her. We'll probably always be best friends, but I don't have romantic feelings for her anymore. Swear to God, we are *not* getting back together—not now, not ever."

"Fair enough." Trish folded her arms and nodded indulgently. "But you have to realize Stefan is a guy with a clean slate. Sure, he's had an iffy start as a tennis bum but he's settling down now, learning his job and becoming a family man who won't cause the company a lot of drama."

"Come on, that's bullshit. Uncle Jack's a so-called family man too, and look at all the drama he's caused. Two ex-wives and he's probably cheating on the third one as we speak."

"And he's not CEO, is he? Your father is."

"In name only." She'd always assumed that was because her dad was two years older, the natural heir. "Dad says they make the big decisions as equals."

"Which is exactly how they'll decide the succession plan, so you can't count on your father to put his thumb on the scale." All-business Trish always spoke in a sales voice that was cunningly persuasive. "For what it's worth, Gianna, Jack's comments about your lifestyle are totally off-base. I know for a fact bankers don't care who you sleep with. What they *do* care about is smart, predictable leadership at the very top. I don't think you'll run into any problems there as long as you keep your nose clean."

Gianna made a mental note to talk with Trish someday about how being gay was an identity, not a lifestyle. This wasn't the moment for a lecture on woke semantics. Trish was an ally whose opinion was widely respected at all levels of the company, and she seemed to be on board with Gianna moving up to CEO one day.

"I know you love Jaz, but that woman's got a ton of baggage. I'll take your word for it about not getting back together, but you need to make people see that. You're thirty-four. Maybe you should give some thought to settling down too, make a family if you want one—and wipe out Stefan's advantage."

The idea that settling down was a prerequisite for being CEO was almost as infuriating as the assumption that a straight man was better suited to the job. "And what if I'm not cut out for that kind of life? Not everybody wants to get married, you know."

"That would be a horse of a different color, but you obviously like having someone special in your life. Or you wouldn't have spent so long with Jaz. Either way, you need to solve that problem. Make it clear the two of you aren't just on hold. I'm serious here, Gianna. Paul's not much of a fan and Jack can't stand her. Your whole career could hinge on this."

In her heart, she knew Trish was right. She'd said to herself only a few days ago the only way Jaz would get the message their breakup was final was if she started dating someone else. What she hadn't realized was that others knew it too.

"So…what now? I take out a want ad?"

"Don't knock it, kiddo. 'Lonely widow seeks handsome guy who can fix a running toilet.' I hit the jackpot with Greg. See me if you need help building a marketing profile that sells."

Gianna playfully kicked at her, banging her sore toe on the chair instead. "Ow! Look what you made me do."

Jaz returned and dragged another chair close to Gianna. "What's so funny?"

Trish abruptly stood and squeezed Gianna's shoulder. "Romance and toilets. I'll let Gianna fill you in. Catch you later."

Gianna's mind raced for ideas on how she could possibly explain the cryptic reply without revealing the nature of their talk.

"This I gotta hear," Jaz said. "Unless we're talking TMI. If Trish's taking booty calls in the john, I don't want to know about it."

"She doesn't strike me as the type."

"I like her. Smart as fuck, you know? Probably the smartest person in the whole company. Present company excepted, of course."

Gianna wondered how she'd feel to know the "smartest person" at TriState was urging Gianna to ditch her and start seeing someone else. Trish was right, of course. Jaz was reliable and fun, the friend who always had her back. To her credit, she'd surrendered to terms for a strictly platonic friendship, though it was obvious she hoped someday for more. Gianna accepted this loyalty without returning it, arguably taking advantage of knowing Jaz would do anything for her.

"How were the bridesmaids?"

"Ughh. If I die, please don't let me come back as a straight chick. They're all so fucking dull."

"*If* you die?"

"You know what I mean. They're over there talking about *The Bachelor* like it's real. Makes my ears bleed."

Gianna considered Trish's advice, already agonizing over how Jaz would react to a chill in their friendship. Their lives were entangled in myriad ways. They had all the same friends, and she was well-liked by Jaz's mom and sister. Jaz even had a key to her apartment. Taking those things away for no real reason would be cruel and hurtful. Maybe if she started dating, it would happen naturally. Worth thinking about.

CHAPTER FIVE

This time last week Keenan had hardly been aware of the forum's chat function. Now she couldn't leave it alone. The problem was that both parties had to be logged in at the same time to use it. She'd checked off and on all weekend and never once caught Gianna online. It crossed her mind to send a text asking her to chat, but another invitation so soon after asking her to meet for a walk might make her seem needy. She'd had a tough day and could have used a friend, but it was up to Gianna to reach out next time if she wanted to be friends.

Sitting at the bar in her neat kitchen, she scrolled through the day's forum posts, taking note of new member Aquarian Soul, a thirty-five-year-old man who'd lost his best friend to suicide. Only one post so far, a reply to her recent photo of Bennie.

AQUARIAN SOUL: *Meh.*

Keenan sighed. Anger was a well-documented stage of grief. Some came to the forum so angry they rejected comfort and support from others. Still, it was hard not to be offended he'd stooped to lash out on his very first post. Aquarian Soul might have a difficult time making friends on the forum.

A quick scan of other recent threads revealed no more posts from Gianna. Just one and done.

"Maybe Gianna's got all the friends she needs, Bennie. What do you think?"

He wagged his tail at the mention of his name but didn't rise from his perch on the ottoman. His trained ear knew when she was talking aloud to herself versus talking to him.

In all likelihood, Gianna was just being polite. She'd started their conversation when she was feeling low and probably felt obligated to continue until she could respectfully disengage. Keenan ought not make that difficult with repeated intrusions.

The bigger question was why Gianna's potential friendship mattered so much to her all of a sudden. One minute she was questioning the wisdom of answering a stranger's chat request and the next she's obsessing over chatting with her again. There was little doubt what changed—these feelings took off when she realized Gianna was gay.

Of course, it was possible Gianna already had a partner. Women that pretty ought to have them lined up around the block. However, dykes with partners didn't trade photos with other dykes online. If she had, she'd be bad news. On the other hand, Covid had carved at least two years of holes in people's social lives, so Gianna might have put that part of her life on hold the same way Keenan had after Annabel died.

Twelve years. That's how long it had been since she felt the first spark of attraction for someone. She'd met Annabel when they both were sophomores at Ohio State. Annabel, so funny and sweet, always sharing M&Ms in microbiology class, pretending the red ones were mutant cells that caused all kinds of mischief. Keenan still remembered her thrill at being invited to a women's basketball game on campus, but it was only when Annabel took her hand that she knew for sure it was a date. Her whole world shifted on the spot. They were inseparable for the next nine years.

Now, based only on a photo and a very brief cyberchat, she was feeling that same inkling of interest, the kind that set her imagination alight. No matter what happened with Gianna, one thing was astoundingly true: She could see herself dating again. *Dating, kissing, sex.*

"I'm losing it, Bennie." She closed her laptop and spun around on the stool. "Let's go for a walk."

* * *

The evening breeze off the Allegheny River was among the many things Gianna loved about her downtown apartment. Dramatic sunsets from her balcony, first-rate amenities. She could walk to the cafes and bars at Market Square, to galleries and concert halls, to sporting events across the river on the North Shore. Best of all, she could rollerblade for miles along the Three Rivers Heritage Trail. Her skate today had been hampered by her crushed toe from the collision with Bigfoot. The worst part wasn't the pain, but an annoying reminder of an evening she'd like to forget. Nothing like being bombarded with all the things wrong in her life.

Her phone had certainly had a busy day. Three texts, two missed calls, one voice mail, all from Jaz. She felt mildly guilty for not picking up but Trish's voice in her ear made it feel like the right thing to do. Moving on from Jaz meant she had to actually *move*, as in do something else.

With her feet propped on the balcony rail, she scrolled through her phone to the forum, smiling to see Keenan online. That's who she should have called today. They could have met for the drink they missed last week.

HALF-A-SET: *Hey!! Good weekend?*

She quickly scrolled through recent posts to gauge the mood of the forum. It wouldn't do to sound too cheery if the tenor of discussion was somber. Only thirty minutes ago Keenan had posted a photo that instantly brought tears to Gianna's eyes—the corner of what obviously was a granite headstone. Tiny Bennie sat in the grass alongside a small lavender candle that looked homemade, baby's breath melded into the wax.

Today would have been her 32nd birthday. I never want to forget how much she loved candles.

HALF-A-SET: *Oh God I just saw your post. Keenan, I'm so sorry.*

Dots appeared to let her know Keenan was typing a response.

WINGÈD SERAPH: *Thanks. Just a quiet day, Bennie & me. Never thought I'd be one of those people who goes to the cemetery to talk to a dead person but here we are. It being her birthday and all. Suppose we all have our little rituals. I've only done it a few times though.*

HALF-A-SET: *How did it feel?*

WINGÈD SERAPH: *Today was the first time I didn't get angry that she gave up. I'm trying to forgive her … guess that means I'm trying to forgive myself too. Told her I was glad she was at peace, said I was doing better. Covid's been a good excuse not to do stuff but I'm looking forward to it now. Don't know what exactly but I feel like I'm ready to venture out into the world again.*

Since Keenan was already going places with Bennie, venturing out had to mean something different. Especially if her visit to the cemetery today had given her a kind of closure.

HALF-A-SET: *Have you traveled anywhere since the pandemic?*

WINGÈD SERAPH: *Bristol TN & Elkins WV. Pop-up clinics for people who can't pay. I'm a dentist, so's my dad. Mom's a dental asst. We sign up at least once a year. Got one coming up next month at Big Stone Gap VA.*

For a second, Gianna wondered if she was being jerked around. She didn't know anyone so selfless that they would spend all their free time visiting nursing homes and giving out free dental care. Maybe Keenan had a weird complex that made her want to be a martyr.

HALF-A-SET: *I've heard of those. Never knew anyone who actually worked at one.*

WINGÈD SERAPH: *It's something my parents always did. They were into docs w/o borders for a while. I went with them to South Africa & Haiti a few years ago. Now it's only rural stuff. Amazing how much need there is right here in the richest country in the world.*

Sure sounded like Keenan was the real deal.

HALF-A-SET: *A dentist, huh? I bet you took one look at my diastema and said "I can fix that."*

WINGÈD SERAPH: *NO!!!!!! Don't you EVER mess with that!! It's beautiful just the way it is.*

Gianna caught herself grinning. If that wasn't flirting, it was one of the most exuberant compliments she'd ever been paid.

HALF-A-SET: *Want to make this a video chat?*

* * *

Keenan bought some time saying she had to take Bennie out. In truth, she'd hurriedly straightened up her kitchen and living area, and changed into a clean polo shirt and shorts. Even Bennie got a brush-up. She finished to find Gianna standing by on WhatsApp.

"Hey, is this good?" Gianna asked, her voice surprisingly deep and throaty. "Can you hear me okay?"

"I hear you fine." Based on nothing at all, she'd expected Gianna to sound soft and demure. Perhaps it was her girlish name, or the emotional dependence she described with her brother. Stupid, sexist stereotyping, she grudgingly admitted to herself. "This was a great idea, especially since I've gone all day without talking to anyone. Unless you count Annabel's ghost and Bennie."

"Where is this famous Bennie?"

"Ah, the *real* reason you wanted to video chat."

"Heh, my secret's out. I have a crush on your dog."

"Don't worry, I'm used to it." She moved from the kitchen bar to the couch, where Bennie immediately climbed into her lap. "Meet Bennie McEvoy. He's the center of attention everywhere we go. As it should be."

"Oh my God, he's so cute."

She explained how Bennie came into her life. "His mom's a toy poodle. The poor girl basically lived her whole life in a cage, birthing one litter after another. Now she's living her best life with Brady and his husband, the princess she was meant to be. Little pink toenails, bows on her head."

Gianna fussed over Bennie and his cuteness as he tried to lick the phone.

"Looks like you're downtown. I see a building in the reflection behind you."

Gianna turned her phone around to share what appeared to be a majestic river view after sunset. "I probably should have asked where you lived. I'm going to feel ridiculous hanging out on WhatsApp if you're down the hall."

"No worries there. I'm in the 'burbs. Westwood."

"Westwood...swanky."

"Yeah, I'm all about the swank. I try not to brag...since I happen to live in my parents' basement."

"Hmm." Gianna cocked her head. "Oh-kay."

"Now, now, don't judge. I moved back home after Annabel. We lived in Mt. Washington but I couldn't bring myself to stay there anymore. Hell, I could hardly dress myself, let alone take care of a house."

"Of course, I get it. Sorry I made fun."

Keenan played it back in her head and realized she'd probably come off as too defensive. "No, you're fine. Honestly, I didn't intend to stay here this long. But with Covid dragging on so long, I couldn't get motivated to get out there and find a new place. I bet it's fun living downtown."

She listened with envy as Gianna described a hip urban lifestyle that included concerts in the park and meeting friends for happy hour. "To be honest though, most nights I come home and crash."

Gianna then described her work as regional account manager of her family's healthcare supplies company, a job that had her out of the office on the road a few days every month. It sounded interesting until the part about the glass ceiling.

"TriState. You're the blue and white bins, right? I've been unpacking those at the dental clinic since I was a kid."

"Are you kidding me? I probably packed them back then."

They talked until long after dark without even a moment's lull, comparing music and streaming interests. From there they spoke of college, work and family. It was especially poignant to hear Gianna talk about growing up with Gabe, though she never broached the subject of his death. Nor did Keenan offer up any details of Annabel's suicide.

Touching on the subject of past relationships, she learned Gianna had been in three she considered significant, the most serious with a woman named Jazmine, whom she now considered her best friend. And who apparently was complicating her life.

"Long story. I'll spare you the details."

"No way. I want the A-version with *all* the details."

Gianna groaned. "It's a total train wreck. Where do I even start?"

"Day one."

"Day one was ninth grade. Gabe and I both were fed up with Catholic school so that year we started at Allderdice High. I didn't know that many people there but Jaz was in a couple of my classes and we hit it off. It dawned on us pretty quickly what we had in common, since we were the only girls who weren't drooling over pimply-faced football players."

Keenan was envious to hear they'd discovered their sexuality at such an early age. Her own high school years had been filled with awkward, frustrating dates with boys as she tried to figure things out.

"We started dating, Jaz and me. My parents lost their freaking minds but convinced themselves it was just a phase. I was getting decent grades and working after school at the warehouse, so they decided to ignore it. But then our junior year"—she winced as if embarrassed—"Jaz got caught with cocaine in the school bathroom. Just a tiny amount but zero tolerance, yada yada, so they got the police involved. She got sent to an alternative school. They stuck her in a diversion program with counseling and community service. But no jail, no fine. She wasn't allowed to contact anyone from our school so we broke up, much to my parents' delight. We stayed friends under the radar."

"I think all parents freak out when it comes to drugs. If they had any idea how easy it was to get drugs at school, we all would have been homeschooled."

"Isn't that the truth! Anyway, after Jaz I was with a woman named Vanessa for a couple of years when I was at Pitt, then with Kaitlyn for about a year. Both of them ended up going to grad school somewhere else. I stayed here and took over the warehouse. Once Jaz got her record expunged, she was looking for a job so I hired her to pack bins. Eventually we started dating again. Got an apartment together, the first time I ever lived with someone."

"How old were you?"

"Mmm…twenty-five?"

By that age, Keenan and Annabel had been living together six years, with Annabel working full-time at a pediatric clinic while Keenan finished her last two years of dental school.

"But after a couple of years we broke up again over something to do with work. Which was my fault because I shouldn't have been her girlfriend *and* her boss in the first place. Then I moved from running the warehouse to account manager, and eventually we got back together. Second apartment. Things were good. After the Supreme Court said gays could get married, Jaz was ready to do it that day, but then…" Her voice had suddenly become somber, and she drew a deep breath as if reluctant to go on.

"Hey…I get it already. Something really bad happened and blew it all to hell. Whatever it was, you don't need to relive it for my benefit."

Gianna laughed softly. "That's a pretty good summary. The B-version, as you'd call it, is she got arrested with cocaine again, but you're right, I don't want to relive it right now. One of these days maybe. It's one of those secrets you keep so people won't find out how stupid you are."

Remarkably, whatever humiliation she'd suffered hadn't been enough to make her stop caring about the woman she still called her best friend.

"That was three years ago, right before Covid. We broke up—for good this time. Her probation officer made her move back home with her mom. TriState kept her on so she wouldn't go to jail, but I refused to have anything to do with her. Then a year ago, Gabe happened." She wiped her eyes as her voice grew stronger. "My mom totally shut down. She's like a zombie. And my dad, a week after the funeral he's back to normal. Hardly ever says his name. Jaz was the only person I could talk to."

"Gianna, I am so sorry. I can't imagine having to go through losing Annabel without my family there every step of the way. I'm glad Jaz was there for you."

"Yeah, she's a true friend, I'll give her that. I'm always going to love her and care what happens to her, but the romantic feelings aren't there anymore. I'll never trust her again."

Keenan gave her a moment to say more if she wanted, recognizing that she didn't know enough about their obviously complicated relationship to offer an opinion beyond what she'd already said.

"I'm really glad you joined the forum, Gianna. You'll find some really nice people there if you need someone else to talk to…including me. And if you're ever in the mood to sit around with a furry ball of comfort in your lap, say the word. We deliver."

Gianna's weak smile was unsettling, a likely sign she was disappointed that Keenan had circled back to the forum and support for her loss. It was a clumsy end to a two-hour chat in which they both had shown interest in getting to know each other beyond the group. Keenan couldn't let her leave thinking she only wanted to be forum friends.

"This was so much fun, Gianna. It's the first time in two years I've talked to anybody this long that it wasn't all about grief. Seriously, this was awesome."

"Same here."

"Maybe next time we can do it in person?"

"I'd love that." Gianna grinned this time, obviously pleased.

They left it with a promise to follow up in a couple of days.

After signing off, Keenan fussed playfully over Bennie while admitting to herself that her excitement had less to do with him than with Gianna. For the first time since Annabel died, she found herself interested in someone.

CHAPTER SIX

Years ago, Keenan's father had set up a picnic table in a shady spot beside the gentle creek that flowed behind their dental clinic. Or *crick*, as they called it in Pittsburgh. She'd been forced to unlearn that pronunciation when she got to Ohio State, along with a few other expressions unique to western Pennsylvania.

Brady had stopped by in his police cruiser with a couple of hoagies she'd bought online for him to pick up. He sat atop the table with his feet on the bench. "Earth to Keenan."

"Oh, sorry. I was just remembering how when I moved to Columbus I had to start saying creek instead of crick. When we moved back here, Annabel told me she'd leave the only home she'd ever known, she'd even start rooting for the Steelers, but she would *never* use the word yinz for you guys."

"I don't know, we made a yinzer out of Chad and he's from South Carolina. And he *loves* calling people jagoffs. She probably would've come around too."

"Maybe so." She smiled wistfully at the memory, one of the rare moments of humor in their last year together. "She tried so hard, Brady. Exercise, medication. I don't think I gave her enough credit for all the work she put into trying to get better."

Other than Keenan's mom, Brady had probably logged more hours than anyone listening to her sorrow. He and Chad were the only ones outside her family who knew the horrid details of that day and the ugly events leading up to it.

Brady said, "You know, my job has me pretty well trained to go after people who steal stuff, or who sell drugs or assault somebody. But hardly anybody on the force feels equipped to handle people having a mental health crisis."

"Looking back on it, I think Annabel did the best she could."

"So did you, Keenan. There probably wasn't anything you could have done to stop what happened."

She was slowly coming around to that belief. Hearing Gianna talk about her guilt made her realize how arrogant they were to believe they could have willed Annabel and Gabe to live. She'd heard that assertion repeatedly from her therapist and those closest to her, but it only hit home when she saw it in someone she'd begun to care about.

"If I haven't said this enough, Brady, I really appreciate you. Not just for all the stuff with Annabel or for bringing me this little sweetie pie." She leaned under the table and fed Bennie a bit of kibble from a plastic bag she carried everywhere. "You're a good person. I'm proud to have you as a friend."

"Stop…you're making me blush." He flipped a sliver of salami to Bennie, whose leash was looped around the table's leg.

"I know, it's cute. And stop giving my dog people food."

"Are you going to tell me what this is about? Don't get me wrong, I'm always happy to pick up a free lunch, but this has ulterior motive written all over it."

He knew her too well. "Fine, Sherlock. I wanted to get your honest take on something. I can't ask Mom. She's too big a cheerleader and I know what she'll say."

"You've got me curious. Shoot."

"It's an easy question, really. How do you think I'm doing?"

Easy or not, it appeared to catch him off guard. "Why ask me? You know yourself better than anybody."

"Yeah, you'd think that. But I might be biased. I'm asking you because of that talk we had about a year ago. You said I was—"

"Checking all the boxes, I remember. You were seeing a counselor, you signed up for that support group…"

"And I got Bennie in the therapy dog program so we could start getting out to meet people." She'd argued at the time that all this was proof she'd recovered, ready to begin her life anew. "Come to think of it, I was feeling pretty good about myself back then."

He laughed. "Till I came along and pointed out you were faking it. You couldn't name a single person from that dog class. Not one!"

Because she'd barely spoken to anyone. "Come on, it wasn't exactly group therapy. I was there to train Bennie."

"And when I asked what advice from your therapist you found most helpful you looked at me like I was talking French."

"I speak a little French, I'll have you know." She couldn't resist sticking out her tongue. "See, this is why I'm asking you now. You see things other people don't. Hell, you see things *I* don't. So again, how am I doing?"

He studied her with one eye closed, a skeptical look if she'd ever seen one. "I think you're probably better."

"Probably?"

"You're still hiding stuff, Keenan. Like whenever dispatch comes over the radio and freaks you out. You did it when it squawked just a minute ago. I get it, you're remembering all those cruisers at the house that day. What I don't get is why you feel like you have to go somewhere and hide while you talk yourself down. It makes me wonder what else you're hiding."

"You're right, it still sets my teeth on edge, but that's basically the only thing that still triggers me." She stared at her folded hands as she told him of her visit to the cemetery. "I'm not going to be mad at her anymore, Brady. I don't believe she was taking the coward's way out. I'm not saying it was right, but for her it was a completely rational choice."

"Because she hurt so much."

"Exactly. I don't think any of us can imagine her pain. I was absolutely gutted by it, but I don't think it was even a fraction of what she felt. That kind of betrayal from her own mother... who gets over it? So I forgave her. What choice did I have? Now I feel like I can finally get on with my life."

After a long, penetrating silence, Brady cleared his throat. "If that's where you are...then I think you're doing just fine, kid."

She smiled and leaned into his knee affectionately. "I'm older than you...*kid*."

Her intention today had been to tell him about Gianna and ask if he thought she was strong enough emotionally to start dating again. It truly was a question only she could answer.

* * *

It was all Gianna could do to keep her mind on work today, with her thoughts darting back to Keenan. Her impression after their video chat had surprised her. Keenan was nothing like the stylish femmes she'd dated before. None of them had her sweet personality. It was nice to meet someone whose first thought was helping others.

"Are you following me, Gianna?" the voice on the phone asked.

She snapped her attention back to work, adjusting her headset to hear more clearly and explain TriState's new product policy. The split screen on her computer reminded her she was speaking with the procurement manager at the regional hospital in Fairmont, West Virginia, Amanda Biggerstaff.

"We're dropping their whole IV line, Amanda. Effective immediately. We're just getting too many complaints about leakage and broken valves. We still offer six other brands, all of them more expensive, unfortunately. But after you factor in spoilage and the time you spend changing out a damaged IV, you're probably better off spending a little more anyway."

If it were up to Gianna, she'd drop all the discount lines. The vast majority of customer complaints arose from cheap medical supplies. They just didn't perform as well as the tried-and-true brands, like Bryson or McKesson.

Her cell phone chimed with several text messages but she resisted checking it while Amanda worried aloud about costs. "Our budget's fixed for the year. I'll need to make adjustments somewhere."

"You might be able to offset it with wound care supplies. I can send over some recommendations. Check your inbox by close of business today. I'll give you another call on Thursday and we can talk about replacements."

As they ended the call, she notched a checkmark for Fairmont and opened the file for her next customer, the health department in Clarksburg. She was about to place the call when she remembered the text. Three of them, all from Jaz.

You need to come over to the warehouse asap!

Rudy's supposed to be supervising but he's out on the dock checking bins! There all just sitting around on their asses for an hour like its break time.

Pls don't say I texted you.

Gianna went to her window, which looked out on the loading bays. One had a panel truck backed up for loading, its driver out front waiting for the signal to roll. At the farthest bay, several of the crew were sitting outside on an open dock, laughing and smoking.

It was late in the day for a delivery truck to be going out, which probably meant someone had screwed up the morning's order and the driver had brought it back to restock. Rudy, who was Uncle Jack's handpicked hire as Stefan's assistant, had been left in charge while Stefan was on his honeymoon. Rudy could have delegated the task of checking the bins to one of the crew, but he probably felt responsible since the error had happened on his watch.

She acknowledged the text and considered whether to respond. It probably wasn't the emergency Jaz made it out to be, but there was no excuse for the crew to be goofing off while Rudy was making good on an order. A surprise visit from the office would let them know someone was watching.

Trish exited the ladies' room and stopped her in the hallway. "Where are you going in such a hurry?"

"Jaz texted from the warehouse. The mice are playing while the cat's away."

"Hmm…I thought Jack left Rudy in charge."

"He did, but apparently Rudy's busy fixing an order."

"Gianna"—Trish released a frustrated sigh—"this is exactly what I was talking about at the wedding. You can't go running every time Jaz calls."

"This isn't about Jaz," she snapped, immediately regretting her tone. "I can see it from my window. There's a bunch of guys hanging out in the bay. They're supposed to be packing tomorrow's orders and setting them out to load." She didn't appreciate that Trish was making her defend herself. "You know, if Jack wanted the warehouse to run the way it's supposed to while Stefan's gone, he would have put Jaz in charge. She knows it better than anyone out there."

"Except we both know those guys won't listen to her."

Gianna felt her face getting hot with the same rage she'd felt listening outside her father's office. "Then they ought to find a job somewhere else, Trish. The only reason they get away with this shit is because we don't put up a big enough fight. TriState's not a democracy, and if I'm ever…" She didn't have the stomach to finish, since her chances of being in charge someday were slim.

"You're right, go! Kick their asses for me too."

Now steaming mad, Gianna bypassed the elevator and took the stairs to the side exit that would allow her to cross the lot and enter the back of the warehouse without being seen. On any given day, the crew numbered about thirty, men and women, most in their twenties and thirties. She recorded the scene on her phone as she walked by rows of towering shelves, counting only six workers pulling orders—all of them women. The first group of men she spotted were in Stefan's office crowded around his computer monitor, yucking it up over something on the screen. Coming up behind them, it took her only a moment to realize they were watching porn.

No one noticed her until she icily said, "Give me one good reason why I shouldn't fire everyone in this room."

Her appearance set off a scramble for the door despite the fact that her video had them identified dead to rights. When she pressed escape to close their file, it collapsed into a folder marked "Urgent Care Vendors." A quick perusal revealed loads of similar videos, with last-used dates going back a year. Stefan's office, Stefan's computer…Stefan's porn.

From there she marched to the last bay of the loading dock, catching more than a dozen slackers. "I assume all of you are clocked out?"

The foot shuffling started immediately as the group headed back inside en masse.

"That's what I thought," she called after them. "Your coworkers could use a hand packing bins for tomorrow."

One of the women who'd worked there for years grumbled something about Jaz under her breath as she walked by.

"Look up, Katie." Gianna pointed toward the building. "I saw you from my window."

Her next stop was the bay where the truck was being loaded. She crossed the ramp into the truck and was greeted by three inches of Rudy's butt crack as he crouched over several open bins, shifting items between them. A scanner gun was on the floor between his feet.

"Hey, what's up?"

He sprang to his feet and took a step toward her as if to block her from walking deeper into the truck. "Gianna…just one of those days. Orders get fucked up, stuff gets put in the wrong bins. You know what it's like."

"Oh yeah, I remember. That's why we went digital. But you shouldn't be the one out here mopping up. You're the boss this week."

He wiped his neck with a bandana and grinned sheepishly. "You know what they say. You want something done right, do it yourself. I'm just trying to get this truck back out on the road."

"I get it. I figure that's why you're out here working late some nights. We appreciate the extra effort."

"Gotta stay on top of it."

"That's why I came to talk to you. I looked down from my office and saw a bunch of your crew goofing off down at bay nine. I came over to tell them to get their butts back to work and caught half a dozen more in Stefan's office watching porn."

He shook his head with disgust. "You'd think these guys could just do their jobs without their mama and daddy standing over them but obviously not. I'll straighten 'em out."

"All right, but make it quick and get these folks back to work." As she stepped off the truck, she noted the tag on one of the sealed bins. "This truck's for Butler Memorial. I'll tell Trish to reach out, say it's running late today."

"No need, Gianna. I already called Terry in Receiving, told him there's a minor issue. He knows to be on the lookout."

"Still, it's Trish's territory. She might want to touch base." After one last glance she added, "You know, we paid a lot of money for the inventory software so we wouldn't keep having these screwups. It would help a lot if yinz used the scanners when you packed the bins."

Walking back through the warehouse, she gave a small nod to Jaz, who was sitting behind her worktable in a corner of the cavernous space. No matter how much she annoyed Stefan or Jack, neither of them could fault her work ethic or her dedication to the company. Stefan in particular could take a lesson.

* * *

Keenan and her mom had commandeered the dining room table for their thousand-piece jigsaw puzzle of a Thomas Kincaid cottage. Her father sat nearby with his laptop.

"Do yinz want to stay in the parking lot at the fairgrounds?" he asked. "It says here they'll have a water truck and electricity. Or I can make a reservation at the RV park. It's about twenty minutes away. Your call, Connie. Doesn't matter to me one way or the other."

She looked at Keenan, her head cocked to elicit an opinion. "Don't ask me. I'm just along for the ride."

This would be their second trip to Big Stone Gap in southwest Virginia, the first one two years ago right after Keenan and Annabel had moved to Pittsburgh. This clinic was dental services only so they wouldn't have to compete with other medical professionals for space and resources. Still, these rural destinations usually had few options for overnight lodging so her father had rented an RV. Keenan was secretly convinced that was his real motivation for doing the rural clinics, so he could try out different RV models in preparation for buying one when they retired. After the clinic, they were taking a week to check out a lakeside campground near Roanoke, which meant Keenan would have to follow along in her car so she could come back to Pittsburgh for work.

Her mom shrugged. "I'd just as soon stay at the fairgrounds. It's not as if we'll have time to do anything but eat and sleep."

"What kind of RV did you get, Dad?"

"Just a twenty-footer. But it's got a toilet and shower. And there's a fridge, a cooktop and a microwave." That meant they could pack their own food instead of eating six straight meals from a volunteer-provided buffet of scrambled eggs or barbecue and baked beans. "Bunkbeds in the back, so there's an extra bunk if Cassidy decides to go."

"Cassidy's a no for that weekend," her mom said. "She has to babysit her brother's kids. Too bad, 'cause we could always use another dental assistant."

The McEvoys had taken part in humanitarian projects for as long as Keenan could remember. She'd started in her teens once she'd gotten some training in her after-school job as a dental assistant. For a while, they'd traveled abroad with a global relief organization, but after withdrawing from the Ecuador trip, they decided to stick closer to home. No matter, since there was plenty of need in Appalachia.

"I think I'm with Mom on this. That's about a seven-hour drive. We don't want to get in late and have to check in and set up. And it's better to wake up and be right there, especially if we're starting at six a.m. like we did last time."

Her dad closed his laptop and announced it was time for *NCIS*, which he hadn't missed in its nineteen-year run.

Keenan wondered how much longer they'd do these pop-up clinics as a family. Pulling twenty-two hours on a weekend wore her out. The physical strain had to be even harder on her parents.

The challenge was more than physical for Keenan, who faced an onslaught of memories each time they went out. The first time her parents had met Annabel, it was at a clinic near Zanesville, Ohio. She and Annabel had used it as a chance to rack up community service points toward their respective degrees. Keenan remembered like it was yesterday sitting in the break tent with her mom at the Muskingum County Fairgrounds, telling her Annabel was the one. Happy times, now buried deep so she wouldn't slip into longing and sorrow.

Right on schedule, the click of toenails on the hardwood floor announced the arrival of Bennie, who must have sensed her sudden melancholy. At times he knew her better than she knew herself. She hoisted him onto her lap and scratched his ears as he licked her chin. "My sweet boy."

"It's too bad we can't take Bennie," her mom said as she placed six fitted pieces of the thatched roof inside the puzzle's border. "He'd be a big help with the kids. So many of them come in there scared half to death."

"No can do. I'd never be able to keep up with him with that many people around. Besides, Brady and Chad are already stoked about dog sitting. You can imagine how much the dogs love playing together."

"You tell Brady I saw him out there in the yard today. Big baby. I haven't forgotten he missed his last cleaning. He'll lose those pretty teeth if he doesn't take care of them."

Pretty teeth made her think of Gianna. So did lots of other things.

CHAPTER SEVEN

After twenty minutes at a quick pace, Gianna dropped the speed on her elliptical, prompting Jaz to lower her speed on the treadmill. On rainy days such as this one, she sometimes invited Jaz to work out with her in the fitness center of her apartment building. Today she had an ulterior motive—breaking the news to Jaz that she'd met someone she might start dating. She hoped being in a public place would cut down on the possible fireworks.

Jaz hadn't yet given her an opening. She'd been grousing nonstop about the misery of sharing a bedroom with her thirty-year-old sister. "It feels like I'm back in junior fucking high. Sabrina makes me turn off the light at ten o'clock no matter what I'm doing. Just because she has to be at work at six o'clock doesn't mean I don't get to have a life. But if I don't turn it off, she screams bloody murder so Mom will hear, and then Mom yells at me for starting a fight."

Gianna had heard it all before and always gave the same advice. "If I were you I'd clean out that room in the basement, fix it up like an apartment. You'd have your own bathroom down there. Get a couch, a TV, a fridge. There's even a private entrance so they don't know when you're coming or going."

"Ugh. It's like a cave down there. Besides, only losers live in their parents' basement."

Gianna smiled but stopped herself from saying she knew one who wasn't a loser. "It's not just losers, Jaz. Everybody faces hardship at one time or another. Financial, emotional, health-related...whatever. You're lucky you have a family who can give you a place to go."

"It's not like they gave me a choice," she grumbled. "But I'll be off probation in December so I won't have to live with Mom anymore after that. If I could move to an apartment like yours all the sacrifice would totally be worth it, you know?"

As soon as they'd broached the subject, Gianna knew exactly where the conversation was headed. Anticipating Jaz's inevitable question, she dialed her elliptical speed back up, knowing Jaz would follow suit and they'd both be too breathless to talk. It worked for all of three and a half minutes before Gianna's lungs were screaming for air.

"Why do you...do that to me...beeyotch?" Jaz shut hers down and stepped off, while Gianna slowed for a cooldown. After a long swig from her water bottle, Jaz picked up where she'd left off, still gasping. "I was thinking...your rent here's like...fifteen hundred, right? That's a little out of my league, but I might could swing eleven. Maybe twelve if I cut back on some other shit. They've got some two-bedrooms here that are only twenty-four. What if we—"

Never. Gianna hopped off her machine, shaking her head.

"Come on, Gi. I'm talking roommates, nothing else. I'll take the little bedroom, and I promise to keep the whole place clean...and do all the laundry too. I did that when we lived together, remember?"

There was nothing Jaz could possibly say that would persuade Gianna to take her on as a roommate. "We're both past the roommate stage, Jaz. You need your own apartment, whatever you can afford. I like having a place that's all mine, where I can have someone over and not have to worry that it's going to bother somebody else."

It was the perfect segue for the conversation she needed to have. The mere mention of her seeing someone else would no doubt ignite Jaz's jealous streak, but she was girded to hold her ground regardless of Jaz's reaction.

As she toweled off, her phone vibrated with a text message.

On my way to Carnegie Library at West End with Bennie for Paws to Read. Could be done by 8 but can't promise. Your call.

Gianna studied the text for a hidden message in response to her invitation. Did Keenan want to come over or was she just trying to be accommodating? It was Friday already and they hadn't yet found time to meet in person, twice because of Keenan's pet therapy commitments and twice because Gianna had to see clients in West Virginia and didn't get home until evening. Tonight was doable, it appeared, but iffy. Gianna wanted more than a tired visit at the end of a long day. She tapped back her answer. *Let's just make it Sunday at the health fair 4 sure. I'll come to your booth.*

Perfect! I'm there from noon to 2.

"Who you texting?" Jaz asked, craning her neck to get a peek at Gianna's phone. "If that's Shanice, tell her I got a Groupon at that nails place if she wants to go tomorrow."

She hesitated, pretending to read. Once Jaz knew she was talking to Keenan, she'd want to know every detail, including questions Gianna couldn't yet answer. "It's that woman from the support group I told you about. We've been trying to get together this week but looks like it's not happening tonight."

"Get together for what? Yinz gonna start having meetings in person?" There would be no end to her questions as long as she drew breath.

"I don't know about the group. I think some of them are meeting up but we've been trading private messages online. The other night we chatted for a couple of hours on WhatsApp. We were going to try to meet for a drink or something tonight but she's busy."

The inevitable conversation was officially underway, and if Jaz's sour frown was any indication, it promised to be difficult. Gianna couldn't avoid it any longer, especially now that the table was set.

Pressing the button for the elevator, she asked, "You want to come up for a bite? Trish brought me half a quiche. Apparently Greg's one of those manly men who won't eat it. You'd be doing me a favor so I won't have to eat it three nights in a row."

"Yeah, sure." The invitation did nothing to quell Jaz's obvious suspicion. "Mom's making that disgusting bean soup with spinach. I saw her put it in the crockpot."

"Yum. I love that."

"Good, I'll bring you a gallon." In a clear sign she was agitated, Jaz poked the button for their floor again and again. "What's up with this person you're texting with? Is she, like, your sponsor or something?"

Gianna didn't dare laugh. "We don't have sponsors. It's not that kind of group. People just talk about what they're going through and try to help each other cope."

"You can talk to me anytime, Gi. I knew Gabe and I know you. That has to count for a lot."

"It does, seriously. But it's nice to talk to somebody who's had more time to process their grief so I can know what to expect. Like the fact that the first year's the hardest. First birthday, first Christmas, so on."

"I coulda told you that. That's why I got the girls together on your birthday."

"Yeah, that was good."

Once inside her apartment, she went to work immediately on dinner, wrapping the quiche in foil for the oven and assembling the ingredients for a salad. Jaz took a seat at the kitchen bar and began scrolling through her phone.

"What's she like, this woman? How do you know she's even real? Creeps sometimes hang out on those sites trying to scam people. Like, they ask you to send them money and stuff."

"I told you, we did a video chat. I saw her."

"Yeah, but that doesn't mean anything. She could be anywhere."

"She's in Westwood across the river. Don't be so suspicious. I'm not stupid, you know." She decided not to admit she was the one who reached out to Keenan, not the other way around. "You want pine nuts in your salad?"

"I don't care," she replied sharply, now furiously scrolling. "What's this for, you meeting up with her? How old is she? What's she like?"

Gianna continued with dinner prep, which meant she could talk without actually having to make eye contact. "She's about our age…very nice. And she's gay. Her partner committed suicide a couple of years ago. That's why she's on the forum."

"Talk about a big red flag," Jaz muttered.

"What a horrible thing to say!" She whirled and slapped both hands on the counter. "That's so unfair. You must think it's my fault too that Gabe died."

"I'm not saying it about you."

"You should *never* blame the people left behind, Jaz. The world's already dumped enough shit on their heads. Either they didn't see it coming, or they saw it coming and couldn't stop it."

"Fine." She went back to her phone.

"What's so fascinating on your phone?"

"Nothing," Jaz said as she laid it face down on the counter. "What is it with this woman, Gianna? Are you going out with her or what?"

"We're meeting up…if we can ever get on the same page. That's all." Given Jaz's already surly mood, she briefly considered playing it down. That would only postpone this unavoidable confrontation. "If we like each other and it has the right vibe, then we might have a couple of dates to see what it's about."

Jaz's eyes went wide with fear. "Wait, they say you shouldn't do that with somebody from your group, that it's like a crutch. The thirteenth step, they call it."

"This isn't like your Narcotics Anonymous, Jaz. It's a support group, not an addiction group. We're not trying to stop ourselves from doing something. It's fine for us to be friends."

"But it's still about the group. Whatever it is you're feeling with this chick, it ain't real."

"I'm not really feeling anything…I barely know her. But I like her enough that I want to get to know her better."

"Why do you want to be with somebody else when I'm sitting right here? You and me, Gi"—she waved her hand between them—"we already have that vibe you're talking about. Always have, always will."

Gianna shook her head, not vehemently but resolute. "We used to have it, Jaz. But that's over now. Come on, we've been through this."

Jaz folded her arms defiantly, her face flushed with unshed tears. "Don't do this, Gianna. For chrissakes, all our friends. It's gonna be so fucking humiliating if you start showing up with somebody else. Is that what you want? To rub my nose in how I'm just your *friend*?" She said it as if it were a childish insult. "Fuck that shit."

Gianna pulled a bar stool over to sit beside her. "I'm sorry if this hurts you. It probably feels like I've sprung it on you and that's my fault. I've been saying for a while that I wanted to start dating again. But I never followed through, so I can see why you might think I wasn't serious about actually doing it. What with Covid, and then work's been really busy this year…" No, she needed to be honest. "But I guess the main reason is I hadn't met anyone interesting until now."

"I can't believe you went behind my back like this."

"What the—" Gianna checked herself before she got angry. "Just because I kept something private doesn't mean I went behind your back. I know this is hard to hear, but you don't have a right to know everything I'm doing. God, you make it sound like I'm cheating or something."

Jaz jabbed her in the shoulder with an index finger. "You belong with me, Gi. Your heart knows it no matter what you try to tell yourself. There's never gonna be anyone who'll love you as much as I do. And I'm never gonna love anybody else—period."

"I know you believe that. We've been through a lot together, and I love you—really. But it's not the kind of love you want. I just don't feel that way about us anymore. I'm sorry." She rested a hand on Jaz's shoulder and felt the tremor of a silent sob. "It's time to let go, Jaz. We can't tie each other up with false hopes that something will change because it won't…not for me."

"How do you know? Have you tried?"

"I don't *want* to try. We had some good times, but this isn't what I want anymore."

"*Good times*, huh? That's what you call it?" she spat with sarcasm. "And now you're just *done* with me?"

"I'm not done with our friendship. That part has always been rock-solid. But I can't keep using it to fill the gap while I wait for someone else to come along. That's not fair to either of us. If I gave you the impression there was still a chance for us to get back together, I was wrong."

With tears falling freely now, Jaz fired back, "I've been there every goddamn time you called, Gianna. Running to you like your stupid puppy dog. Don't pretend you're sorry, 'cause if you were truly sorry you wouldn't be doing this."

Gianna had practiced pieces of this conversation in her head, how Jaz had so much to offer the right person and that whoever won her heart would know what real love felt like. In the moment though, she didn't dare patronize her with the suggestion that she start looking for someone to date too.

"I've been spinning my wheels for three years, Jaz. I need to get on with my life. I can't just say it—I have to do it. I hope you can find a way to accept it so it doesn't hurt our friendship."

"Some friendship." Jaz buried her face in her hands and growled, "How much more do I got?"

"How much what?"

"You know, goddamnit. How much?"

"Oh…" The court-ordered restitution. "I haven't looked lately but I think it's down to nine hundred and change."

"That's why you've been stringing me along, isn't it? Pretending to be all nice and sweet. Because I still owe you money. Admit it, that's the real reason you won't let Stefan fire me. It's probably why you keep telling me I should live at Mom's—so I have enough to make restitution. I bet the second I pay you off"—she smacked her hands together—"I'll never even see you again."

"Jesus, Jaz. Do you have to keep dredging this up? I'm not the one who ordered you to pay me back. That was the judge." She was tired of having this conversation every time Jaz felt like wallowing in self-pity.

"Oh yeah? Then give it back to me. The court won't know the difference." She held out her hand. "You're always saying you forgive me. Go ahead, prove it. It's two thousand at least. Look at how much you spend on this place. I know you can afford it."

Beneath Gianna's cool facade she was seething. This game was familiar, with Jaz casting herself as a victim of Gianna's cruelty or neglect. For too long she'd responded patiently with reassurances, concessions and promises, knowing all along she was being manipulated but willing to do whatever it took to help Jaz through her ordeal. She'd seen for herself how little emotional support Jaz got from her family, with none of the financial advantages Gianna sometimes took for granted. At that moment, however, her game had become tiresome.

"I *did* forgive you, Jaz. I believed you were genuinely sorry, but every time you bring it up this way, it makes me wonder. You throw it around like you're being persecuted. You're not. You stole three thousand dollars out of my account and used it to buy drugs. Even when you got caught, you lied about where the money went. If you want to be forgiven, the least you could do is own up to it and show a little remorse. Anything less is just cheap words, like you're laughing at me behind my back for being such a sucker."

"How could you even think that? I love you, Gianna. I'd lay down my life for you." She sniffed loudly and clutched her head with both hands. "It's gonna break my fucking heart if you start seeing somebody else."

Whether deliberately or out of desperation, Jaz seemed determined to make this as difficult for Gianna as she possibly could.

"Look at me, Jaz." She gently pried her hands from her face and held them fast. "What we had together was special. Nobody can ever take that away. But now it's time to figure out what kind of friends we're going to be. You need to let go of us being anything else."

Jaz refused to meet her eye as tears streamed down her cheeks. "I can't, Gi."

"Yes, you can. We've already been doing it for the past three years, right?"

"*You* have. I only acted that way so I could still be with you, but I've still been in love with you the whole time."

Gianna sighed, admitting to herself that she'd known that all along. "I don't know what else to say, Jaz. Maybe we need some space for a while—"

"No! Please don't do that, Gi. I'll do whatever you want. Just don't push me away."

"If you mean that, here's what I want." Here was her chance to lay it out like she meant it. "I want us to be the kind of friends who cheer each other on. I'm so proud of you for staying clean... you have no idea. If you can do that, Jaz, you can do anything."

Jaz had yet to look at her but it was clear from the slight upturn of her lips that she relished the praise.

"But you have to accept once and for all—right here, right now—that friends is all you and I will ever be. Whatever dreams you have of us getting back together, it's never going to happen. I know it as sure as I know my name." She hated how cruel that sounded, but it had to be said. "I realized these last couple of weeks that I'm excited about dating again. You're my friend and I want you to be happy for me if I find somebody...just like I'll be happy for you. If you can't handle that, then we'll have to put some space there. I can't deal with you losing your shit if I go out with somebody."

"Fine," she snapped. "Just not this forum person. You don't need somebody else's misery in your life. You deserve a clean start."

Gianna considered letting that go since she planned to ignore it anyway. But as she went back to preparing their dinner, something told her not to let Jaz get away with dictating who was or wasn't acceptable. With her back to Jaz, she said, "I'm going to decide on my own what sort of person I need in my life, and right now, that's the woman from the forum. Her name's Keenan."

She wasn't entirely surprised when the door slammed behind her.

CHAPTER EIGHT

Keenan raised her face to the faint spray blowing through their covered booth, courtesy of the towering fountain at Point State Park where the Allegheny and Monongahela Rivers came together to form the Ohio. The fountain's mist was all that kept fairgoers from sweltering on an unseasonably warm fall afternoon. At least her two-hour shift would be over before the afternoon heat kicked in.

This was her first year at Pittsburgh's sprawling health fair, where she and other volunteers were helping raise awareness of the myriad ways certified pets could provide unique therapy to those in need of comfort and companionship. In between talking to visitors she watched for Gianna, who'd texted her earlier that she might be late.

"It's my turn to pet him," a girl of about four pleaded to her brother, who sat cross-legged on a mat with Bennie in his lap.

"You both can," Keenan said, dropping a second mat beside them. She let go of his leash, feeling sure she could collect him in a hurry if needed. "I've got some books you might like. Would you like to read to Bennie? He's a great listener."

As the child took her seat with a book, her brother scrambled across the booth to pet Murphy, a docile golden retriever handled by teen Jamie Haines. Jamie's father lingered in the background as Jamie patiently showed the boy how to win Murphy's attention.

"Your daughter's a natural, Mr. Haines," Keenan said. "I've run into her and Murphy a couple of times at the children's hospital. I can't think of many teenagers who'd give up their weekends to do what she does."

"It's personal for her. We had a visit from a therapy dog like Murphy when her mom was home with hospice three years ago. Meant a lot to her."

Keenan blinked back sudden tears triggered by her own path. "I got there kind of the same way. Dogs are angels when it comes to broken hearts."

Also in the booth today were Lola, a lively border collie still in training, and Zeus, a gorgeous chinchilla rabbit. No matter the company, Bennie always held his own. Not only was he small and soft, he relished the attention. Nursing home patients in particular lit up to see his tiny tail wag as they petted and cooed.

A commotion outside the booth announced the arrival of Duke, a gentle gelding from a therapy riding stable in nearby Butler County. Chestnut red with a white diamond on his forehead, Duke was a favorite at Oakberry Court, wandering the lawn on sunny days to nuzzle residents and eat bits of apple from their hands.

The little girl who'd been petting Bennie shot past on her way to join the growing crowd of spectators surrounding Duke. Keenan spun to secure Bennie before he followed and wandered under the horse's hooves. Instead, he'd turned his attention to a surprising newcomer.

"I take it this little cuddle machine is Bennie?"

"Gianna!"

"Keenan!" she mimicked with a grin. Somehow she'd sneaked into the booth and taken a seat in a folding armchair, offering her lap to Bennie. Unlike most fairgoers, she was dressed smartly in dark blue ankle pants and a white shirt, its sleeves rolled to her elbows.

"I was beginning to think you weren't coming."

"Sorry, we have a hospitality booth over by the Block House, and I couldn't leave until my cousin got there." That explained her business look.

"I should have realized you'd be here. D'oh, it's a health fair. You probably have customers all over the place."

"A few." Gianna tucked a fallen strand of glossy dark hair beneath the Versace sunglasses atop her head before nuzzling Bennie's snout. "None of them as sweet as this little guy. I think he likes me."

"He does, I can tell." She didn't have the heart to tell her Bennie treated everyone that way. "You got here just in time. My shift's up in about two minutes. Any chance you'd be up for a walk over to the Water Steps? It's probably Bennie's last chance to play before it turns cool." The cascading water feature was located across the Allegheny in North Shore Riverfront Park, an easy walk from the fair.

"Sounds like a plan." Still focused on Bennie, she asked, "Does this little guy have any idea how cute he is?"

"Considering how many times a day he hears it, I'll go with yes."

The booth suddenly bustled with the arrival of the last shift, which included another golden retriever and a pair of tabby siblings.

"That's our cue," Keenan said, scooping the children's books into a neat stack for the next person.

As they exited the park, she explained how libraries used therapy dogs to help children grow comfortable with reading aloud. "They're perfect listeners and they don't laugh when you make a mistake."

"I should borrow him so my cousin can practice giving his reports at our staff meetings. He leaves all of us scratching our heads." Nearing the Roberto Clemente Bridge at Sixth Street, Gianna hesitated. "My apartment's a couple of blocks from here. Mind if we take a side trip so I can change into something a little more casual? It's okay to bring Bennie. They allow pets. Or I could run up real quick and then meet you over there."

"No, we'll come up. I've been curious about these new apartment buildings downtown. Their ads are all over Facebook. It might even inspire me to leave the nest again."

They entered the lobby of an apartment tower on Seventh Street less than a block from the Andy Warhol Bridge, the second of Pittsburgh's suspension bridges across the Allegheny. Gianna led them into an elevator where she pressed a button for the sixth floor.

"You should have been here the other night for the fireworks when I told Jaz I was meeting up with you this weekend. Unless you're allergic to dyke drama, that is."

Dyke drama was the last thing Keenan wanted in her life, but she couldn't picture Gianna being the dramatic one. "Are you sure she understands the word ex?"

"I've sent her the memo plenty of times, but she keeps ignoring it."

At the end of a narrow hallway, Gianna swiped a keycard, opening the door to a corner apartment with hardwood floors, red brick walls and exposed ductwork along a high ceiling. The furnishings were modern, in muted colors that took nothing from the room's architecture. In a word, hipster.

"Oooh, nice." She held tight to Bennie's leash as he took in the new smells. It would be just her luck he'd hike his leg on the sectional sofa, despite never having done such a thing. "This is exactly the sort of place I pictured you living in."

"Oh yeah? Why's that?"

"Just an impression. Urban chic."

Gianna cocked her head and nodded. "Yeah, that sums it up pretty well. It's kind of small but I like it." A tour through the entire apartment took only a few steps: a black granite counter with stools that served as a dining table and divided the living area from the kitchen, and a bedroom with a walk-in closet and bath.

"My basement cave isn't much bigger than this and it definitely doesn't have the wow factor." She followed to the small balcony where Gianna had been sitting for their call. It faced northwest overlooking the third bridge, the Rachel

Carson. "I'm getting a serious case of apartment envy. This is fantastic."

"Thanks. I took one look and wrote them a check. I always wanted to live near the center of the hive so I could walk to places like Market Square and the North Shore. There's concerts, sports…practically anything you'd want right out the door. And the Heritage Trail—a great place to rollerblade. Plus this building has all the usual amenities: a fitness room, dry cleaning service, a rooftop bar you can rent out for parties."

Keenan instantly saw the appeal and tried to imagine herself in such a place. She and Annabel had gone straight from their shabby student apartment to a three-bedroom starter home in one of Columbus's middle-class neighborhoods. Had she moved downtown after Annabel died instead of back with her parents, she might actually have a social life beyond the folks she met fleetingly through her outings with Bennie.

"Sometimes I feel like I'm living inside a dating app," Gianna said. "I steer clear of the happy hours up on the roof so I don't get hit on by guys. Speaking of happy hour…you want a drink or something?"

"No, I'm good. Bennie would take some water though. I brought his bowl."

"Help yourself while I change."

She fished a collapsible bowl from her backpack and filled it from the sink while Bennie danced with excitement. "It's just water, Bennie. Try not to lap it all over this nice lady's floor."

"Don't worry about it," Gianna called from beyond the open bedroom door. "My cleaning lady comes on Mondays. And yes, I just admitted to being too lazy to clean seven hundred square feet."

"It's okay, I get it. My parents won't take rent money so I got a housekeeper to do the whole house once a week. I pretend it's for them."

Gianna reappeared, now wearing a blue Pitt T-shirt with yellow running shorts. She'd swapped her Versaces for wraparound sports shades. "All set. Do I look like the Facebook ad?"

"Exactly." She looked amazing, trim with well-toned legs. Little wonder she got hit on. Her looks weren't the only thing Keenan found attractive. Gianna had an air of self-confidence that was captivating.

* * *

Dozens of pleasure boats—from kayaks to pontoons to river yachts—dotted the waters below the Andy Warhol Bridge. A perfect Sunday outing, Gianna thought, mentally chiding herself for not taking advantage of the perks of living downtown, the very ones she'd been bragging about.

"That trip you mentioned for the clinic, the one in Virginia? I might be able to help out."

"That would be awesome!" Keenan said as they strode across the bridge with Bennie in the lead. "If you want to come with us, I can definitely arrange it."

"Whoa! That's not what I had in mind. I was talking about sending supplies. We're discontinuing some of our discount lines so it's a good time to get rid of our inventory."

"That's too bad—no, I mean it's great. Supplies are always welcome. What I meant was we could use some volunteers with your kind of experience."

"What experience? I've never done anything like that in my life."

"Sure you have. You said you've been packing bins since you were a kid. So if I yelled for a double-ended curette, you'd know exactly what to bring me."

"True," Gianna conceded. "But you might be overestimating my usefulness. I've never had to work with actual patients. Sounds a little too adventurous for me. But I'll think about it."

"Fair enough. It's two weeks from now and we'd need to leave around ten o'clock on Friday morning, back on Monday afternoon."

"That could work actually. When would you have to know?"

"We've got the space, so anytime. Are you really interested?"

"Oddly I am. It sounds like a great experience. It's not something I'd do on my own but if I could tag along with people who'll tell me what to do, then sure, I'll consider it."

"Gianna, that would be so amazing."

As they descended the stairs to the waterfront walkway along the North Shore, Gianna's phone pinged, the fourth time since they'd left the apartment.

I see your car. Where ru?

"You aren't going to believe this. Jaz is in my parking garage trying to figure out where I could be if my car's there but I'm not answering my phone. She can't stand not knowing where I am." Under her breath she added, "Or who I'm with."

"That's a little creepy if you ask me. Sounds like you two need some space from each other."

"I couldn't agree more. She's already texted me half a dozen times this weekend acting like her little bitch-fest the other night didn't even happen. This morning she said to come over because her mom cooked something special just for me. I told her I was busy all day and she texted back how she hoped her mom's feelings wouldn't be hurt."

"Wow." Keenan visibly shuddered. "That's pretty manipulative."

"Yeah, but only if it works. I refuse to get sucked into any more of her games. My friend Trish from work, she says—" Gianna stopped abruptly. "What am I doing? You don't want to hear about Jaz. She's my problem, not yours. Let's talk about you."

"That's very sweet. But I want to talk about you too, and this is obviously on your mind."

"I don't want her on my mind." She gestured toward a kiosk advertising ice-cold drinks. "Wait here. You want one?"

"Sure, it's hotter out here than I thought."

As she waited for her credit card to go through for two bottles of water, she studied Keenan from afar. Five-six or seven, slim build with straight posture, short blond hair. From here one couldn't tell whether she was a woman or a man. But up close her delicate features made it obvious, as did her soft voice.

So different from Jaz, who was full-figured and into glorifying her femininity with makeup and accessories.

Keenan's appeal went well beyond her appearance. Her kindness and gentle manner were on display in everything she did. Gianna found it alluring.

She returned just as her phone dinged again.

I'm coming up.

"Oh great, now she's going to let herself into my apartment and wait for me." Heading off Keenan's judgment, she quickly added, "I know. You're thinking why does my ex have a key to my place. Because she's still my best friend. You'd give your best friend a key, right? How was I supposed to know she'd turn into a stalker?"

"Where did you leave things the other night?"

She related the gist of their argument, all the points she'd made to drive home the message that their romantic relationship was over but she hoped they'd always be friends. "I've said it all before. What's different this time is I told her I'd met someone I liked. That's you, by the way . . . in case you didn't catch that."

Keenan grinned and tugged on Bennie's leash. "Did you hear that, Bennie? The nice lady likes us."

Gianna felt a wave of excitement over having said it out loud. "Yes, the lady does."

"The feeling's mutual, isn't it, boy?" Bennie had spotted the Water Steps and was tugging at his leash. "We're not afraid of lunatic stalkers."

She appreciated that Keenan was able to joke about Jaz's horrid behavior. Or maybe she was laughing off real concern over what Jaz might do. "Sorry if this is freaking you out. I'm pretty sure she'll turn her temper on me, not you."

"I'm not worried. About the only thing I fear is a patient who tries to bite me while I'm checking their teeth. Other than that, Bennie helps modulate my freak-out scale."

It was at least the third time Keenan had invoked Bennie in her reply, like a reflex or defense mechanism. Gianna made a mental note to notice it going forward. For now, her giddy brain was celebrating the fact that this friendly walk was now a date.

The Water Steps were a jagged stack of blocks over which fresh water cascaded, forming small pools of varying depths until it drained at the bottom to be pumped back up. As usual for a summer day, kids splashed their way from top to bottom while adults perched along the side soaking their feet.

Keenan stopped to swap out Bennie's harness for a rainbow collar. He then wasted no time jumping into the lower pool, which was barely deep enough to reach his belly.

"Up here, boy," she said, tugging him up the step to a deeper pool. As he thoroughly soaked himself, she kicked her sandals to the side and waded in. "You coming?" she asked Gianna.

Gianna sat to remove her trainers and socks, then gingerly slid her feet into the cool water. "I can't count the times I've been by this place on skates. Today's the very first time I've ever put my feet in."

"Are you kidding me? What would be the point of living downtown if not to play in the Water Steps on a hot day? You have a civic duty to appreciate public parks."

"All right, already. I'm appreciating as fast as I can."

Trish said u left the booth 1 hour ago. Where r u?

She shoved her phone inside her shoe and sat down on a dry block by the edge. Bennie immediately splashed his way into her lap, where he shook himself before jumping back into the water. The three-second greeting left her soaked.

"Oops…sorry about that."

Gianna sneered and kicked a stream of water in Keenan's direction. "You are not."

"You're right, I'm not." Still holding Bennie's leash, Keenan picked her way over a small waterfall to sit on a concrete block across from Gianna. "I take it she's still texting."

She was surprised by Keenan's return to the subject. "She's trying to find me. It's infuriating that she won't leave me alone. If she thinks this stalking crap is going to make me want to come back, I've got news for her. It makes me want to run in the opposite direction."

"Obviously I don't know her like you do, but it sounds like she wishes she hadn't run off. Maybe she just needs some reassurance that things are still okay between you two."

"That depends on her definition of okay. If she's ready to accept our relationship has changed and it's never changing back, then yeah, we're okay." Gianna regretted the bitterness and sarcasm in her voice. "Do I sound like an asshole?"

"No, you sound frustrated. You have a right to be. Look, if you…"

"What?"

Keenan shrugged. "If it's really bothering you, why not text her to come over? It would put her mind at ease to see us just hanging out with Bennie. You'd be showing her that you aren't going to cut her out of your life. And you wouldn't have to worry about facing her when you got home."

"No, absolutely not." It was a gracious offer but Gianna was tired of placating Jaz. "In the first place, it's not up to me to put her mind at ease. She needs to face reality. Badgering me all day isn't going to change anything. If I text her now, she'll think all she has to do is keep it up and eventually I'll give in. That's not the message I want to send."

"Yeah, good point. You can't let her set the terms, not when you're trying to be friends and she's trying to get back something that's gone."

"Exactly. She can sit in my apartment and torture herself if that's her thing. I'm not going to let it ruin my day. Or Bennie's day either." She snapped her fingers to call him over, laughing to herself at how she too had used him to deflect, this time from a loose end to their conversation—*and in the second place*—which was that she was enjoying her time with Keenan way too much to let Jaz crash it.

Keenan tugged Bennie toward her and lifted him out of the falls onto the dry steps alongside, where he shook vigorously. "I can't let him get too tired splashing around or I'll have to carry him home—wet."

Gianna lumbered to her feet and bent to give him a scratch. She liked the feel of his soft tongue licking her fingers. Everything about Bennie was gentle. "I never would have guessed I'd like being around a therapy pet. He's so calming." Laughing, she added, "Maybe he's trying to tell me I need therapy."

"He's pretty good at taking the edge off a tough day. Just shoot me a text if you're ever in the mood for some canine company. We'll be right over."

"Careful what you ask for."

As they strolled back across the bridge toward home, Gianna played back the day's conversation in her head. Keenan had complimented *her* apartment and probed about *her* troubles with Jaz, all while giving away little about herself. Other than her mention of the clinic at Big Stone Gap, she'd mostly let Bennie carry her end of the conversation. Gianna couldn't say for sure it was by design, but it was clear she'd done a lousy job of getting Keenan to open up.

"I'm glad we finally got to meet in person," Keenan said. "I was pretty sure you weren't a Nigerian troll but it's nice to get confirmation."

"Ah, but I will gratefully share to you the proceeds of my inheritance if you would kindly provide your bank information," she replied, laughing. She crouched to pet Bennie. "I'm so glad I got to meet this little guy too. And I really apologize for all the interruptions from you-know-who."

"Hey, that's life. I don't envy the rest of your day though. Think she's up there watching us?"

"I doubt it. You can't see this bridge from my balcony." Gianna had an evil thought. "I should catch an Uber to her mom's house, see what she cooked for me."

"Man, that's cold. And kinda perfect."

They stopped when they reached the end of the bridge where Keenan would break off toward the city parking garage. Gianna was reluctant to see her leave but she couldn't very well invite her back up with Jaz waiting in her living room. "I was thinking...there's this Pride concert in the park next Friday night. One of the bands is VeraDid. It's a girl band. Their—"

"Yeah, I know all about VeraDid. Their new CD, *Once or Twice*." She seemed to recall that two of the band members were queer.

"That's right. A bunch of us were talking about meeting up. We bring chairs, blankets. You should come."

"Friday?" Keenan squinted, as if visualizing her schedule. "I may have something already, a Bennie visit. I'll try to reschedule though. You think it would be all right to bring him? He could use some practice being with crowds."

"Absolutely. My friends will love him. I'll text you the details." Before their goodbye could become awkward, Gianna leaned in and laid a quick kiss on Keenan's cheek. "Let's do the WhatsApp chat again too. I like talking to you."

"We'll be waiting, won't we, Bennie? We'll get all our arguments lined up to convince you to come with us to Big Stone Gap."

"It might not be necessary. I'm already leaning that way."

"Fantastic!" Keenan replied with a grin. "Come on, Bennie. Let's get out of here before she changes her mind."

Gianna was no psychologist, but it didn't take a trained eye to see that Bennie wasn't merely a therapy pet for others—he was also Keenan's emotional support. Whether she realized it or not, she used Bennie to buffer interactions. Whatever she was afraid of, Gianna felt an almost aching urge to help. So much that she'd all but promised to help out at a volunteer clinic in the wilds of Virginia. Something about Keenan had really made an impression. Or rather something made her want to impress Keenan.

Nearing the parking garage, she looked up just in time to see Jaz's faded red Toyota roll up to the exit. With a quick sidestep, she hid behind a van until it was gone.

CHAPTER NINE

Gianna waved to Stefan as he exited Uncle Jack's office. On just his third day back at work after his honeymoon, one would think he'd still be tackling the stack of work on his desk. She couldn't help being annoyed at how much time he spent in his dad's office instead of at the warehouse. It really wasn't her business—except screwups in the warehouse were everyone's business.

Summoned by text to Trish's office, she rapped lightly on her open door. "Hey, what's up?"

"Shut the door and get in here."

"Oh boy, somebody's got some good gossip."

Trish, looking casual in a denim shirtwaist dress, came around her desk and gestured toward the small round worktable she used as an overflow desk. "Not a word leaves this room, swear?"

Gianna hastily took a seat and folded her hands in anticipation. "Tell me everything."

"Guess who just got headhunted?"

The ramifications hit her all at once. "Forget it, you can't. Who was it? No, it doesn't matter. You can't leave, Trish. What did they offer? I'll tell Dad he has to match it."

Trish laughed. "Relax, I'm sure it was just a random call from somebody perusing the LinkedIn pages. They wouldn't say who the company was, just that the job was in the Phoenix area."

"Phoenix! Why would you want to go to Phoenix? It's hot as hell there. Doing what?"

"Regional accounts manager. Pretty much the same thing I'm doing now but with a larger area and"—she rattled a fake cough—"two full-time assistants. For a national health supplies company."

National. That probably meant somebody big, like Bryson Solutions or McKesson. Or Johnson & Johnson. It would be a lot more responsibility—but a hell of a career move. Not for Trish though. She wouldn't uproot her family, not with her parents getting on in years and her youngest son starting college at Duquesne. And her husband. "Hey, what about Greg? He'd never leave his law firm."

"Don't bet on it. He's originally from Albuquerque. I think he'd move west in a heartbeat. But like I said, it was just a random chat. He left a number, said to call him if I wanted to talk some more."

"But you aren't going to do that…right? Of course not. You just called me in here to give me a heart attack."

"Yeah, I did kinda want to see the look on your face. Here, help me eat these." Trish fetched a bag of Skittles from her desk drawer and shook several into Gianna's open palm. "What's funny about these calls—I've gotten them before—is they don't actually ask if you're interested. They ask if you know someone who might be. I usually blow them off but this one made me stop and think, on account of that little chat we had at the wedding. You were talking about how you'd feel if you knew they were going to make Stefan CEO. That no matter what you did, no matter how qualified and prepared you were, you'd never get the top job. Remember that?"

"Every damn day, Trish." She thought again of Stefan roaming the halls of the executive offices as though he had nothing else to do.

"I've worked here at TriState for twenty-six years, Gianna. Made regional manager when I was thirty-two, and I've been stuck in the same job ever since. It was a damn good job when I was a single mom raising three kids. But I always knew it was the top of the ladder for me here no matter how hard I worked. You and Gabriel and now Stefan were always going to get the top jobs."

All of that was true.

"The point is, sometimes I wonder if I should have listened to some of those offers. Not now—I'm not going anywhere so don't worry—but eight or ten years ago when I had more room to grow." She leaned over until she was only inches from Gianna's face. "Now why am I telling you this?"

"Come on, I'm not going to leave my own family's company."

"Even if it means working for Stefan someday?" Trish glanced over at the closed door before continuing, "Or more likely, working your ass off behind the curtain, running the company and cleaning up all the messes while he sits at the head of the table and gets all the accolades. You don't deserve to be Stefan's number two, Gianna."

She couldn't deny that scenarios such as that one had plagued her since the accidental eavesdrop outside her father's office. They also had taken a toll in terms of her smoldering attitude toward Stefan, whom she'd always loved.

"All I'm saying is you should talk with one of these headhunters and see what else is out there. You know this business, Gianna. The most you'll ever be at TriState is a big fish in your own pond—and maybe not even the biggest fish. Imagine the possibilities in a company where there's room to grow. How about I call this guy back on Monday, tell him I thought of someone who might be interested?"

"You know I can't leave TriState. I'd be walking out on my whole family. I couldn't do that to my father, not after what Gabe did."

Trish flipped her hand as if swatting a fly. "What your brother did was selfish. But just because he left you holding the bag doesn't mean you have to keep holding it."

Gianna couldn't defend her brother's final act, no matter how forgiving she tried to be. "Forget that I brought up Gabe, Trish. For the record, I'm not going anywhere. I'm staying right here until they *beg* me to be CEO." She rose and snatched one more handful of candy. "Which they will."

"All I'm saying is think about it."

Gianna was already at the door but turned to say, "If it makes you feel better, I don't ignore *all* your advice. I had that talk with Jaz...and then I went on a date with somebody else." She left it there, closing the door behind her before Trish pummeled her with questions she wasn't ready to answer.

By the time she reached her office, she was torn between anger over Stefan and TriState's glass ceiling. Then came a wave of excitement that she had met someone who could make her forget about such irritants. Friday was too long to wait to see her again.

She fired off a quick text, *Any chance we can have dinner tonight?*

* * *

Vincent's was the McEvoys' go-to place for Italian food, located less than a mile from the dental clinic off the Penn-Lincoln Parkway. Keenan had sampled most of the menu during the Covid lockdowns, when they'd picked up dinner there once a week. She'd suggested it to Gianna because its tables were well-spaced and the family atmosphere was good for conversation.

It took a moment for her eyes to adjust to the darkness inside the restaurant to find Gianna waving from a table in the corner. Like Keenan, she'd come straight from work, dressed smartly in a tight black skirt with a gray blazer, the sleeves pushed to her elbows. Stylish, professional. And *sexy*, she realized with delight. No one had triggered that reaction in years.

"Hey, you been waiting long?"

"About ten minutes. No big deal."

They quickly ordered Sierra Nevada pale ales while perusing the menu, eventually agreeing to split a spinach pizza.

When their drinks arrived Keenan asked, "How's your week going?"

"It's better now, thanks," Gianna said, raising her bottle to toast. Her smile was tight, almost grim. "Thanks for meeting me on such short notice."

"Is everything all right?"

"Yeah, I just wanted to see you. Is that okay?"

"Absolutely." Keenan smiled and studied Gianna's ambiguous expression. "I was worried you might be having problems with Jaz."

"Believe it or not, she's actually one of the few people who's not on my last nerve right now. She's about the only person in the warehouse I trust to do her job the way it's supposed to be done." She went on to describe her frustration with her cousin and his shoddy work ethic, and her anger that he was destined to be the family's choice for CEO. "Trish is probably right. I'd have a better career if I went to work for a big company like Bryson Solutions—but then I wouldn't own any of the business. Who walks out on a deal like that?"

"It matters that you're happy there. The future matters too. It might not be so great to own part of a business if it's losing value and prestige because the person who's running it isn't competent." Before Gianna could respond to that cynical prospect, Keenan switched tacks. "Have you ever thought about leaving Pittsburgh?"

Gianna shrugged. "Can't imagine where I'd go. As long as I can remember, my work life's been geared toward being ready to take over someday. I learned all the departments, studied the financial guts of the business. Stefan though…honestly, I don't think he even cares. He just does whatever his dad tells him to do."

"No wonder you're frustrated. Who wouldn't be?"

"I'm doing it again. I swear I didn't ask you to dinner so you could listen to me go off on another rant. It feels like that's all I do when we're together. I want this to be more than that."

Keenan appreciated that Gianna was conscientious about how they communicated, though she didn't want her to feel constrained in what she could talk about.

"Gianna, for the"—Keenan counted on her fingers— "fourth time, is it? If it's on your mind, you can always feel free to talk about it. It so happens we have this family perspective in common. I grew up working after school in the dental clinic, went to dental school, all with the expectation that I'd come back here and take over my dad's practice when he retired. Except I didn't stick to the plan—at least not at first—because Annabel's whole family was in Columbus. She wanted to be near them so I went to work at a public clinic there. If her family hadn't all turned out to be such bastards, we'd probably still be there." It was the first time she'd hinted to Gianna of the events that had set Annabel's suicide in motion. Even the barest mention caused her voice to shake. "And she'd still be alive."

"You're saying they caused her to take her own life?" Gianna seemed to realize she was struggling with the subject and covered her hand. "Here's where I say you can talk about whatever's on your mind—but only if you want to. Believe me, I know how hard it is to open some of these boxes."

Keenan was blindsided by the swell of emotions, especially the rush of anger she thought she'd gotten under control. "It's been a while since I talked about it. I wasn't expecting it to hit me that way."

"It's okay." She held out both hands for Keenan's. "We don't have to go there at all. Just take a few deep breaths, clear your head."

"That's the one thing I can't do. It doesn't go away. Once I start thinking about it…" Keenan shook her head, her anger growing. "Annabel's family betrayed her. Every goddamn one of them. There's nothing they'd like better than for people not to talk about it. So yeah, every time I tell the story it hurts. But it hurts even more not to talk about it because that's what they want. That's how they got away with what they did."

Gianna caught the waitress as she walked past and handed her a credit card. "Would you mind fixing our pizza to go?"

* * *

"Annabel had a history of depression but she managed it pretty well, usually with diet and yoga. If it dragged on she'd take medication until it went away. The one thing she refused to try was therapy. I thought it might help to talk about it, but she always said there was nothing to talk about, she didn't have any deep-seated problems from her past to deal with."

Sitting side by side on the L-shaped sofa in Keenan's basement apartment, Gianna listened intently as Keenan slowly opened up about Annabel. The anger she'd exhibited at the restaurant appeared to subside almost as soon as Bennie climbed into her lap.

"Annabel was close to her family, especially her mom. When she graduated with her nursing degree, Nancy even got her a job at the same pediatrics practice, so they saw each other at work every day." She paused, her face pensive. "If you want to know the truth, it bothered me sometimes, her being closer to her mom than she was to me."

Gianna couldn't help but guess where this story was going. It must have been a serious falling out since they'd left Ohio to get away from it.

"We talked about it once, Nancy and I. One of those teen pregnancies. It was just the two of them till Joe came along. They got married when Annabel was eight, and Nancy said she got clingy after that, like she was afraid of being left out. Normal kid stuff, she said, but Annabel never really grew out of it."

It wouldn't have been normal in Gianna's home. Her mother had missed out on the warmth gene, except when it came to Gabe.

"Her problems kicked off about a year and a half before she died. She and her mom went to one of those recertification seminars on how to recognize signs of childhood sexual abuse. She ran out right in the middle of it, then came home practically hyperventilating, said it triggered a memory from when she was a little girl, being in a room with Joe and her cousin Lisa." Her expression turned to disgust. "Joe was having them play some kind of game that involved inappropriate touching."

"Oh my God, that's revolting. Her own stepfather." Gianna shuddered. "Please tell me her mother divorced him. Or shot him. Even that would have been too good for him."

"Annabel didn't tell her right away. She was worried it might be a false memory that got planted by something she heard. But then she talked to Lisa and she remembered it too, exactly the same way. And Randy—that's Joe's son by his first wife—he has two little girls, so Annabel and Lisa decided they had to confront Joe. Annabel even told him she could live with it if he'd just admit what he did and say he was sorry, and swear he wasn't still doing it. She just needed to know the little girls were safe."

"And let me guess. He denied it."

"Viciously. He said Annabel needed to be in a mental hospital and Lisa was just a brainless idiot who'd agree with anyone because she couldn't think for herself."

Gianna shook her head slowly in disbelief. "That's what they do, isn't it? Blame the victims, gaslight everyone."

Keenan huffed. "That's not even the worst part. Annabel eventually told her mom. She took Joe's side, told Annabel to stop spreading lies. Then Randy heard about it and all hell broke loose. One night there was this commotion outside our house. We looked out and Annabel's car was on fire. There went Randy's truck down the street. Two days later Lisa recanted, said she remembered them playing some kind of innocent sexual game with Annabel but that Joe wasn't there."

"Randy must have scared her."

"Hell, he scared me too. I have no doubt next time it would have been the house. That's when I talked Annabel into coming back here and starting over. She was torn up at work because her mother wouldn't speak to her, so that seemed like the best thing to do. We packed everything, and then the day we left Annabel wanted to stop by their house and say goodbye. Nancy wouldn't even come to the door."

Hearing Keenan's voice become shaky again, Gianna slid closer and wrapped an arm around her shoulder. "Sounds like you did everything you could to protect her."

Keenan shrugged. "I wasn't much help to be honest. Mom and Dad loved her, so when we got here they tried to step up. A new family, all that. But I underestimated how much it hurt when Nancy took Joe's side against her. She wouldn't take Annabel's calls, blocked her on Facebook. It broke her heart."

It sounded as if it had broken Keenan's as well. "I can't even imagine how much that must have hurt. A lot, obviously…to do what she did."

She laid her head on Gianna's shoulder. "The real kicker was six months later. Annabel wasn't getting any better so I suggested we go back for a visit. I thought if she could sit down with her mom and their minister, they could start to heal their relationship. Annabel was willing to do anything. I called Lisa's mom to see if she could help set it up, and she said Nancy was killed in a pile-up on I-70 a couple of weeks after we left."

Gianna twisted to look her in the face. "Two weeks? And nobody even bothered to tell you?"

"That's Joe for you. He told the family he called Annabel and she said so what, her mother was already dead to her. Of course, it wasn't true. She didn't give a shit what any of them thought of her, but it destroyed her that she didn't get to make peace with her mom." Keenan wiped her eyes with her wrists but it wasn't enough to hold back her tears. Even Bennie seemed to notice, rising up to lick her chin. "She came apart so fast after that, like she lost all hope of ever getting better. But it never crossed my mind she'd do something so final."

It was one of the saddest stories Gianna had ever heard, and it got even worse as Keenan shared the horrific details of her suicide. "I can't even fathom what it must have been like for you to find her that way. Bad as it was to lose Gabe, I count my blessings I wasn't there to see it."

They sat quietly for a couple of minutes, with Gianna ever conscious of their physical closeness. She hoped her mention of Gabe hadn't been insensitive. A few weeks lurking on the forum hadn't yet prepared her for the duty to comfort others. Was it best just to listen or try to relate? She had no idea what Keenan needed from her right now, but the impulse to hug her was overpowering. "I'm so sorry you went through that. I wish I could have been there for you when you needed it."

"You're here now, Gianna." After wiping her face and nudging Bennie out of her lap, she grasped Gianna's free arm and pulled her into a loose embrace. "Obviously I still need a hug every now and then. Especially when I tell that story."

"I'm here for that," Gianna said, tightening her grip. With their foreheads touching, she gave in to the urge to seek out Keenan's lips for a gentle kiss that lasted all of three seconds before the shock hit her and she pulled away. "I'm so sorry. I don't know what I was thinking." She covered her face with her hands to hide her embarrassment.

"It's okay, Gianna."

"No, it's not. I can't believe I did that. It's like I was taking advantage."

Keenan scooted up beside her and hooked their elbows. "I didn't feel that way so you shouldn't either. I didn't pull away."

"I know." She nodded, feeling less embarrassed but still regretful. "It's not the way it should have happened, is all. It doesn't change the feelings behind it though. I like you… and I've been wanting to do that. Just wish I'd picked a better moment."

"Look at me, Gianna." Keenan took her face in her hands and drew her close, delivering a soft kiss of her own. "I get where you're coming from, and maybe you're right about the timing. But speaking for myself, it's a nice reminder that I can choose not to wallow in pain. If it makes you feel better, we can pretend it didn't count. Which means we get to do the whole first-kiss thing over again, right?"

Keenan's forgiving smile held so much promise, Gianna almost kissed her again.

CHAPTER TEN

Holding tightly to his leash, Keenan let Bennie lead the way past the Fort Pitt Block House to the massive lawn surrounding a granite outline that marked the former site of Fort Duquesne, which the French had burned to the ground rather than surrender it to the British. The concert stage was erected at the western point of the outline with the fountain towering behind it. Gianna had said to meet near the southern point.

After a quick dash to Marshalls at lunchtime, her wardrobe now included pre-shredded skinny jeans and a funky gray sweater that was longer on one side. Plus a pair of black-striped Toms she'd scuffed a bit so they wouldn't appear new.

To say she was nervous was an understatement. Some of that was anxiety over making a good impression with Gianna's friends, since they might become her friends too. However, her main source of uneasiness was the prospect of meeting Jaz, a woman who probably hated her guts just for drawing breath. Last weekend she'd been ready to prove to Jaz that she wasn't a threat to her friendship with Gianna. Now that she and Gianna were dating, she probably *was* a threat—or at least Jaz would see it that way.

Dating! Calling each other, agreeing to meet, having fun. In anyone's book, that was called dating.

"Whoa, little man." She squatted to pet Bennie, soaking up his soothing presence. "I just realized I'm doing something I haven't done in about twelve years, so let's you and me get on the same page. You need to be sweet and charming and I need to remember my name and try not to behave like a social misfit. Think we can manage that?"

She looked up to see Gianna jogging toward her in trainers, tights and a snug zip-neck pullover that showed off her figure.

"Hey, you made it." Gianna dropped to a knee to greet Bennie, who welcomed her with obvious delight.

Fresh from her epiphany, Keenan recognized an annoying sensation she'd last experienced in high school when she'd tried to date boys, an inability to relax and be herself. She was about to become preoccupied with trying to say the right thing, smile the right way, laugh at the right time. What happened to their easy rapport from two nights ago?

"No stealing my dog," she managed, alarmed at the shakiness of her voice.

"We have a spot near the stage. Come meet everyone." Gianna gestured at her new jeans and suddenly yanked a tag off. "Nice jeans. Oh sorry, were you planning on returning these after tonight?"

Keenan sighed and turned her back. "Better check the sweater too."

"Nah, you're good." She lifted Keenan's backpack and slung it over her shoulder. "It's too bad you missed happy hour, but I told everybody about Bennie. They can't wait to meet him."

"And me, Gianna? Did you mention me?"

"Uh…" She grinned.

"He can't drive himself, you know. You might have dropped my name at least." She didn't mind Gianna's playfulness when it came to Bennie. While it was true he needed more training in crowds, the main reason she'd wanted to bring him was to buffer her interactions with others. In particular, with Gianna's ex.

"By the way, a heads-up. Our friend Nick used to be Nicole but he's been transitioning for about a year. Just wanted to let you know so you won't get confused if someone screws up his pronouns."

"Cool. I never knew Nicole so Nick he is. Is, uh…is Jaz here?"

"She is," Gianna replied, nodding pensively. "She's actually in a pretty decent mood considering I told her you were coming. Maybe she's finally gotten the message. I don't want to freeze her out but I will."

Which message? Keenan wondered. Gianna hadn't shared how she'd handled Jaz stalking her over the weekend, nor how she'd resolved Jaz's blowup from the week before.

"Let's hope it doesn't come to that," Keenan said. "Twenty years is a lot of good times. It would be a real shame if all those memories were lost to hard feelings. I'm not trying to tell you what to do. But I wouldn't want to see either one of you slam the door on the other. It's painful." She figured Gianna was smart enough to realize that was a reference to Annabel's falling out with her mom.

"I don't think I'd ever go that far, but sometimes I think some space might do us some good. She's been living rent-free in my head long enough. I can't let myself get worked up over her feelings all the time. I'd never do anything to hurt her deliberately, but I need to get on with my life and let her worry about herself."

It sounded as though Gianna had done some serious soul-searching, but Keenan had a feeling her resolve would be tested. She was too nice a person not to care if Jaz was hurting. "She's going to be threatened by me, don't you think?"

"Probably, but she doesn't get to dictate what happens. I'll introduce you and let you take it from there. Don't feel you have to go out of your way to make friends with her—especially if she gives you a bad vibe. Just talk to the others instead." She nodded toward Bennie. "What am I saying? We both know this little guy's going to be the center of attention."

Keenan laughed, wondering if anyone ever noticed how she sometimes used Bennie to avoid having meaningful conversations. "It's okay, Gianna. I've still got a few social skills I can dust off."

They reached a small group already set up for the concert in lawn chairs.

"Hey, I want yinz to meet a friend of mine." Gianna began with a Black couple, Nick and Shanice. Shanice immediately dropped to her knees to nuzzle Bennie, who was only too happy to nuzzle back. "Nick's a dental hygienist. I told him about the clinic at Big Stone Gap."

"That's impressive," Nick said, standing to nearly six feet tall. He wore his hair short and sported a faint mustache. "Gianna said yinz do this a couple of times a year, hundreds of patients. That's pretty intense."

"It's definitely an adrenaline rush. Want to come along?"

He held up his hands. "Not me. I go twice a month to Hill House. Same clientele but I don't have to leave town. You should try it sometime." He looked down at Shanice and back to Keenan, rolling his eyes. "Look what you did bringing this dog out here. I guarantee it's going to start the second we go walking back to the car. She's going to want a dog."

Keenan laughed and replied, "Surrender now and save yourself the headache. I promise you'll never regret it." She unfurled a blanket from her backpack. Part of her wanted to drop to the ground with Shanice, but Gianna was waiting expectantly to introduce her to the others. She'd already gotten a glimpse of everyone and knew right away the pretty one standing on her own—long dark hair, brown eyes and full-figured—had to be Jaz.

Vic and Dani were a sporty couple who'd ridden to the park on their bikes. Ellen and Fran were a bit older than the others, mothers of teenagers who wouldn't be caught dead at an "old people's" concert.

"And this is Jaz, who's been my best friend since ninth grade." Gianna wrapped an arm around her shoulder and squeezed with obvious affection, while Jaz delivered a side-eye that suggested she was less than satisfied with her meager status. "And this is Keenan. She's a dentist in Westwood."

Keenan almost laughed. Gianna definitely could use some help with introductions.

"A dentist…" Jaz said, crinkling her nose. "I couldn't do that, sticking my hands in somebody's nasty mouth."

Gianna tells me you're on probation. How's that going? The thought of asking that question triggered what had to be a shit-eating grin, resulting in a mask of confusion on Jaz's sour face. "You have a gorgeous smile, Jaz. A lot of my patients would love to have teeth as pretty as yours."

Her mouth opened and shut twice before she finally managed, "Thank you."

Gianna said, "Don't look now but I think Shanice is stealing your dog."

As they returned to the blanket, Keenan asked Jaz, "Do you like dogs?"

She shook her head and contorted her face as if she'd encountered a foul smell. "No, they bite."

"Not Bennie," Gianna said as she joined Shanice on the blanket. "He's a sweetheart. Keenan takes him to nursing homes. He's never bitten anyone, right?"

"No, I've never even heard him growl. He's really laid back."

"I thought dogs didn't like loud stuff. It hurts their ears. Bet he goes apeshit when the music starts."

"He needs to get used to it. Sometimes therapy dogs have to go to places where there's a lot of noise. I think he'll be all right but I'll take him home if he gets stressed."

Shanice patted the blanket beside her. "Sit right here and talk to me. You grow up here?"

"Graduated from Brashear High. Then I went to Ohio State, so I lived in Columbus for ten years. But I moved back here about three years ago."

"Just in time for Covid to turn all of us into hermits." Shanice continued to pepper her with questions, most of them casual but a few that were probing. "Were you and your partner married?"

"It was on our to-do list but we never got around to it." Keenan had raised the subject of marriage a couple of times after the Supreme Court case made it a possibility, but it never got much traction in their house. Annabel hadn't ruled it out though, a fact that had left Keenan hoping it might happen someday. It sure would have made life easier when she died. She'd been forced to deal with Lisa as next of kin to settle Annabel's estate. "What about you and Nick?"

"Their wedding was gorgeous," Jaz said as she sank to the blanket, apparently realizing it was that or be left out of the conversation.

"Nicest wedding I've ever been to," Gianna added.

Jaz then launched into a litany of details and anecdotes that had the others laughing. Something about her smug glances at Keenan made it clear she meant to exclude, to remind Keenan she wasn't part of their group because she didn't share their experiences.

Nick rose and peered off in the distance. "Concessions stand's open. Who wants something to drink?" He recorded everyone's orders on his phone and tugged Gianna to her feet. "Come with me, girl."

Before Keenan could panic about being left alone with Jaz, Shanice nudged Bennie across the blanket. "Go ahead and pet him, Jaz. He's a sweetheart."

Despite looking as though she'd swallowed quinine, Jaz held out her hand to Bennie. His tail wagged as he inched closer until finally he was close enough to curl up next to her and lay his chin on her lap.

"Is he like this with everybody?" she asked, her fingers tickling a spot behind his ear.

"No, it has to be somebody he trusts. Looks like he has a good feeling about you."

"Don't know why…I don't even really like dogs."

Shanice said, "Let me tell you something about Nick. He's not easy to impress but Gianna told him about this thing you're doing, these free clinics out in the middle of nowhere. He thinks that's damn cool."

"It's a phenomenal experience, Shanice. Most people have no idea how much need there is in rural America for services like these. Everything's so fast-paced…it's exhilarating. I've been trying to talk Gianna into coming with us. She's considering it, or so she says. She'd be a big help."

"Wait a damn minute," Shanice said. "Are you telling me Gianna might be going on this trip too? To do what? She's not a dentist."

"No, just as a volunteer." Keenan had only mentioned Gianna's interest to make her story more relatable. She realized too late its potential to make Jaz jealous, especially if she thought Gianna wanted to come to be with her. "Once she told me what kind of work she did, I practically begged her to come. It's not often we find someone who knows how to put together instrument trays and keep forty stations supplied. Plus her company's donating a bunch of supplies."

"This is going to give Nick ideas. He'll be hitting yinz up to do a clinic in Stanton Heights."

Keenan handed Shanice a business card from a pouch on her backpack. "Tell him if he builds it, I'll try to come. I can put him in touch with—"

Suddenly Bennie yelped, followed by a flurry of growling and snapping as Jaz shoved him from her lap.

"Ow! That little shit just bit me."

* * *

Gianna dropped her armload of soda cans on the blanket and looked around to try to catch a glimpse of Keenan. "Which way did she go?"

"That girl's long gone by now," Shanice said.

"She damn well better be," Jaz snarled, nursing her hand. "I'm lucky the little bastard didn't break the skin. I'd have to get all those rabies shots in my stomach. She shouldn't be bringing him to a place like this anyway with so many people around. Especially if she's not going to watch him."

Gianna wanted to stand up for sweet Bennie, to say he wasn't at all vicious, but she hadn't been here to see what happened. Whatever he'd done, it clearly had been serious enough for Keenan to take him home right away, not even sticking around to say goodbye.

A roar went up as VeraDid took the stage to the thump of a bass guitar. All the attention to Jaz's dog bite gave way to excitement over "Once or Twice," the band's hottest hit. They followed with two more high-energy rock tunes before slowing it down with a soulful ballad by lead singer Tina Best.

The music wasn't enough to distract Gianna from her concern over Keenan. How embarrassing for her that this had happened the first time she met new friends. Gianna was so preoccupied with worry she didn't notice Shanice had wriggled her way through the others to stand beside her.

"Gi, I'm sticking my nose where it doesn't belong but that little dog got a raw deal. There's no way he just up and bit her. I didn't see what Jaz did to him but I know she did something."

Of course! That was the only thing that made sense. "Did Keenan see it? Did she say anything?"

"No, but I'm telling you, that dog yelped before he snapped at her so she must have pinched him or pulled his ear or something."

Suddenly all she felt was rage. She wanted to get in Jaz's face, to shove her to the ground and pinch her until she bruised, asking her how she liked it. Instead she stormed off across the park toward her apartment building and tried to no avail to raise Keenan on her phone.

She was passing through Commonwealth Park, a grassy canyon that parted high-rise hotels and condo buildings, when Jaz caught up with her. "Gianna, wait. Where you going?"

"Do *not* follow me, Jaz!" she shouted, whirling to face her. "I can't believe you'd do something so low. And why? For attention? So Keenan would have to leave?"

Jaz straightened her back and put a hand on her hip, a defiant stance. "What are you yelling at me for? I'm the one who got bit."

"That's a lie. I spent all day last Sunday with Bennie and I know for a fact he doesn't have a mean bone in his body. The only reason he would've snapped at you was if you'd done something to hurt him. A *puppy*, for God's sake!"

Stubbornly feigning innocence, Jaz said, "All I did was pet him and he bit me for no reason."

"That's bullshit and you know it," Gianna snarled through gritted teeth as she walked away.

Jaz caught up with her again, catching her elbow. "If I did hurt him, it was an accident. Maybe his fur got caught in my bracelet or something and I didn't realize it. I don't even like dogs, but she was like, 'Oh, everybody likes Bennie. Here, pet him.' I was just trying to be nice."

"That's right, Jaz. It's always someone else's fault, isn't it?"

Jaz sneered. "Look at you, acting like your shit don't stink. 'Cept we both know better, don't we?"

Gianna glared at her, daring her to say another word.

"Yeah, that's right. What would all our friends think if they knew what kind of person you really were?"

"Are you threatening me, Jaz? Because it's not going to get you what you want. What it *will* do is end us as friends. You hear me? *End* us! So you go do what you've got to do, say what you've got to say. Just know there's no coming back from it—ever."

* * *

Keenan wasn't surprised by the WhatsApp chime, though she was mildly disappointed it hadn't come sooner. Apparently Gianna had tried calling her earlier but then hung around to enjoy the concert with her friends instead of following up… which admittedly wasn't a cardinal sin. She owned her part for running off without saying goodbye. Given how upset she was, it probably was for the best.

"Hi there."

"Keenan…I don't know what to say." Gianna was sitting at her kitchen bar, her face scrubbed and her hair held back with a headband. A half-glass of red wine dangled from her fingertips. "How's Bennie?"

"He's officially in doggie jail, which means he's not allowed to work as a therapy pet for now. I'll have to cancel Oakberry on Tuesday, and probably the library the week after we get back from Big Stone Gap."

The agency that had certified Bennie had a strict policy on incidents of aggression. Failure to report one was grounds for dismissal from the program.

"But it was hardly anything. It didn't even break the skin." Gianna sounded tired...or maybe a little drunk. "How would they even know?"

"We're all on the honor system. I had to submit a report to the behavioral team at the agency telling them what happened. I did that when I got home. They'll review it and recommend a course of action."

"What are the possibilities? They won't pull his...whatever, will they?" Her words had a detectable slur.

"Someone sounds a little tipsy."

"Yeah...maybe a little." She pushed her glass aside and blew out a breath through the side of her mouth. "I needed to chill. I'm not usually much of a drinker, promise."

Keenan guessed there was more to the story, and it probably had to do with Jaz. "I doubt they'll yank Bennie's certification for a first offense, but it's complicated by the fact that I don't have a statement from Jaz about her injuries or what provoked him to snap at her."

"Best leave Jaz out of it." Gianna sighed and shook her head. "Shanice said he was just sitting with her. She thinks Jaz pinched him or pulled his ears or something. Whatever it was, I'd bet you a thousand dollars she did it on purpose."

That was Keenan's guess too but she didn't want to accuse someone without evidence. "I wondered about that. Too bad the form I filled out didn't have a space for 'jealous dyke.'"

"See? Didn't I tell you? As soon as I heard what happened, I left. I tried to call you and say it was all bullshit but then Jaz followed me and we got into this huge fight on the sidewalk. I fucking lost it with her. Started yelling and...Keenan, I am so, *so* sorry this happened."

"You don't have to apologize. I won't hold you responsible for something you didn't do."

Gianna's pained expression said otherwise. "Just because I didn't do it doesn't mean I'm not responsible. I feel like I'm the one who made Jaz the way she is. She's manipulative, argues all the time…she's possessive. She owns me and she knows it."

"What does that mean, she owns you? She has something on you?" From the extended silence, Keenan concluded the answer was yes. "Do you want to tell me about it?"

"I don't want to but I probably should," Gianna finally grumbled. "See, Jaz and me started hanging out in ninth grade when all the other girls"—she made a face of disgust—"they were all boy-crazy. We'd make fun of them. I could tell Jaz had it pretty rough at home. Single mom, food stamps, all that. She used to love coming over to our house because I had my own room and we had all the latest stuff…big TVs, video games. I liked going to her house because she was out to her mom. I hadn't come out to my parents yet so I felt more relaxed at her house, like I could be myself."

"You were lucky to have that."

"Yeah, Mrs. Sadowski was like a second mom…except better, considering my real one kinda sucked."

Keenan snickered. It actually explained a lot about her bond with Jaz, which had proved remarkably resilient given the ups and downs Gianna had described.

"Anyway, our sophomore year in high school…a lot of the kids were messing around with drugs by then, and since I was the one with the cash"—she looked away and sighed again—"I bought some coke off this guy. Half a gram, that's all. Just enough so we could both try it. We thought we were so tough, you know?"

"Nope. I can honestly say I have no idea what that feels like."

"It feels like we were ignorant little shits. Hiding out in the bathroom during biology lab. I went into a stall to pee and next thing I know the vice principal comes in and catches Jaz cutting lines on the windowsill. Soon as I heard her, I climbed up on the toilet so she couldn't see my feet."

Keenan pictured it and laughed. "You must have been scared shitless."

"I was shitting bricks. But Jaz took all the blame. She figured she was caught, there was no point in both of us going down."

"That was decent of her. And now you're forever in her debt."

"Yes…and no. She stayed two whole nights in juvie before they released her to her mom. Then she had to go to court. It took her two years to jump through all their hoops—community service, fine, probation—but when she turned eighteen she got her record wiped clean, like it never happened." Gianna continued while twirling the wine glass by its stem, as if too embarrassed to meet her eye. "I went to bat for her with Dad and Uncle Jack to help her get a job at the warehouse. Second chances, all that. We weren't dating anymore but I felt like I owed her. I *did* owe her. That could have been me…my whole career down the toilet."

"Teenagers screw up all the time. If they gave Jaz a second chance, I'm pretty sure you'd have gotten one too."

"Mmm, maybe. But they probably would have stuck me in the warehouse forever. I tell you, it woke my ass right up. I never did anything like that again, not even weed. But Jaz… man, she kept messing around with it. I had no idea. We got back together, nice apartment by Schenley Park. Four or five years…or six, however many…it was good. Then Dani called me one night when I was at a workshop in Cleveland. Jaz was out dancing at Cattivo and she OD'd."

"Oh my God!"

"I drove back here and went straight to the ER. They got her stabilized, and then the second they discharged her, the cops came in and slapped on the handcuffs. It was fucking surreal."

Keenan could only shake her head. "You must have felt so betrayed."

"That wasn't the half of it. Not only was she using behind my back, I found out she'd gone on my computer at home and was sucking cash out of my savings account to pay for it—over three thousand dollars."

"Holy shit. That's some nerve. I can't believe you're still speaking to her, let alone calling her a friend."

"I hear that every day. Everybody thinks I'm insane. I broke up with her, obviously. But like I said, I felt like I still owed her because she never told anybody it was me who bought the coke that first time. So I paid for a lawyer to help get her a deal. He got her off with probation and twenty-eight days rehab, but the court's making her pay me restitution. And I begged—I mean really *begged*—them to keep her on at the warehouse, 'cause that was part of her deal. Lose your job, go to jail. I still care about her, you know? But man, she's pushing it with this bullshit. I figure we're even now. I'm not saving her ass ever again. If she didn't know that before she knows it now."

"That's…wow. Does she have any idea how lucky she is to have a friend who'd do all that for her? And after she stole from you? I can't imagine."

"And now she's threatening to tell all our friends that *I'm* the reason her life's fucked up." She jabbed her chest with her thumb. "Sorry, wine gives me a potty mouth."

"Is she acting out like this because of me, Gianna?" Of course she was. Jaz hadn't disguised her hostility at the park, dissing her work and cutting her out of conversations, to say nothing of what she'd done to Bennie.

"Yeah, probably. But you know what? I don't give a shit. It's not going to change what I do."

All of Gianna's past efforts at making Jaz a sympathetic figure crumbled in the face of this new information. Not only was Jaz a stalker who likely had provoked Bennie to snap at her, she was spiteful enough to threaten the one person who'd stuck her neck out to help.

"What will you do?"

"Guess I need to tell Dad and Uncle Jack what I did. It's better if it comes from me, don't you think?"

"It certainly would neutralize her threat, but—"

"They'll be pissed as hell. Not because of the coke—that was forever ago—but because they'll know it's why I made them keep her on all this time."

"I wouldn't rush in there on Monday morning and spill my guts if I were you. Jaz has to realize she could lose her job without you standing up for her. She may have second thoughts."

"Doesn't matter…I still have to tell them. And I'll have to come clean with our friends, break it to them that I don't do stuff out of the goodness of my heart."

"Except you do. And you also happen to be the victim of a blackmailer. One doesn't cancel out the other."

Gianna sighed. "It feels good to finally get that off my chest. I never actually told anybody that before. Does that make you want to run screaming in the opposite direction? It's okay if you do. Well, not okay…but I understand."

Keenan almost laughed at her pitiful demeanor. "I'm not running anywhere. In fact, I think you need to get away from all this stress for a few days. Come with us to Big Stone Gap next Friday."

"Okay."

It was cruel to extract such a promise with Gianna in her compromised state. "That's great, but I'll call you in a day or two to make sure you mean it. I'd really love to have you."

Gianna raised her glass again and said, "And I'd love to have you. Is that okay to say?"

This time, Keenan did laugh. "I think it's fine. In fact, I'm going to go to bed now and think about what it means."

"I should probably do that too." Her face lit up. "Hey, let's have lunch tomorrow."

"I'd love to but I think we're going to need a rain check."

Gianna's face drooped with disappointment. "Aww…how come?"

"Because you're going to have a hangover tomorrow. How about I take you to brunch on Sunday? I'll call you, okay?"

"Not if I call you first."

Keenan ended their call and laughed again. After all the things that had gone wrong today, she sure was happy.

CHAPTER ELEVEN

The Sunday brunch crowd at City Works was an eclectic mix of couples, families with children, and small groups of friends. Gianna recognized a few faces from her apartment building, people she crossed paths with in the elevator or fitness room. The weather still was mild, but a front was on the way that finally would bring fall temperatures.

Keenan stood out as she walked back to their patio table from the restroom. She wore tan cotton pants rolled twice at her ankle and a pink, slightly wrinkled, short-sleeved shirt tucked in with a thin brown belt. No obvious makeup or jewelry, though Gianna had noticed tiny gold studs in both ears plus a braided gold ear cuff in one. Completely charming, whether she realized it or not.

"Are you watching the sky across the river?" Keenan asked. "Thunderstorm coming our way."

Gianna dismissed the waiter who tried to refill their coffee, asking for the check.

"No, I invited you. I'm supposed to pay."

"Old-fashioned, are you?" Gianna felt emboldened after their kiss five nights ago. "What if I promise to let you pay next time? That guarantees us another date."

"You've got yourself a deal. Let's see, Big Stone Gap...I think there's a Dairy Queen."

"That's five days away. Surely we can find time to go out before then." She was tempted to add, *Unless going out wasn't what you had in mind.*

"Gianna? Gianna Del Vecchio?" A man appeared at their table, his bearded face vaguely familiar. "Rob Blanchard. I was a friend of Gabe's."

"Oh, right. How are you?" She glanced at Keenan and decided to skip the introductions. She barely knew Rob and didn't expect him to hang around.

"I'm good. I thought about yinz not long ago. One of those Facebook thingies popped up, you and Gabe and Amy at the birthday party at the Tavern." He tapped his forehead. "Sorry, probably shouldn't have brought her up. I'm thinking she's not one of your favorite people after what happened. Anyway, good to see you."

She nodded her goodbye and rolled her eyes as he walked away. "People can be so fucking clueless."

"What's that about?"

Leave it to Amy Tyler to spoil a pleasant Sunday brunch. As if she hadn't destroyed enough.

"Are you okay, Gianna?"

After hearing Keenan's wrenching tale of Annabel, Gianna knew she ought to find the courage to talk about what happened to Gabe, painful though it was. "Amy Tyler is the reason Gabe is dead. Maybe not the main reason but definitely the trigger. At least that's what Uncle Jack says."

Keenan leaned forward and lowered her voice. "Are you saying your brother killed himself over a woman?"

"A two-timing bitch," she said bitterly. "She's one of Trish's clients, runs a home health company in McKees Rocks. Uncle Jack introduced her to Gabe and they hit it off. Gabe was so in love with that woman. Said he couldn't believe how lucky he was."

"But you didn't like her?"

"No, I did. We all did." She slumped back in her chair, staring absently at her lap. "My mom was over the moon when they got engaged. She pushed them to set a date. Gabe tried but it's obvious now why Amy kept putting it off—because she was still seeing her old boyfriend."

The waiter returned with her credit card and the check, giving her a welcome reprieve. Telling the story again took her back to when it happened, when she'd shared the news with all her friends over tears and beers.

"It's bothering you to dredge this up, I can tell," Keenan said. "You gave me a choice the other night whether to talk about Annabel or not. I'm giving that to you now."

"No, I don't mind. It just makes me so angry." She took a sip from her almost-empty water glass, admittedly a stall tactic as she readied herself to go through it again. "Gabe had been wound up about work for weeks...orders getting screwed up, that kind of thing. Our birthday party—he didn't even want to go. He only did it because of me, but I could tell his head was off somewhere else all night. I wondered if it had anything to do with Amy but they always seemed crazy about each other. About a month later we were in Cincinnati at a trade show and he up and left a day early, took a flight home and left me to drive back by myself. When he got home that night, he apparently caught Amy half-dressed with her ex and went ballistic, started screaming and trashing the place. The other guy took off. Amy locked herself in the bathroom and called Uncle Jack. By the time he got there, Gabe was out on the balcony threatening to jump if she didn't come out and face him. I never would've dreamed he'd lose it like that."

Keenan's expression was a cross between horror and disbelief, the same Gianna had seen on practically everyone as they heard the tale.

"Uncle Jack said it must have triggered some kind of mental breakdown, that he was yelling things that didn't make sense. He kept talking to him and trying to get him to come back inside. But then all of a sudden he just yelled out that Amy was a liar and he jumped."

"My God, it almost sounds like a psychotic break."

"Exactly. And that's what kills me. All the signs were there, the agitation about little stuff at the warehouse. Obsessing over mistakes, even ones that were easily fixed. But I should've picked up on it. We were twins, for chrissakes. He must have been standing on the edge all that time and I didn't have a clue."

"Sounds like he really wanted to punish her."

"That's what Uncle Jack said, that he yelled something about how she was going to remember it for the rest of her life." But even after hearing Uncle Jack's tearful recounting, Gianna couldn't make sense of her brother losing it that way over Amy. "It kills me that I didn't realize he was capable of that. My own twin. All I know is *I'm* not capable of it."

Keenan took her hand as they started back to the apartment, then tucked it into her arm in a way that felt protective. Clearly the story of Gabe's death had moved her.

They walked hastily from the restaurant but made it only a block before being pelted by raindrops.

"It was stupid not to take an umbrella," Gianna said, pushing the water through her hair as they finally entered her apartment lobby. Seeing that Keenan was soaked through her shirt, she quickly added, "I've got dry clothes if you want them. We can throw yours in the dryer."

A loud clap of thunder seemed to shake the whole building, causing the lights to flicker and die.

Keenan snorted. "Something tells me your dryer might not be working right now."

* * *

Keenan stood aside to catch her breath while the doorman unlocked Gianna's apartment with a master key. With power off in the building, all the keypads were useless.

"Yinz have a nice day," he said.

"Thanks, Mario." Gianna—not the least bit winded after climbing six flights of stairs—led the way inside, where the sliding balcony door provided scant light from the darkened sky. "Wait there, I have a flashlight."

She returned with a pair of towels, and moments later, a T-shirt with yoga capris that Keenan guessed would be a size too large.

"I lit a candle in the bathroom if you want to get changed in there."

From the dim light, she took notice of Gianna's choice of organic soap and lotion. Trendy stuff, all natural. Not surprising, really. Gianna's overall tastes ran basic without frills, from her fashion to her apartment furnishings. She seemed to live an uncomplicated life.

Keenan hung her pants, shirt and camisole over the shower door and ran her hands through her hair in hopes it would dry without sticking up all over her head. When she returned to the living room, she saw that Gianna had changed into similar togs and had turned part of the sectional sofa and ottoman around to face the balcony. The sliding door was open and a towel was on the floor to catch the rain splatter.

"May as well watch the light and water show. It'll get stuffy in here soon with the AC off." She fetched a keycard from the counter. "By the way, I made you this magic key in case we decide to meet here after work or something."

"A key to your apartment?" It struck Keenan as awfully soon to be trading keys. "Are you sure you want me to have this? Bennie and I might start hanging out while you're at work. He'll demand I raid your fridge."

"Good luck with that. I hate grocery shopping."

Keenan held up the card and asked, "Does this happen to be the magic key that used to belong to Jaz? Because the last thing I want is to be-bop in here and find her sitting at your bar. That might be hazardous to my health."

"It's your very own code, but you don't have to worry because I disabled hers. I programmed yours in, hers out. I do it all on my phone. My cleaning service has a code too. But if you sneak in and steal stuff, I'll know it was you because my phone records it."

"Ah, in that case"—she set it inside her wet shoe—"I'll keep it. But I really think you should disable it until you know I'm coming over. I may be tempted to throw wild parties while you're at work."

Gianna laughed. "Sorry, but I can't picture you throwing wild parties. You're as straitlaced as I am. Minus my occasional propensity to down an entire bottle of wine."

"You were really upset about Jaz the other night."

"I was livid. The wine though…that's your fault. I didn't want to keep calling you while you were driving so I had a drink while I was waiting for you to get home. And then another one while I decided whether or not to confess my teenage sins. I was worried you'd think I was a cokehead."

"Liquid courage, huh?"

"I actually realized that I wanted to tell you…in case it was a dealbreaker. You had a right to know."

A dealbreaker. That meant Gianna was thinking ahead, probably asking the same questions as Keenan. The same questions anyone would start to ask when they met someone they liked spending time with. Could I have a future with this person?

"Stupid teenage mistakes are not a dealbreaker, but I'm glad you told me. It helps me understand your loyalty to her."

"You should know that my loyalty has a limit. She's not going to control my life, and she definitely doesn't get veto power over who I date."

Keenan stacked her feet next to Gianna's on the ottoman and took her hand. "Does this mean we're officially dating?"

"It sure looks that way."

She wanted to ask if Gianna was dating anyone else too but thought it would make her sound too clingy. On the other hand, she didn't want to go too far with someone who was playing the field. That would be her dealbreaker, especially if they had sex. "I think you might be right about me being old-fashioned. If there's been a dating revolution over the past decade, I've missed it, so you'll have to bring me up to speed."

"What does that mean?" Gianna brought their laced fingers to her lips. "Dating is whatever we say it is, if that's what you mean. I like you so far. I want to get to know you better."

"You already know more about me than most people."

"I could say the same." Gianna leaned over so their heads were touching as they continued to watch the rain. "But I think you should be the one to set the pace. I don't want to rush you into anything like I did last week."

Keenan turned and gently tugged Gianna's face toward her for a kiss. It lasted only a few seconds, but she left no doubt that she was ready for it. "Consider it set."

"Well, then…"

Thunder rumbled as they fell into another kiss, this one long and slow. Mesmerized by the sensations, Keenan couldn't help flicking her tongue over the gap in Gianna's teeth.

"I know what you're doing."

"It's what you get for kissing a dentist who thinks your little diastema is sexy as hell."

Invoking the word *sexy* seemed to raise the temperature in the room ten degrees, and Gianna responded by wrapping her in both arms and pulling her close. Another kiss…another. Mouths open, tongues exploring. The smell of rain, the crack of thunder. All of Keenan's senses had come alive at once.

When Gianna's fingertips brushed the skin beneath her T-shirt, Keenan remembered she wasn't wearing her camisole. She was running out of time to slow this down because in only moments Gianna would—

Gianna abruptly withdrew to look her in the eye, her expression a silent plea. "I can stop if you need me to."

"I need you *not* to stop." She pulled Gianna's hand to her breast and held it there, savoring the intimacy. All she could think was how much she wanted Gianna to be the right person to touch her this way.

* * *

A knock at the door jarred Gianna from her nap and she instinctively drew Keenan closer beneath the sheet. They couldn't have been asleep for more than a few minutes. It was clear from the hum of the AC that the power was back on.

"You have company," Keenan murmured sleepily.

"Only if I answer the door."

The knocking persisted, followed by the distinct sound of the door handle being tried. That could only mean—

"Gianna!" The knocking became pounding. "Come on, Gi. Open up."

"Is that who I think it is?" Keenan whispered as she sat up and pulled the sheet to her chest.

"Relax, I'm not answering it."

"I'm sorry, okay?" Jaz's muffled voice cried through the door. "I'll never tell a soul, Gianna. I swear. *Please* let me in."

Gianna stretched across Keenan's lap for her phone, which she'd muted after Jaz's first text two hours ago. Speaking quietly, she said, "Someone's been busy. Thirteen texts, seven missed calls, two voice mails. Sorry, sorry, sorry."

"It's like last weekend on steroids."

"Doesn't matter." She set her phone aside and tugged the sheet down to plant kisses on Keenan's warm belly.

Keenan pulled the sheet back up, clearly anxious. "Do you think she knows I'm here? Of course she does. My car's in your visitor space."

"If we don't answer, maybe she'll assume we're out."

When the annoying racket finally ceased, Gianna tiptoed to the door and looked through the peephole to find the hallway empty. By the time she returned, Keenan was getting dressed in the bathroom with the door ajar. Jaz's presence obviously had made her uneasy.

Gianna slipped on her shorts and T-shirt and tapped lightly on the door. "Is everything all right, Keenan?"

"It's great," she replied, opening the door to confirm that she was, in fact, fully dressed, though it was obvious her clothes were still damp.

What a disappointing end to such a lovely afternoon, she thought, as if the spell that had driven them to bed was broken. "This was the best day I've had in a long time. I don't want it to end."

"Me neither," she said with a quick smile that seemed almost perfunctory. "I just realized it's almost seven thirty. I have to get home to Bennie."

"I thought he stayed upstairs with your parents when you were gone."

Keenan moved her mouth as if to speak but stumbled over her reply. "He…technically, I'm sure he's fine. But he hasn't had a walk today. And I won't get to see him as much tomorrow because, you know, doggie jail so he can't come to work with me."

Gianna caught her by the arms and spun her gently to sit on the bed. "I know you're upset about Jaz coming by."

"Freaking out, actually. It's creepy. What she's doing—the way she's demanding your attention—that's not healthy, Gianna. And I have to admit, after what she did to Bennie I'm a little worried about getting caught in her crosshairs."

"I get that. I'll deal with her, I promise. What I care about right now is if you're feeling okay about us. About"—she gestured toward the rumpled bed—"this."

Keenan clasped her face and kissed her hard, once again swirling her tongue through Gianna's teeth. "I hope that answers your question. If not, I can come back tomorrow after work to show you."

"That was *such* a right answer." Gianna walked her to the door, where they shared another kiss and a long, satisfying hug. "I'll be sure to activate your magic key."

Gianna closed the door behind her and leaned against it, still smiling at Keenan's insistence on their next date. She'd never dreamed this one would end in bed, but Keenan had been as eager as she was. If Keenan felt half the excitement she did, this relationship had a real chance of becoming something special.

The next moments were a happy blur. Turning on a few lights, pushing her furniture back in place, and deciding to sleep on the sheets they'd shared. Her cleaning lady would change them tomorrow.

Another knock startled her.

"For chrissakes, Jaz," she grumbled, this time stalking to the door. Through the peephole, she saw not Jaz but Keenan. "Miss me already? Or did you forget something?"

Keenan's face was several shades of annoyed. "Someone smashed my windshield. Any guesses as to who?"

CHAPTER TWELVE

Sitting in her father's SUV at a nearly deserted dog park, Keenan gave an impatient Bennie a scratch. Brady was late to meet her but he'd texted he was on his way. "Let's give him two more minutes, Bennie."

The cool crisp air was welcome, and she lowered a window as she waited. The weekend forecast for Big Stone Gap called for frost, a tidbit she'd already texted to Gianna. What she wouldn't give to be a fly on the wall at TriState today, where Gianna planned a showdown meeting with her father and uncle later today, followed by a confrontation with Jaz over the incident in the parking garage. Keenan texted her once more for luck and stowed her phone as Brady's patrol car slid into the space next to hers.

He opened her passenger door and commenced a rowdy love-fest with Bennie, who jumped from the vehicle so he could run to a fencepost and relieve himself.

"I'm over here, you know," Keenan said drolly.

"You need your belly rubbed too?"

"That's a hard no."

She climbed out with a thermal lunch bag and Bennie's leash, though he didn't need it once Brady opened the gate into the fenced area for small dogs. Bennie was greeted instantly by a pair of terriers he'd played with before. She waved to their owner as all three dogs began the sniffing ritual.

"You're looking pretty jolly for somebody who got her car trashed," Brady said as he tossed his cap back inside his car. Then he snatched the bag from her and peered inside. "This better be the chicken tetrazzini you promised."

"It was hot when I left the clinic but you were late." They found a bench in the sun and she emptied the bag and handed him the larger of two bowls.

"So what's this favor you wanted? Something to do with your windshield?"

"Let me start with the good news. I'm now officially dating a gorgeous woman named Gianna"—she sucked a breath between her teeth—"and I don't want to jinx it but it feels like it might turn into something. I really, *really* like her."

"Whoa!" Brady's eyes widened above an enormous smile. "Keenan, that's fantastic. That means we get to meet her, right? Chad's going to want to have a dinner party ASAP. You know how excited he's going to be."

Chad was addicted to cooking shows. The mere mention of new friends meant the opportunity to try out recipes by his favorite chefs.

"In good time. We're still getting to know each other but I definitely want her to meet my two favorite guys." Sharing the news made it real—surreal, even. It wasn't even two weeks ago that she'd given herself permission just to think about it. "I know you're going to like her. She's our kind of people."

"Why's that? You talk, I eat. This stuff's good."

Bennie and the terriers came over to wind around their feet before tearing off again to play.

"She's three years older, so thirty-four. Went to Pitt." She described Gianna's job and the family company, adding, "As soon as I realized she knew all about dental supplies, I asked her to volunteer with us at our next free clinic in Virginia. I just threw it out there. I couldn't believe she actually said yes. She's coming with us on Friday, said I inspired her."

"I have to agree with her there. It's inspirational what yinz do. I read a post on Facebook about those free clinics, how desperate some of the people are. Makes me wish I had skills like yours. I think I'd want to do it too."

"That's what's so great about Gianna. Once she realized she had something to offer, she stepped up just like that." She snapped her fingers. "So when she called me inspirational, it felt real. Not like lip service."

"Ah, so I'm lip service. Got it."

She sighed loudly. "Everything's not about you, dipwad. I'm just saying she feels genuine. I like that about her. There's just this one problem—her ex is a little unhinged. A lot, actually."

She went on to share some of what she knew about Jaz, ending with the behavior she'd witnessed personally. Stalking Gianna when they were out together, provoking Bennie at the concert. And the incessant pounding on the door.

"So you think she's the one who smashed your windshield?"

"I don't think it. I know it." She showed him a screen grab from the garage's security footage on her phone taken just as the windshield on her Subaru was being smashed. Though the area was dimly lit, the image plainly showed a woman in a wide-striped top wearing a ball cap with her ponytail pulled through the back. "Gianna sent me this a little while ago. The power was out after the storm but the security cameras in the garage were hooked up to the emergency backup generator."

"It's pretty dark though. You can't really tell who that is."

She advanced to the next photo. "This was forty-five seconds later at the exit. Same top, same cap."

"Oooh, I'd say you've got yourself a case. Is that the favor? You want me to go pick her up? You have to swear out a warrant."

"Believe me, it's tempting. But no, the favor was just to have you look at it and tell me if it's enough evidence. I don't want to escalate this on my end, but it's good to have some leverage against her to make it stop."

"It's a misdemeanor so you have two years to use it."

"More like a couple of months if I really want to stick it to her. She's on probation till December for possession of cocaine."

"Unbelievable," he muttered, shaking his head. "Anybody stupid enough to do something like that when they're on probation deserves what's coming. She could end up having to serve her whole sentence and then some."

"I don't want to do that to her over some broken glass, but I'll keep it in my hip pocket. I just want her to knock it off."

"She might not leave you a choice. Girl doesn't sound too smart."

"Gianna's meeting with her this afternoon. It'll help that she can dangle this over her head, especially the probation part. Either she cuts the shit or I call the cops."

Brady finished his lunch without talking, but a frown had settled on his face.

"What are you thinking?"

"You're not going to like it." Avoiding her look, he snapped his fingers for Bennie, whose friends had left with their owner. "What you said about Jaz being on probation for drugs... Doesn't that raise a red flag about Gianna?"

"No way." She shook her head vehemently. Gianna's high school exploits weren't relevant, and there was nothing else pointing to a flirtation with drugs. "I know for a fact she's not into drugs. She had no idea Jaz was using three years ago, and she broke up with her as soon as she found out."

"Still...if there were drugs inside her circle, it could mean she's hanging out with the wrong people. I should check her out."

"You will *not* check her out!" She gave his shoulder an emphatic shove. "Come on, Brady. We aren't responsible for our friends. Besides, she's hanging out with *me*, and I'm about as clean as they come. If you don't count smoking weed in high school."

"You smoking weed?" He grabbed her elbow. "I'm running you in, girl."

"Statute of limitations!" she wailed through her laughter and his. "I'm not bringing her for dinner if you're going to arrest her, you *stasi*."

"All right, but years from now when you're both sitting behind bars at Muncy, they'll trace it back to this moment when you chose a life of crime."

"You're such a nut, Brady. Though it's nice to know I have my own personal police force to carry out my grudges."

"Call me if you change your mind, you hear? About Jaz, I mean." He bent down to pick up Bennie, whose muddy feet smeared his black trousers. "If I were you, I'd be more pissed about what she did to this little guy than the car."

"Trust me, I am." She checked her phone and started repacking her lunch bag. "I need to get back to work. Thanks for coming on such short notice."

"No problem. Tell your folks I said hi. And tell your mom her tetrazzini's out of this world."

"I better not mention it...considering you just ate their lunch."

* * *

Gianna waited solemnly for a response from her father or Uncle Jack to her long-overdue confession. From their grim faces, it wasn't her behavior twenty years ago that bothered them, but what it implied about why she'd pushed them to hire Jaz.

"I cannot tell you how much this disappoints me, Gianna," her father finally said. "That you'd expose this company to risk because you were being blackmailed by Jazmine Sadowski—"

"I wasn't being blackmailed, Dad. I just felt that I owed her my loyalty. What do you think would have happened to me back then if she'd told the police where she got the coke? They probably would have let her go and I'd be the one with the police record. She took the whole rap for me. And because of that, I was able to get into Pitt with a clean slate. And I can meet clients in the medical field without that shame hanging over me. She deserves my help."

From behind his desk, her father shook his finger at her. "That's no excuse for keeping this from your uncle and me. Do you have any idea the risk we took putting a known drug user on our payroll? You vouched for her and she went out and got herself busted again."

Gianna was immensely glad she hadn't told anyone in the family about Jaz also stealing from her bank account. When that thought crossed her mind, she recognized that her behavior was indeed indefensible, at least from a business standpoint. Jaz had shown she couldn't be trusted, yet Gianna had fought for her to keep a job where she could easily embezzle goods for resale or redirect shipments to the wrong people.

Uncle Jack poured a scotch for himself and her dad. "It was twenty years ago, Paul. I'm hardly a fan of Jaz, but we don't have any reason to suspect she's done anything wrong here at work. Is that right, Gianna?"

She was nearly floored to get Uncle Jack's support but she wasn't looking a gift horse in the mouth. "A hundred percent. She's always been an asset to TriState. My loyalty to Jaz goes beyond what she did when we were kids, Dad. We were in a relationship for eight years and I still care about her. I didn't want to see her in jail any more than you'd want to see me there. So yes, I went to bat for her when they said she'd go to jail without a job. God knows no one else was going to help her."

Her father rose, pushed his hands in his pockets and rocked back on his heels. "I'll say it again, Gianna. I'm disappointed in you. Running a company is about making good decisions. It should go without saying that we'll take this into consideration when we lay out our succession plan."

You can't be serious. She was relieved to realize she hadn't said it aloud, no matter how much she meant it. Now wasn't the time to argue for a promotion, since she no advantage to press. In retrospect, she'd shown extremely poor judgment.

"I believe," she said as she rose and started for the door, "that when the time comes for you to make that decision, there won't be any doubt as to who's best equipped to lead."

She was shaking as she walked to her office down the hall, where she found Jaz sitting across from her desk. Legs crossed, foot swinging, a finger to her chin. She looked like a bratty teen in the principal's office.

Gianna closed the door and went around the desk to her executive chair, leaning on its authority. "I've just come from a meeting with Dad and Uncle Jack. I told them what happened in high school, how I bought the coke and you took the rap for it."

Jaz sat up straight and looked at her with alarm. "Gianna, you didn't have to—"

She held up a hand. "It's done. They were the ones I was most worried about finding out, so I'm glad it's not hanging over my head anymore. Tell whoever else you want."

"I was just spouting off and you know it. Why would I tell a secret I've kept for twenty years?"

"Why would you threaten me with it? You can't throw it in my face ever again, Jaz. More importantly, I can't protect your job anymore. They won't listen to me. If you want to keep working here, you need to make nice with Stefan and convince him he can't get along without you."

Jaz folded her arms and stared at her with strained defiance. "Will that be all?"

"That's just the work stuff. We need to talk about our friendship."

"What's to talk about? You obviously hate me."

Gianna was sorely tempted to leave it there, just close the conversation and send Jaz on her way. It would only be a temporary solution, however, since Jaz would be back in a matter of days if not hours.

"I don't hate you, Jaz. Although you seem to be trying hard to get me to. In just the last two weeks, you've stormed out of my apartment while I was fixing you dinner. You've harassed me with text messages and calls after I told you I had plans. You were very rude to Keenan."

"Because her fucking dog bit me!"

She continued calmly, "It doesn't take a genius to see why you're doing all this. It's because we're seeing each other."

Jaz shrugged and looked away. "If you say so."

"What do *you* say, Jaz? Is there another reason you're behaving this way?" She wished Jaz would try to talk to her in a reasonable way so they could find a way forward that didn't result in more hurt feelings and acting out. "I'd really like to know what's going on."

"This is so fucking ridiculous. You know exactly what's going on." Jaz rose and began to pace, finally stopping beside the window that looked down on the loading dock. "Friends hang out together. They pick up the goddamn phone and answer each other's texts. But not you. You're ghosting me like I don't even exist anymore."

"Because you're calling me when I'm with someone else. And when I don't answer right away, you go crazy and blow up my phone. Or you go on a hunt to physically track me down." To say nothing of letting herself into her apartment. "It's too much, Jaz. Even if I weren't seeing Keenan, you'd be smothering me."

Jaz's nostrils flared with anger. "So was that your official announcement? Very sensitive of you."

"For chrissakes, if that's news then you haven't been listening. Yes, we're dating." She'd hoped to get through this conversation without getting angry but Jaz seemed to relish provoking her. "I believe you'd like Keenan if you gave her a chance. She's one of the kindest—"

"Sorry, but no fucking way."

"She's one of the kindest people I've ever met. And she certainly didn't deserve to have her windshield smashed with a lug wrench." She swiveled the monitor on her desk around and showed Jaz the photo from the surveillance tape.

Jaz looked away and muttered, "I have no idea what that is."

"No? Maybe these will help." She paged through six more screen grabs taken by various security cameras as Jaz's Toyota rolled through the garage, culminating in the exit photo, a clear image of her face. "And one more, the license plate reader, in case there's any doubt about who this is."

Gianna's anger roiled under the surface as she watched Jaz process being caught, and then toss her chin as if she didn't care.

"You know what else I see in this picture? *You* violating your probation."

That definitely got Jaz's attention. She threw up her hands and whined, "I didn't mean to, okay? But I had a right to be pissed off. If you'd just answered your fucking door, it wouldn't have happened."

Jaz would find out soon enough that her door was a moot point, since the card that allowed her into the garage and onto the elevator had been deactivated by the building manager after he saw the security tape.

"You are not in charge of my door, Jaz. Or my phone. You don't get to dictate when I answer. While you're throwing your tantrum, maybe you'd like to know that Keenan's best friend is a cop. You know what he said when she showed him these photos? 'Yeah, that's definitely a VOP. Want me to go pick her up?' VOP means violation of probation, in case you didn't know."

She relished the sudden look of horror on Jaz's face.

"How's that for some irony? At this very minute, your staying out of jail depends on whether or not Keenan wants to extend her kindness to you."

Jaz scurried back to the chair. "Gianna, I—"

"It's not up to me, Jaz. It wasn't my car you vandalized, just like it wasn't my dog you provoked. If I were you, I'd be falling all over myself trying to figure out how I could make this right. All she has to do is decide to press charges and you're going to jail."

"Fuck." Jaz blinked several times and wiped her eyes with her wrists. "I'll pay her back. I'll write her an apology, whatever she wants." She quickly added, "But you have to give it to her."

"You don't have the guts to face her?"

She covered her face and broke down in sobs. "Please tell her not to go to the police. I've only got two more months, Gianna. I've done everything they said. No drinking, no drugs…I share a room with my fucking sister. I promise I won't do no more shit like that. I just was…I can't stand thinking about you with somebody else. It eats me alive."

"And you thought if you made her life miserable enough, she wouldn't want to date me. Is that it?"

"You know how my temper is. I can't control it sometimes, but I swear I'll try harder. Just please don't let her report me."

"Your temper isn't some out-of-body ghost that takes over. It's you, so you need to be the one to fix it." She allowed Jaz to wallow in her misery for a few moments longer before handing her a lifeline. "You'll be relieved to know that for now, Keenan isn't going to press charges over this. But she wants this harassment to stop, and so do I. If it doesn't, she *will* press charges. Is that clear?"

The icy silence was probably the best she could hope for.

"She really is a kind person, Jaz. If you got to know her, you'd be amazed by how much she does for others. I like being around that kind of energy."

Jaz pulled herself together and walked to the door. With her hand on the knob, she turned back and said, "Like I said, I'll pay for the damage but it might take me a little while to get the money. And I'll write a note saying sorry, but you have to give to her. 'Cause I don't want to be her friend."

It probably was as close to a truce as they'd get. Keenan wasn't likely to get her money without prodding, since Jaz's stubbornness would prevent her from following through. Still, Jaz was cornered and she knew it so she had no choice but to back off.

Though Gianna had forgiven her betrayal two years ago, she wasn't sure their friendship would weather this. The last thread that held them together was ready to snap.

CHAPTER THIRTEEN

The small stone cottage sat at the end of a private road that climbed past sloping meadows that only three months from now would be swarmed by skiers. The back of their wraparound deck faced a wooded area, affording privacy for both the hot tub and the floor-to-ceiling glass of the great room. Laurel Mountain was a perfect romantic getaway no matter the season, and only ninety minutes from Pittsburgh.

Gianna captured Keenan in her arms from behind as she wiped the last of their dinner dishes. "This was such a great idea. I forget how nice the mountains are in the fall. Do you ski?"

"Does once count?" Keenan tilted her head, baring her neck for a kiss. "But I'm a big fan of sitting by a roaring fire drinking hot chocolate."

"A girl after my own heart." She latched her lips onto a sinewy muscle, barely resisting the urge to suck. Hickeys were for teenagers.

"Am I?" Keenan asked.

Gianna played the words back and realized what she'd said. It sure seemed that Keenan was on the verge of stealing her heart. "Maybe. I should be asking you, though."

"Hmm." She broke free, and with Bennie on her heels, walked out on the deck and stooped to test the swirling water of the hot tub. "I think it's ready."

Piece by tantalizing piece, she removed her clothes as Gianna watched transfixed. She had to know how sexy that was.

"So are you?" Gianna asked as she shed her clothes and followed her into the tub. "After my heart, that is."

"I think I could be. Isn't that the object of the game?"

"Ah, so it's a game, is it? Bennie, your mom's toying with me."

"Don't say his name! He'll try to jump in." She held up her hand like a stop sign, and he obediently stayed put. "And actually no, it's not a game. But it's the objective, isn't it? At least it is for me."

"Splanify."

"I never play Scrabble with people who make up words."

"Scrabble's a game, you know. So I guess you *do* play games." Gianna couldn't decide which one of them was deflecting. Did either of them really want a serious conversation about what was happening between them, or were they content for now to drift along and see where they ended up?

With only a slight tug, Keenan floated Gianna into her lap and began massaging her backside. "This is not a game, naked lady. It's a process. You meet someone, you date, you get naked... and if you're lucky, you fall in love. Once I get to the naked stage, it's safe to say my heart's not far behind."

Touched by her frankness, Gianna held Keenan's eyes for several seconds before closing in for a kiss. "I'm glad to know that."

Keenan's arms tightened around her and she rested her head on Gianna's shoulder. "I'll be honest with you though—it scares me. Just a little. I worry that I haven't asked myself the hard questions. That could be because right now I don't care about the answers."

"You're losing me. What kinds of questions?"

"For example…" Keenan lifted her head and, without making eye contact, began stroking Gianna's sides. "What should I compare my feelings to? How I felt with Annabel or how I felt the week before we met when I wondered if I might be alone for the rest of my life?"

"Ahh. Good to know I'm not the only one who thinks about things like that."

"Who do you compare me to?"

"Nobody. I was referring to being alone. After I broke up with Jaz the second time, I started to think I really sucked at picking girlfriends. Either that or I sucked at being a girlfriend. The difference between you and me is I *have* thought about it, and I—" She caught herself and took a moment to ask if she really wanted to put herself out there. If she didn't, Keenan probably wouldn't either. How else would they know where they stood? "Honestly, when we met up that day and walked to the Water Steps, it crossed my mind that I might be getting another chance. And I've felt that way ever since. So whatever you have to go through, take your time, do it right. I will too because I believe you'll be worth it."

"Oh, Gianna."

"I hope that wasn't too much too soon. You've got a whole lot more emotions to sort through with Annabel and all. I promise I'm not going to rush anything."

Keenan clutched her head and held her for a long, deep kiss that seemed filled with words she couldn't say. When her hands began to roam beneath the steamy water, it was clear they were done with words for now.

* * *

"You don't have to do this," Gianna whispered, holding the phone behind her.

Keenan held out her hand. "I want to. Let's get this over with."

Jaz had texted that morning asking for Keenan's number, a request Gianna absolutely refused. But then Jaz had offered to call her on Gianna's phone, as she was eager to extend an apology.

"Hi Jaz, this is Keenan," she said flatly.

She'd rationalized taking the call by pointing out that she held all the cards, so Jaz wasn't likely to go on the attack with so much at risk. The potential upside was a burying of the hatchet, which not only would end the frightening physical attacks but also would take the stress off Gianna and restore her social life with her friends without worrying Jaz would erupt again. Keenan's main concern was that Jaz would extend an apology that was patently insincere, daring her to refuse it and risk looking like an ass.

"I'm sorry about your car. It was stupid what I did."

Keenan drew a total blank for how to respond. Should she agree?

"Gianna probably told you I can go off whacked sometimes. I don't mean to. I just…sometimes I can't control it."

"Come on, Jaz. If you can't control it, who can?"

She didn't answer, as though taken aback by the challenge.

"You came after me twice, once with my dog and then with my car. That's not temper, that's a vendetta. And it needs to stop."

"I didn't hurt your dog on purpose, I promise. I told Gianna, I was petting him and I guess his fur got caught on my bracelet or something. It was an accident."

Keenan knew a lie when she heard it, but this one she could use. "Great, then could I get you to do something for me? For Bennie, actually. I need you to go online and fill out a form saying exactly what happened so the pet therapy group will clear him to work again. I'll have Gianna send you the link. Odds are they're going to clear him anyway but I don't like having an incident like that on his record when it wasn't his fault."

"O-okay, whatever," she stammered. "And I looked up how much it costs to fix a windshield. It's like…two hundred dollars?"

"It was three, plus another hundred to tow it to the shop." She paused a beat to let Jaz absorb the seriousness of what she'd done. "I'm willing to forgive that, but like I said, this has to stop."

"Forgive it, you mean…?"

"You don't have to pay me back. But I do need you to fill out that form. Today if possible. It may not seem like a big deal to most people, but the folks at the nursing home really enjoy it when Bennie comes to visit. He can't do that until he's cleared."

"I'll do it, I will. Thank you so much. God, four hundred dollars. That's like a whole week's pay almost. For me, anyway."

"It's not exactly chump change for me either, so I want my money's worth in that note."

As Jaz apologized one last time, Keenan gave Gianna the thumbs-up sign and nodded. Gianna responded with the throat-slashing gesture, meaning she didn't wish to talk to Jaz again.

"Uh, I'm not sure where she went. I'll tell her to give you a call." When she was certain the call had ended, she sneered at Gianna. "I just lied for you."

"And I appreciate it. That four-hundred-dollar gift was awfully generous. I already told her she had to pay you back every dime."

Keenan scrolled through Gianna's phone. "It's worth it to me to get the letter that gets Bennie out of jail. I'm sending her the link now."

"She owed you both."

"And now she just owes me. Maybe she'll think about it the next time she gets jealous and buys dynamite or something."

Gianna had changed into hiking sandals and was standing by the door holding Bennie's leash. "Don't you have any crazy friends or twisted relatives? I feel like I'm carrying the load here."

As Keenan slathered on sunscreen, she ran down her short list of friends, which included Brady and Chad, and Kristy from her high school. "I don't see Kristy all that much—she's got a baby now—but we were close enough back in the day that we can still relate. Like the years haven't changed who we are."

Keenan shouldered a backpack containing sandwiches and water for a hike that began on a rocky path off their back deck. From the map they'd found in their welcome packet, it zigzagged uphill for half a mile before joining a trail leading across a ridge to a ski area vista. Four miles round trip.

"Your friend, did she know Annabel?"

"They met a couple of times, but I wouldn't say they knew each other. Kristy came to visit in Columbus for the Penn State game and it happened to be during one of Annabel's dark spells. She stayed in bed practically the whole weekend."

"Did that happen a lot?"

"One or two episodes a year, but they usually came in clusters when her meds needed adjusting. And honestly, they weren't all that bad until the last year. Here in Pittsburgh, she worked at one of those nurse temp agencies where they call you to fill in. Every day was a crapshoot about whether she'd answer the phone or just stay in bed."

The narrow path forced them to walk single file with Bennie in the lead.

"Were you ever scared to leave her alone?"

"I should've been," she mumbled, feeling suddenly nauseous from the familiar gut punch. "The truth is I wasn't worried about her that way. Annabel never tried to hurt herself, never even threatened to. We used to talk about it and she always said her depression wasn't like that. She wasn't hopeless or despondent, she was just paralyzed. And it always passed. A couple of days down and she'd be back to herself."

"Wait, are you saying you didn't even know she was suicidal?"

"Of course not. I'd have put her in the hospital or something. I thought she'd work through it like she always did. Some days she was fine." Even to her own ear, her voice sounded defensive. For the last two years she'd berated herself for having her head in the sand. "Maybe I just looked away because I knew I couldn't stop it."

Gianna stopped and turned around. "Do I sound like that, Keenan? I hope not because it's absurd. Rationally, we have to know we aren't to blame for what they did."

"The thing is, though…there was this one time…about a week before it happened." She hadn't told a living soul what she was about to reveal, not even her mom. "We were taking a walk through the neighborhood before dinner like we usually did. We passed this house that had a ton of cars out front, and when we got closer…there was this big arrangement of white flowers on the porch."

"A funeral."

"Yeah. I didn't say anything when we were walking by because we'd only found out a week or so earlier about Annabel's mom, and I knew she was really upset about not getting to go to the funeral." She could picture Natchez Street as if it were yesterday, the houses squeezed together, the grass growing up through cracks in the sidewalk. Mostly she remembered their silence, like a solemn nod to the grieving family inside. "When we passed the house, Annabel said, 'Whoever he was, he's lucky.' And I said, 'You mean because he had so many friends?' And she said, 'No, because he isn't here anymore.'"

Gianna slowed and wrapped an arm around her waist as they continued their uphill slog. With a quick kiss to her temple, she said, "And you think that was a warning?"

"If it was, I obviously didn't take it seriously. And frankly"—the knot in her throat nearly stole her voice—"that's going to haunt me for the rest of my life."

* * *

"I have to lie down," Gianna moaned as she stumbled from the shower and grabbed a towel. She couldn't remember the last time she came that hard standing up. On the heels of their five-hour hike, it sapped the very last of her energy reserves. "How old is too old for unconventional sex?"

By her grin, Keenan was obviously pleased with herself. "That was hardly unconventional. Wait till we try it in an RV with my parents asleep only twelve feet away."

She wagged a finger. "I will not be doing that."

"Go on, lay your knackered self down. I'll bring us a snack."

Gianna fell across the bed and reached through the open door of Bennie's crate to give him a scratch. He was tuckered out from their hike, even though Keenan had carried him most of the way back from the vista.

It hadn't escaped her notice that Keenan had gone all out to make their weekend special, packing gourmet snacks and meal kits, and two bottles of what she said were her favorite wines. Cinched in a short sexy robe, she arrived in the bedroom carrying a fruit and cheese tray and a chilled bottle of dry Riesling with two glasses.

Gianna smoothed the blanket so she could place the tray on the bed. "Stop spoiling me! It's causing me great anxiety because I don't know how I'm going to top this when it's my turn."

"You'll think of something." Keenan placed a strawberry between her teeth and offered Gianna a bite. Predictably, it turned into a very wet kiss that left both of them laughing.

"When am I going to find out something about you that I don't like?"

"Who says you will? I have oodles of likable traits."

Gianna carved a sliver of brie and shared it on an apple slice. "How many traits to an oodle?"

"Mmm...six. But it's up to you to make the list. It wouldn't be appropriate for me to brag about my oodles. That would be in poor taste."

"Nothing about you is in poor taste. I know because I've tasted it." She scooted close enough to wrap her arm around Keenan's shoulder. "I was halfway serious about finding out something I don't like. Don't you have some bad habits you need to warn me about? Secret vices? Unhealthy obsessions?"

"My only vice is red wine that stains my teeth but it's canceled out by my *healthy* obsession with dental hygiene."

"Uh-oh, are you going to nag me to floss?"

Keenan sat up and looked at her with alarm. "Oh God, please don't tell me you"—she leapt up and retrieved her overnight bag from under the bed. "This will never work. I can't be with someone who doesn't floss."

"Calm *down*. Jesus, all this time I figured your dealbreaker would be drugs or embezzling or kicking puppies. Turns out it's flossing."

"It's best you know now."

Gianna grumbled, "Fine. It so happens I do floss." *Most days.*

"I'll be watching." She pushed her bag back under the bed and crawled up with another strawberry in her teeth. After a shared bite, she snuggled back under Gianna's arm.

"Seriously, Keenan, do you have any real dealbreakers I should know about? I don't want to do anything stupid."

"I guess just the obvious one, same as everyone else."

"Which is?" Getting an incredulous look, she went on, "I want to hear how you put it."

"Hmm…okay, this is tricky. I can't just say I don't want you dating anyone else, or kissing or touching or whatever. It has to cover all scenarios." She sat up and hugged her knees as she rocked. "How about this? I wouldn't want you chasing a spark with someone else."

"Chasing a spark?"

"Come on, you know what that means. You're with somebody—it could be someone you've just met or someone you've known for years—and all of sudden you feel this little flicker of excitement. It probably happens more than most of us are willing to admit. But the dealbreaker is if you pursue it. If you act on it."

"You mean if I flirt?"

Keenan pursed her lips and nodded slowly. "But only if you really mean it. People play around, that's no big deal. But if we're in a relationship, having sex, and you're checking somebody out…I really don't want to be on the shit end of that. So break up with me before you go chasing a spark." She jabbed Gianna's thigh. "What's so funny?"

Gianna hadn't realized she was smiling. "Nothing, I just got all happy thinking about us being in a relationship."

"Oh, this is definitely a relationship," Keenan replied, opening the front of her robe. "And now you know the rules."

"No chasing sparks."

"And?"

"Flossing."

CHAPTER FOURTEEN

"Number six to X-ray," the loudspeaker blared.

Six was Gianna. She took a quick look at her supply tables to make sure nothing was askance and raced out the side of the giant tent, which was open all the way around for ventilation. Even beneath the canvas, most wore sweaters or sweatshirts to ward off the fall chill, but running around so much had kept her plenty warm.

Dozens of prescreened patients were lined up outside the X-ray truck, one of several mobile units situated around the fairgrounds. This particular truck was staffed by medical technology students and instructors from nearby Mountain Empire Community College. No one saw a dentist without passing through X-ray.

"Number six right here," she announced with a friendly wave. After two days of shuttling patients to their next stop, the X-ray team recognized her, even with the KN95 mask she wore at all times. Health authorities had loosened most Covid restrictions, but clinic organizers remained concerned about the low vaccination rate in the region.

A painfully thin woman whose weathered look told years of hard luck tales met her, carrying a manila envelope with her fresh films. "Lord help me, I ain't seen a dentist since I was about ten years old. Don't let me pass out on the way in there. You'll have to carry me."

"You don't have to be nervous. All the dentists are very good. I'm Gianna, by the way."

"I'm Sally...Sal to everybody that knows me." She held a hand to her masked jaw, as if to cushion her pain. "I cain't believe this is finally happening. I been here since Thursday night waiting in the car with my friend. I didn't even wanna come but I got so I cain't hardly eat. And I cain't sleep neither 'cause it hurts all the dang time."

"They'll get you fixed up, Sal." She knew better than to add "good as new" since that usually wasn't possible. "You'll need to keep your mask on until your dentist says it's okay to take it off, okay?"

She led Sal into the tent, probably the same tent that housed blue-ribbon livestock during fair week. Folding chairs for patients were set up at the end of five long rows of tables, each with eight to ten dental stations. Rows one and two were staffed by dental hygienists who performed a thorough cleaning. Many of their patients were children who'd come along while their parents or caretakers received more serious treatment. The third row, manned mostly by dental students under the supervision of instructors, was for "drillings and fillings." The last two rows, which included Keenan and her father, were for extractions.

Gianna peeked at Sal's paperwork and guided her to a seat beside Keenan's row. The triage team had already decided that Sal needed to lose the tooth that was causing her so much pain. According to the McEvoys, stories like hers were the norm for rural clinics. Chronic lack of dental care led to patients showing up with teeth so badly decayed they couldn't be saved. Pulling those teeth was the only expeditious way to stop the pain, since anything requiring multiple visits was out of the question. Some patients might be fitted for dentures or bridges, which were being made in a portable lab truck, but most just left with a bloody socket stitched up and packed in gauze.

Over the last two days, Gianna had glimpsed several cases of a condition known informally as "meth mouth," in which multiple teeth were rotted from the prolonged use of methamphetamines. These patients also were given substance abuse referrals, but Keenan said it was just as hard to get drug rehab in poor rural areas as it was to get dental care.

Though surrounded by circumstances she found heartbreaking, Gianna saw hope in the faces of those moving along the assembly line. Many like Sal had arrived two days early to stake out a place in line, afraid need would overwhelm capacity. They slept in their cars, ate from coolers and grocery bags they'd packed for the trip, and used portable toilets and outside water faucets. All this so they could eat solid food again. So they could talk, laugh and sleep without a constant dull ache. So they could smile again and reclaim their dignity.

After showing Sal to her seat, she left to check supplies along the back row, the eight stations assigned to her. Wearing fresh polymer gloves, she restocked bibs, gauze, and rinse cups, and collected the numbered trays of used instruments for the sterilizer. Finally caught up, she paused to drop her mask and take a gulp from a tall travel cup filled with water that used to have ice.

Every chance she got, she stood close to Keenan's station to watch her work. Like all the volunteers, Keenan wore a yellow paper gown, gloves and a headlamp affixed to her face shield. Before treating each patient, she carefully explained what she was going to do, how it might feel, and how it would help them. Then throughout the procedure, she provided steady reassurance. A true professional. Always kind and compassionate, she was the perfect dentist for the anxious patient. Gianna made a mental note to try to hold off seating Sal until Keenan was free.

"Number six to X-ray."

* * *

Keenan stretched and kneaded the taut muscles at the base of her neck. The hardest part of doing extractions for hours on end was having to stand and lean a certain way to get the leverage she needed to pry a tooth from its socket. She envied her dad, whose arm strength meant he could pop one out with a simple twist from the comfort of his stool.

"You just left bloody handprints on your back," Gianna said from behind as she shook out a fresh paper gown. "Looks like you've been hugged by the Evil Dead."

She'd lost count of how many patients she'd seen since six a.m. yesterday, though she assumed her mom was keeping count. Keenan and her dad always worked side by side so her mom could serve as dental assistant to both.

"I feel like the Evil Dead." She discarded her bloody gloves. "Two more hours. Think you'll make it?"

"I'll make it. I'm more worried about you. You look exhausted."

"I am, but..." She tipped her head toward her father, who was working on a patient. He was fit and healthy for his age, but pushing himself at sixty-one wasn't without risk. "Dad's the one we should be worried about. If Mom didn't make him take a break every now and then, he'd go nonstop for twelve hours."

"Coming through," her mom announced, waving a spray bottle and paper cloth.

They stepped aside as she disinfected the station and collected all the used instruments in a sterilization tray.

"I'll take those, Connie," Gianna said. Nodding toward the table behind their stations, she added, "I got you four clean sets. Filled your water, brought you some ice-cold Gatorade and Clif Bars. Let me know if there's anything else you need."

"We're bringing you back, girl," her mom said, then to Keenan, "She's very good at this."

"See what you've gotten yourself into?" Keenan said as her mom walked away. Turning around, she allowed Gianna to massage her shoulders. "She's right, you're really good at this. You have no idea how much easier this job is when your volunteer's a step ahead of you. I can't believe they roped you into escorting too."

"I guess they caught me sitting on my butt once too often. I'm getting a workout now, but yinz are the real superheroes." Gianna held up the gown. "Here, let me help you into your cape."

"This means I have to get back to work, doesn't it?"

"If it makes you feel better, the X-ray line was down to about a dozen. The end is near." Gianna gave her shoulders one last squeeze and said, "Just a heads-up, the woman I'm bringing over next is Sal. She's pretty anxious, said she hadn't seen a dentist since she was ten."

"I'll take good care of her. Thanks for letting me know."

As she watched Gianna greet Sal, her heart swelled with emotion. Gianna had a way about her, whether she recognized it or not. She gave Keenan credit for inspiring her charitable side, but it was obvious to anyone she was naturally compassionate. All weekend she'd treated everyone here with respect, no matter how they looked—or how they smelled—and she was especially kind to those like Sal who were nervous.

"She's a keeper, that one," her mom whispered from behind. "And I'm not just talking clinic."

"Yeah, I know," she murmured, never taking her eyes from Gianna. Over the last three days Keenan had come to realize how much she wanted this relationship to work. That emotion she kept feeling in her heart…it was love.

* * *

Gianna stumbled into the RV and went straight to her bunk to collapse, skeptical about whether a warm shower and hot meal would be enough to persuade her to move again. Organizers were saying they'd served nearly eight hundred patients in two days. She couldn't feel more satisfied if she'd treated them all herself.

Keenan and her parents had to feel satisfied as well. Connie counted sixty-six patients between them, mostly extractions but also filing, scaling, drilling and filling. Keenan said they all felt an urgency to do as much as they could with the patient in the chair since it might be years before they saw a dentist again.

All around her, she'd seen hardship. Poverty may not have caused these people's dental problems, but it certainly made them worse. Many had shared their misfortunes on the short walk from one station to the next. It was bad enough that their decaying and broken teeth were painful. They also were unsightly, which put better jobs out of reach, some said. They were marks of shame for drug use and visual reminders of domestic violence. While tremendously humbled by her own privilege, Gianna was glad to have been a part of something that helped ease suffering and gave people hope.

Keenan emerged from the shower compartment wrapped in a bath towel, then tugged the curtain closed that separated their sleeping berth from the rest of the RV. Her forehead was red and raw from the headgear she'd worn all weekend, and her face sagged with obvious fatigue. She eyed Gianna on the bed and smiled. "I bet it feels good to lie down."

"Heavenly is more like it. I was lying here thinking about this whole weekend. You guys are amazing. I'm never going to forget this as long as I live."

"I'm never going to forget you coming with us. I'm so proud of you. You worked your ass off."

"No more than anyone else. The hygienists, the dental students. All the volunteers. I was really impressed by how many churches pitched in with food and donations."

"Every time we do one of these, it makes my real job seem like such a breeze," Keenan said as she slid into red flannel pajama pants and a gray Buckeyes T-shirt. "You can see why Mom and Dad take the whole week off afterward. It takes a toll, both physical and emotional. They get to put their feet up, enjoy the lake."

"That's great. They deserve it. So do you."

"Someone's got to hold down the fort at home. Besides, I'm kind of partial to taking my time off one Friday afternoon at a time so we can go somewhere." She ducked to catch Gianna's eye. "But not next weekend. I already have appointments on Friday."

"Okay, but I get to pick where we go next time. Deal?" As she gathered her toiletries, Keenan's father announced he was heading into the shower.

"Don't worry, he's always quick," Keenan said. "They're having dinner with friends of theirs, another couple that comes every year. I'll fix something for us. Grilled cheese?"

"Perfect." She was too tired to care what they ate.

"What's the verdict on the weekend? Do you feel like you made a difference?"

She thought of Sal, who'd stopped to thank her on the way out, and to tell her she couldn't wait to eat regular food again. "Definitely. Not like you and your parents, but I feel good about it. What I find so incredible is that yinz know how hard these events are going to be and it doesn't scare you off. You keep signing up for them over and over."

"Is that your way of saying this was your one and only?" Keenan laughed softly. "Don't worry, yes is a fine answer. It's more than a lot of people do."

"I wasn't saying that at all. But I can't get over the level of dedication yinz have to keep doing it. It's profound."

"Thank you."

"I'm not sure I can match it but I want you to invite me again next time—seriously. Obviously I can't commit to anything specific right now, but I'm open to doing it again." Left unsaid was the implication they'd still be seeing each other six months or a year from now when the McEvoys signed up to do another. "But next time I'm following your mom and dad's cue—taking a whole week off to recover. I don't know how I'm going to function when I get back."

"What's your week like?"

"Assuming all hell didn't break loose while I was gone, I'll just be playing catchup on my accounts. Dani's birthday's on Wednesday so I need to put in an appearance at her party. They're meeting at Cavitto's for karaoke."

"Isn't that a girl bar?"

"Depends on the night. Want to come?"

Keenan bobbed her head from side to side as if considering it. "I sort of do because I want to get to know your friends better, and I'd *kill* to watch you sing karaoke. But I also wonder if this might be a good time for you to do something with Jaz, something that shows her you're still her friend."

It was a sweet gesture, but also frustrating since Gianna was still angry over Jaz's threat. "I can't believe you're so nice to her after all the crap she's pulled. No, I take that back. I *can* believe it because I've seen how you treat everybody."

"I'm thinking about both of us. All three of us, actually. Anything that makes her feel more secure about your friendship is good for us."

"Yeah, I know. But I also want my friends to see that I'm with you now. I don't want them whispering behind my back about how Jaz and I are going to get back together someday."

Keenan broke into a grin as she climbed onto Gianna's bunk. "So you're *with* me now, are you? I like the sound of that."

"Get used to hearing it. There are people I want you to meet, including my family. They'll be quite pleased to hear I'm seeing someone who doesn't have a rap sheet."

"I'd love to meet your family, but after the way you've described them, I'm surprised you'd want me to."

Gianna grunted. "True. Right now my family life feels pretty toxic."

"I wouldn't go that far." Keenan pursed her lips. "Trust me, I'm an expert on family toxicity. Yours is dysfunctional…maybe a little noxious. But toxic is when they start firebombing your car."

Or breaking your windshield. Gianna kept that thought to herself, since that was friends, not family, and Keenan seemed determined not to spoil her friendship with Jaz. However both were violent acts meant to intimidate, and in light of all the trauma with Annabel's family, it made sense that Keenan would want to mend the relationship with Jaz before it went totally off the rails.

"You're right, we're not in toxic territory yet. I'd like to keep us from getting there but I don't know what I can do about it. I was thinking the other day that it's time I let go of my grudge over their favoritism toward Gabe. I'm thirty-four years old, time to grow up. The problem is it's still right there in my face as long as Mom keeps acting like she's lost her only child."

Keenan drew Gianna into her arms and kissed her temple. "Half the battle is *wanting* to fix it. Just try to keep the doors open and let me know if I can help. How does your mom feel about dogs?"

"What a fascinating thought. Honestly I have no idea. Wouldn't it be amazing if Bennie came around and broke through her armor?"

"It wouldn't be the first time. The little guy broke through mine."

It was a long shot, she knew. In her family, they'd had a couple of outdoor cats but never a dog. She couldn't begin to visualize her mother with a dog in her lap. But she'd experienced for herself the effect Bennie had on her mood, and it was worth a try. What sort of conversation might they have if her mother wasn't consumed with grief?

"We should try it, Keenan. I'll scope it out. You sure you won't mind?"

"Are you kidding? After all you've done this weekend I'll owe you about six years' worth of favors."

"Six years! That's a lot of favors. And when I run out, all I have to do is sign up for another clinic, right?"

Keenan laughed. "I guess that depends on how long you want me around."

Gianna answered with a mighty hug, worried it was too soon to put her true feelings on the table. She needed to be sure Keenan was ready to move on from Annabel, since the idea of Keenan being in her life for years to come was starting to feel serious.

CHAPTER FIFTEEN

From her office window, Gianna watched as the last panel truck left the bay. "I'm really sorry about this, Ellen. I'll make sure your order goes out today." Along with those of two others who'd left messages yesterday to complain about missed deliveries. "I understand. I promise I'll make it right. Again, I'm so sorry this happened."

There were only a couple of scenarios to explain why three customers on the same route had missed deliveries. Either a truck had broken down or the driver was new and hadn't followed the route. Those bins were sitting somewhere...unless they were delivered to the wrong place, an even worse scenario since they'd have to be retrieved. There wasn't time for that. Ellen's nursing home in Claysville was shorted a bin last week too and now they were low on critical supplies.

When Stefan's number went to voice mail, she called Jaz.

"Are you back?" Jaz asked.

"Yeah, I got back last night." Jaz probably didn't want to hear about her weekend, which was fine because she didn't have time for personal conversation right now. "I'm trying to reach Stefan. Is he around?"

"He's playing golf with Jack. They left about an hour ago."

"Great. Orders aren't being delivered but he's got time to play golf."

"It's what they do, Gianna. I been trying to tell yinz but nobody listens. They make like, 'Oh, it's business. We have to go play 'cause these are our clients.' It's all bullshit."

"Where's Rudy?"

"Called in sick."

"Are you kidding me? Rudy's out sick and Stefan still leaves to play golf?" She knew better than to complain to Jaz about Stefan but she was exasperated. "They missed three orders on the Wheeling route yesterday. Please tell me those went out today."

"I can look."

As Jaz walked through the warehouse, Gianna politely asked about her weekend. Their rapport was more stilted than usual, as though both recognized that Gianna's weekend was not to be discussed. She couldn't help but wonder how long it would take for Jaz to come around to accepting Keenan. Sooner or later she'd have to—because Keenan wasn't going anywhere.

"There's a bunch of bins by bay seven. Let me see..." A pause while she checked the tags. "High Ridge Care Facility, Arden Manor...here's a bunch for Claysville."

"So they didn't go out today either. Damn it!" This was unacceptable. "What the hell's going on, Jaz?"

"Can't tell you, but I checked these bins off day before yesterday so they should've been on the truck. Number seven went to Akron this morning so I guess that's why they didn't go today."

Gianna silently screamed the F-word three times as she grabbed her purse. "I'm coming down there. I need to cram as many of those into my car as it'll hold."

Twenty minutes later she had all of Claysville's order packed into her SUV, but she'd have to make another trip to deliver the rest.

"Want me to come with you?" Jaz asked.

"I'd love the company but you're the only one here I'd trust to run the warehouse."

"Funny, it don't say that on my pay stub."

It was a fair point, one Gianna would raise with Uncle Jack. Better yet, with her father. He'd go ballistic if he found out Jaz had been left in charge.

"Thanks for your help." She paused before getting into her vehicle. "You want to ride with me to Dani's birthday party tomorrow? I can swing by and pick you up."

Jaz's face brightened. "Sure! Wait, are you still…?"

"Seeing Keenan? Yeah, that's going great." She knew Jaz well enough to read the letdown in her face, even as she tried valiantly not to pout. "I want her to meet all my friends but we don't have to do everything together. She knows my friendship with you is important to me and she's cool with us hanging out."

Gianna left it at that. Her relationship with Keenan made her happy. It was up to Jaz to decide how to feel about that.

* * *

Keenan had arrived home last night to an email from the pet therapy association giving Bennie the all-clear to go back to work. While she was leaning toward retiring him—and herself—from library events and visits to care facilities, his work with anxious patients at the dental clinic would keep his certification active. At the moment, he lay curled in the lap of twenty-year-old Ashley Grant, in the chair for her first checkup in two years.

Peering through her goggles, she matched what she was seeing to the X-ray. To her assistant, she said, "Cassidy, I want to do twenty-seven and thirty-one today, then eight through ten at the next visit. Can we get that scheduled?"

"I have to come back?" Ashley whined. "I was hoping I could get it all over with at the same time."

It was clear from her squirming and frenetic petting of Bennie that she was extremely nervous about being in the chair. Or perhaps general anxiety was a trait that carried over into other aspects of her life. That would make sense, given what Keenan was seeing.

"It's a fair bit of work, Ashley. We can do half the fillings today but you're going to need a crown on that tooth that's causing trouble. They have to make it at the lab, so you'll have to come back anyway."

Ashley groaned. "Fine, but let's do as much as we can all at once."

It was good that she was eager to fix her damaged teeth, but it wouldn't matter in the long run if she didn't get her bulimia under control. The acid was doing a number on her enamel.

Keenan tipped her head, a signal for Cassidy to leave the room. When she was gone, she brought Ashley's chair upright and slid the stool around so they could talk face to face. "Bennie likes you. Do you have a dog at home?"

Keenan chatted casually for a moment to strengthen their rapport. Patients were usually embarrassed about being called out for bulimia, but she would be negligent not to confront it.

"Ashley, we need to be frank about what's going on here. I saw you two years ago and your teeth were in great shape. You've lost a fair bit of enamel since then. An alarming amount, to be honest. It's more than what we usually see with sugary snacks and pop, and I don't see any indicators of a physiological condition that would explain it. This kind of damage…I suspect it's caused by stomach acid, which happens when you throw up. Is that what's going on here?"

The young woman continued to pet Bennie, never lifting her eyes to meet Keenan's. "It happens…sometimes."

"I see quite a few cases like this, especially in patients your age. Usually women but not always." Careful not to sound judgmental, she explained the progression of tooth loss if the problem wasn't addressed. "The good news is I think we've caught this in time. You have a nice smile and we want to save it. I can do some fillings and a crown this time, but if it gets worse you could be looking at implants or dentures in a year or two. Let's not let it come to that." She reached in a drawer for a brochure on bulimia and encouraged her to speak with her parents if she felt she would benefit by talking to a counselor.

It saddened her that some of her patients—even girls as young as ten—felt so much pressure about their appearance that they'd do something so unpleasant and harmful.

Ashley pursed her lips, her expression one of defeat. "I guess it would be pretty stupid to lose weight and not have my own teeth."

Keenan chuckled. "We all have things we don't like about ourselves. Want to hear mine?"

"It can't be that bad. You look great."

"Mine started back in middle school when all the other girls in my gym class were getting breasts. But not me. Word got around that I was flat-chested and all the boys started calling me Kenneth instead of Keenan. Funny, huh?"

"That's bullying. It's disgusting."

"When I turned eighteen I got some money from my grandmother, and I actually looked up how much it would cost to get implants." She smiled as Ashley glanced down at her chest. "Nope, didn't do it. I decided looking quote-unquote normal wasn't worth having to wear a bra. I don't even own one."

"Oh, that's rich. You're so lucky."

And my girlfriend likes me just the way I am. Though satisfied with the rapport they'd built, she decided to keep that thought to herself.

"I'm lucky I learned to like myself without changing who I am. But now that I've said all that—and told you my secret—I should also say I'm a dentist, not a counselor. If you want advice from a professional, there's a number on that brochure."

"Can I just steal Bennie? He fixes everything."

"He'd probably be happy to go home with you but I'd miss the little rascal. But hey, there's your answer. If you want a friend who accepts you the way you are, you can't go wrong with a dog."

* * *

It was well after dark when Gianna backed up to bay seven to unload the bins she'd collected on her second run. The bay doors were closed and the employee lot was empty but for

Stefan's fleet SUV, identical to hers but black, and Rudy's truck. Rudy…who'd called in sick today.

After stacking the empty bins, she tried the door and found it unlocked. "Anyone home?"

Stefan emerged from his office, still dressed in golf slacks and a polo shirt with a Callaway vest. His usually perfect hair had a flat ring around it, likely from wearing a visor all day. "Gianna…I was just heading out. You need something?"

His nonchalance enraged her. "What do I need? I need an explanation for why three of my orders sat on the loading dock all day yesterday instead of going out on the Wheeling route. I need an explanation for why, if they were missed yesterday, they weren't rushed out first thing this morning. I need someone to tell me why the hell there wasn't anyone here this afternoon who could answer that."

"Whoa! Somebody needs to chill."

"Don't fucking tell me to chill, Stefan." It jolted her to hear herself yelling at her cousin with such fury. She needed to dial it back for family's sake if nothing else. "Look, I just got back from making two delivery runs because those customers were depending on us. Do you have any idea what happens when a nursing home runs out of adult diapers? The poor patients lose what little dignity they have left, and it's a nightmare for the staff. Meanwhile, the people responsible for getting orders where they're supposed to go are out on the golf course all day." It was a miracle she'd said all that without more cursing.

"I'm sorry, I didn't know what was in their order." At least he had the decency to look embarrassed. "Rudy pulled them off the truck yesterday to make room for something Dad needed to send to Wheeling. He said those bins could wait till tomorrow."

"Why is Rudy working tonight? He called in sick today."

"I don't know. Maybe he felt better and came in to catch up."

More importantly, why was Uncle Jack sending bins to Wheeling? Those were *her* accounts. Suddenly she was the one embarrassed, realizing something must have come up while she was out of town and Jack had taken care of it. And now she felt like a total jagoff.

"Shit…I'm sorry, Stefan. It's probably because I was out of town and your dad had to step in and handle it." She sighed and ran a hand through her hair. "It would have been nice if someone had given me a heads-up—an email or something—but I can see now that it wasn't your fault. And I know you wouldn't do that on purpose."

"No, but it was partly my fault. I knew you were out of the office for two days. I should have checked the order and called them to see if it was a problem. If I'd known what it was, I'd have driven it down there myself. Believe me, I'd do anything to get out of playing golf."

"What? You don't like golf?"

"God, no. I hate it, but Dad says I have to learn so I can schmooze with all the clients. He even signed me up for lessons with a pro."

Gianna had always thought Uncle Jack cared more about image over substance. "I don't know, Stef. I have great relationships with my clients and I've never played golf with any of them. Maybe he's talking about the higher-ups, the decision makers. The ones I deal with care about their products and getting their orders on time."

"You may not believe me but that's what I care about too. How about I give you a heads-up next time something like that happens? That way, we can deal with problems before they become disasters."

"That's a deal. Thanks, man." They shared a fist bump, after which she apologized again. "In the future I'll try not to step on your toes."

She trudged upstairs to her office and sat down to access the system so she could see who it was in Wheeling that had placed the special order. Oddly, there weren't any changes logged to yesterday's manifest. An emergency order that hadn't yet been invoiced? Or more likely, a replacement shipment for damaged products or shipping errors. Whoever it was, she needed to reach out and—

"Gianna!" Uncle Jack appeared in her doorway. Like Stefan, he still wore his golf clothes.

"Christ Almighty, you scared me. I thought everyone was gone."

"What's this I hear about you ripping my son an asshole?" Neither his tone nor expression suggested this was to be a friendly conversation.

"I was upset about three of my orders getting pulled off the truck and no one being around to tell me why. But I apologized to Stefan for losing my temper. I shouldn't have lit into him that way."

"No, you shouldn't. He isn't your underling, Gianna. He reports to me—and so do you for that matter. What happens in the warehouse isn't your concern. If you have any issues, you bring them to me."

She was shocked by his gruffness. "How can I do that when you're out on the golf course and not answering your phone?"

He shook his finger at her. "Did you hear what I just said, Gianna? I'm not accountable to you. And I don't want you down at the warehouse anymore. That's not your job. If you have a problem with deliveries, you come to me. Leave Stefan alone." He turned to leave but then whirled back around. "And you can tell your little friend she's not the hall monitor, calling you up to tattle over every little thing. If she wants to keep her job, she'll stay in her own lane and do exactly what Stefan tells her to do."

Gianna remained at her desk for several minutes after he'd gone, shaken to the point of nausea. In all her years at the company, she'd never been dressed down like that, not even by her father. It couldn't be a coincidence that it had come on the heels of her confession about buying cocaine in high school. Now she had a sinking feeling that Uncle Jack planned to tear her down so he could elevate Stefan.

* * *

Keenan sat cross-legged beneath a fleece blanket with Bennie settled in her lap. He always had fun when he stayed with Chad and Brady, but there was no mistaking whose boy he was. He hadn't let her out of his sight since she picked him up last night.

As she petted him, she chatted on WhatsApp with Gianna, who'd clearly had a day from hell.

"...the whole thing was like a bad dream. I wanted to throw up."

"If you ask me, Jack seems pretty desperate to push Stefan out there whether he's ready or not. Could be that he's kicking you out of the warehouse because you keep finding problems there and making Stefan look bad."

"That makes as much sense as anything. And if I'm honest, the way he yelled at me was no worse than me yelling at Stefan. You could say I deserved it."

"You could...but you'd have to be willing to gloss over the fact that you were right. They screwed up your orders *and* spent a workday on the golf course. What did you do besides put your customers first and run your ass off to make sure they got what they needed?"

"Details, details." Gianna finally smiled. "Thanks for listening. Oh, by the way, I asked Jaz to ride with me to Dani's party. You were right, she seemed glad it was just us. But I did tell her we were dating and that it was going...ahem, really well."

"Did you now? That's such an amazing coincidence because I might have said the same thing to Mom." Actually, what she'd said was that she thought Gianna was *the real deal*. She'd even decided to tell her so but not over a chat app. "Are we still on for going somewhere next weekend?"

"Already made the reservation but don't ask because it's a surprise. Speaking of next week, how would you feel about coming over on Wednesday night? We'll cook dinner together and you can spend the night."

"I'll have to check my very busy social calendar." For three seconds she feigned interest in her schedule. "Well what do you know? I'm free."

"I don't want to be all morbid about it, but it's Gabe's one-year anniversary. I wouldn't mind going through some old pictures if you're interested."

"Oh, Gianna...of course I'm interested. I'd be deeply, deeply honored to spend that evening with you."

Gianna heaved a great sigh and shook her head as if warding off tears. "Good, now I have something to look forward to on that day."

"I'm here for you, Gianna. You won't have to face any of this alone. Not Gabe, not Jaz, not work, not your family. You can lean on me for anything." She started to add that Bennie could help too but thought better of it. This was about more than comfort. She was offering herself—mentally, physically and emotionally—as a partner.

CHAPTER SIXTEEN

"Are you sure it's all right?" Gianna spoke to Keenan through her car's Bluetooth connection as she navigated downtown traffic. "I won't be that long, just one drink across the river at Mike's. She knows you're coming over. I told her yesterday."

"It's kind of sweet Jaz remembered the day," Keenan said. "I just left my office so I can be waiting with dinner when you get home."

"That's great, thanks. I'm going to park at my place and walk over. Oh, you should have seen Jaz's face when I told her she was banned from parking in the garage at my building. Anyway, that means she'll have her car across the river so I may catch a ride back with her. Turning in now…going to lose you. See you in an hour tops."

She was surprised to find Jaz waiting on the sidewalk outside her garage.

"I parked in the city lot around the corner. It's only five bucks after five, not a bad deal."

Wrapped in long sweaters, they headed on foot across the Roberto Clemente Bridge. Game nights often saw a fair bit of foot traffic over to PNC Park, but the Pirates were ending the season on a road trip to Atlanta.

The conversation as they walked began somewhat stilted, with both of them avoiding any talk of Keenan. Gianna asked about Jaz's mom and sister and received the expected string of complaints, though it was nice to hear her speak so proudly of Sabrina's recent promotion.

"I've been thinking about you and Gabe, how much you miss him. It made me realize I'd be really tore up if something happened to Sabrina."

"There aren't any words for how awful it is to lose a sibling," Gianna said. "Thanks for remembering Gabe today. I kept waiting for Dad to come into my office and say something, but I should've known better. He's totally tuned it out. Knowing Mom, she probably hasn't gotten out of bed all day."

"Hard to believe it's been a whole year. Seems like just yesterday we were all at the Tavern for your birthday."

She thought of her encounter with Rob Blanchard and how his mention of that party had prompted her to tell Keenan the story of Gabe's death. "When I told Keenan how it happened, it struck me that I still have a hard time accepting the fact that Gabe killed himself. Don't get me wrong—I believe it. But there must have been more to it than Gabe being jealous and angry. Something we didn't know about, like a chemical imbalance in his brain or something. Gabe could be moody sometimes but I never saw him lose his shit."

"I saw him tear into Rudy once when they had to call one of the trucks back. One of them must have texted Jack because he came down and ripped into both of them."

Gianna sighed. "If they'd just use the damn scanners!" She hadn't told Jaz of her confrontation with Uncle Jack or the fact that she'd practically been banned from the warehouse. "I'm so glad I'm out of there. I'd lose my mind if I had to deal with that crap every day."

"Tell me about it." Jaz eschewed her usual diatribe about the warehouse, perhaps a sign she finally understood she was on her own at work, and it was up to her to make the best of it.

As they neared the bar, Gianna decided she had to broach the elephant in the room. "Jaz, I meant to say this the other night. I really appreciate you calling Keenan to apologize. She did too." Not getting a reply, she continued, "I think you'd like her if you gave her a chance. You have to admit, it takes a really nice person to forgive what you did to her car."

"That was so stupid," Jaz mumbled.

"We all do stupid things when our emotions get the best of us. I hope you'll get to know her. She's important to me, and so is your friendship. It might be selfish but I want to hold on to both of you."

Jaz nodded glumly, still plainly reluctant to accept Keenan's place in her life.

They entered Mike's Beer Bar, a sprawling taproom known for its expansive offering of microbrews. The crowd was modest, normal for a weeknight without a home game.

"Jaz! Over here." In a corner by the window, two pub tables had been pushed together to hold at least a dozen people, all the usual faces from the happy hour crowd.

Gianna eyed Jaz, who was grinning and waving at everyone. "What's this?"

"They wanted to come too so you'd know they didn't forget either."

Overcome with emotion, Gianna approached the table and fell into the arms of Shanice first, followed by Nick, then the others one by one. Ellen and Fran, the older couple, presented her with a small stuffed bear wearing a bowtie.

"Yinz are so sweet. I can't believe you all came."

"We're here for you," Fran said, drawing her into a motherly hug that helped hide her tears. Whispering, she added, "Shanice tells us you've got a special lady."

"Keenan. You met her at the concert."

"Right, with the dog. Where is she?"

Gianna checked the keycard app on her phone. "She's just arrived at my apartment and is getting ready to make dinner."

Fran shook her head. "You should call her, tell her to come on over."

"I told Jaz I'd stay for one drink. I didn't know everybody was going to be here."

"It's going to be longer than an hour." She nodded toward the group. "We're all ordering dinner."

Indeed, the others were speaking to a server over shared menus. In the thick of it was Jaz, who had to have known this would disrupt her plans with Keenan, but chose not to say anything. Gianna couldn't leave her friends after they'd turned out to help her past this milestone.

She stepped outside with her phone and placed a quick call. "Hey, have you started cooking yet?"

"Just waiting on the oven to warm up."

Without throwing Jaz under the bus for purposefully undermining their plans, she explained the situation. "I'd feel bad if I walked out on them."

"I understand." Though she definitely sounded disappointed. "I can pack it all in the fridge and come back tomorrow if you want."

"I was hoping you'd come over and join us."

"Gianna, are you sure? They came to be with you, to remember Gabe."

While that was true, Gianna knew her friends would be happy she was seeing someone new. "All the more reason for you to be here. You can hear about Gabe from friends who knew us together. The Del Vecchio Boxed Set. Plus it gives me a chance to introduce you as my girlfriend."

"I can hardly say no to that, can I?" Keenan's smile was obvious even over the phone.

A new girlfriend. For everyone but Jaz, it was a bright spot on a sad day.

* * *

With every step across the Clemente Bridge, Keenan wished she'd brought her car. It wasn't that the walk was long—not even half a mile—but that she'd changed from the comfortable shoes she'd worn to work into cute flats that went with her outfit.

If the coming blister on her pinky toe wasn't enough, there was also the fact that Jaz had knowingly undermined her plans with Gianna. While she wanted to be irritated, she reminded herself it was the anniversary of Gabe's death. Regardless of Jaz's motives, this gathering was a chance for Gianna's friends to show their support for her loss. Only an asshole would get upset about that.

Besides, it was also another chance to meet Gianna's friends, and tonight would have the special caveat of being introduced as "the girlfriend." That little nugget canceled out any resentment she had about having her plans upended.

All that said, she wasn't looking forward to another face-to-face encounter with Jaz, despite having buried the hatchet over the phone. It was hard to believe Jaz was truly remorseful if she'd pull a stunt like this one. Still, Keenan vowed to make the best of it for Gianna's sake.

Gianna was watching for her, apparently. She immediately left a large table to greet her with a kiss that drew wolf whistles from a couple of men at the bar. "Thank you for coming. I will make this up to you, I promise."

"I have no doubt." She held Gianna's gaze with a broad smile, cementing her status for all to see.

"Come meet the gang. You already know some of them." She clasped Keenan's hand and tugged her to the table. "Hey, everybody! For those of you who didn't get to meet her at the VeraDid concert, this is Keenan. We've been seeing each other for a few weeks and she says it's okay for me to introduce her as my girlfriend. So…meet my girlfriend, Keenan McEvoy."

Spontaneous cries of excitement became muted as eyes furtively wandered to Jaz, who sat at the far end of the table absorbed in her phone. In this case, Keenan didn't mind being ignored. It was better than hostility.

As she greeted each of Gianna's friends in turn, she was most delighted by Shanice. "I knew something was up with you two. I could see it brewing."

"Come on," Gianna said. "You couldn't have known it before I did."

Shanice swatted her stomach. "Don't be so sure about that. Your face is an open book. Time to go change that Facebook status, girl."

The sporty couple, Vic and Dani, joined the conversation, insisting they too had seen Gianna's interest at the concert.

"But it doesn't count unless Keenan saw it," Dani said. "Did you?"

"Kinda." Keenan grinned. "But I thought she had a thing for my dog, not me."

"Come to think of it, I did," Gianna said. Shaking a finger at Shanice, she added, "That's what you saw on my face."

Keenan hated this awkwardness around Jaz. She'd always prided herself in her ability to talk to people honestly, even when it involved difficult subjects. She quietly approached her while the others were teasing Gianna. "Excuse me."

Jaz looked up from her phone and proffered a weak smile.

"Hey, I just wanted to say thanks for that letter you wrote for Bennie. It was perfect. The board approved him the very next day. That's how good it was."

"Yeah, I'm glad it worked. I felt bad when Gianna said he wasn't allowed to go nowhere."

"We put a hold on our visits but he still comes to work with me. Man, he loves that. Some people get nervous at the dentist, but if they're cool with it I bring him in and he sits on their lap while I work. It helps them stay calm, especially kids. So thanks again."

However nervous she'd been about seeing Jaz, it was painfully obvious Jaz was even worse.

"This was a great idea, Jaz. Anniversaries like this are so damn hard. I could tell Gianna was dreading today, but showing up here and seeing all her friends…look at her. Most people in her situation would be crying right now, but thanks to you she's having a good time with people who care about her."

"I was good friends with Gabe. I feel like I lost him too."

"Of course you did. I'm sorry for your loss too. Everyone assumes a death like this only affects family." Keenan didn't want to push too hard but she believed the key to winning people over—whether a bulimic patient who needed to change her harmful habits or a jealous ex-girlfriend whose friendship she wanted—was to start from a place of respect. "Gianna says you were one of the few people she could lean on after it happened. I know what it's like trying to get through a loss like that. I couldn't imagine anyone doing it on their own. She was lucky to have you there."

"I'm always gonna have her back. That's never gonna change—no matter what."

The last was said fiercely, as if a warning, and it was followed by a brief stare down that was broken when Keenan felt an arm slide around her waist.

"I have to borrow this lady," Nick said. "You need to come meet Lesley and Val. Lesley's one of us."

Confused at first, Keenan cocked her head. "Wha—a dentist?"

"An orthodontist, baby. She's raking in the dough."

Keenan returned to Gianna's side to meet the couple, who appeared to be at least twenty years apart in age, with Lesley the older of the two. Their conversation took off when Keenan learned she too had gone to Ohio State.

"I can't believe I'm surrounded by Buckeyes," Gianna said.

While they stumbled over an awful rendition of the "Buckeye Battle Cry," the others rang out a chorus of boos and laughter. In the midst of it all, Keenan glimpsed Jaz slipping out the door without even a word of goodbye. At her place was a neat stack of bills to pay for the dinner she'd ordered but wouldn't stay to eat.

* * *

As a cool breeze blew in off the river, Gianna huddled with Keenan on the sofa rather than close the sliding glass door. She liked the fresh air, and she especially liked that it cooled the whole apartment, meaning she and Keenan could cuddle tonight in bed.

"The day's nearly done, Gianna. A whole year. You're going to make it."

"Thanks to you," she said. They'd spent the past two hours poring over digital photos of Gabe she'd arranged in an album. Christmases, birthdays, school pictures. "Thanks for shaming me into calling Mom. It was the right thing to do."

"When you said your dad basically pretended it never happened, I realized she probably had no one to talk to."

"She was glad to know someone else was missing him too." They'd only managed five minutes on the phone, sobbing through their shared grief. "At least now I know why she keeps to herself. She can't talk about Gabe without breaking down."

"Maybe next time it'll be easier."

"I might go by there one night next week and see if she's up for having us over for dinner. I really want her to meet you. And Bennie. I think she'd like him."

"We're at your service."

Gianna tossed her iPad aside and turned off the lamp, leaving only the city lights to light the room. "Is this okay?"

"Yeah, it's like the night the power went out. That was pretty sexy as I recall." She snuggled into Gianna's arms.

"Until you got to your car and found your windshield broken."

"That kind of sucked, but what I remember most about that day is how I felt when you lifted my T-shirt and made love to my nipples. As you might guess, my breasts haven't gotten much attention in this lifetime. I decided right then I wanted to be yours."

Gianna moaned. "That was exquisite. Does this mean you're mine now?"

"I don't think there's any doubt."

The weight of that settled on Gianna like a warm blanket. "I'm yours too. Although I need to do a better job of being there for you. It feels like I'm always calling you to complain. You have to listen to me gripe about work, about how much I miss Gabe, but you never seem to need me for that kind of stuff. Or maybe you think I'm not up to the task."

"What does that even mean?"

"I don't know, that you don't think I'd give very good advice. Or you don't want to dump on me because I can't handle my own shit."

"I have another explanation," Keenan said as she laced their fingers and kissed her knuckles. "I'm in a pretty good place right now. Work's going well, Bennie's great. I've had two and a half years to process what happened to Annabel, so I'm not constantly tortured by those memories. Plus I've recently met the most amazing woman who I think about all day every day. It doesn't mean I'm breezing through life without a care in the world, but right now my cares are pretty trivial."

As they talked, Keenan's fingertips softly traced her forearm, a mindless gesture that she found surprisingly intimate. Being with Keenan had shown her there was so much more to intimacy than sex. Feather-like touches, smoldering looks. Most of all, the deep truths they shared about loss and life. She was so close to telling Keenan she loved her. All that stopped her right now was this being the anniversary of Gabe's death.

She fell across Keenan's lap and hugged her waist. "Is it okay if we just hold each other tonight? We'll have the whole weekend starting Friday. I think I'd feel weird if we…"

"It's fine, Gianna. More than fine, it's sweet. This is a day to think about your brother. I'm glad you asked me over to be with you."

"I knew it would be easier if you were here. You always say the right thing and you even know when not to say anything at all." She pushed herself up and tugged Keenan to her feet. "I want to show you something."

Keenan followed her out to the balcony, where Gianna wrapped her up from behind and pointed across the river.

"See that building with the red sign lit up on the side? That's the Bancroft. It's where Gabe and Amy lived, on the top floor."

"Oh my God, is that where he…?"

"Yep. I sit out here sometimes and imagine what it was like to fall all that way. I wonder how many seconds he had that he knew he was going to die. I like to think"—she clutched the air—"God grabbed his spirit before his body hit the ground."

"It must be hard to see that every day. I'm surprised you didn't move…or at least change apartments."

"It's just a building. I can't actually visualize it because his apartment was on the other side facing the baseball park. But I like being close…like maybe his spirit is still out there. If you think about it, it's no different than setting an urn on the mantel or going to the cemetery to see a grave."

"Hmm, I guess. Do you think you'll ever make peace with the way Gabe died?"

Gianna had contemplated that question almost every day and was no closer to an answer. "This may sound weird but I hope I never make peace with it. I still can't comprehend the fact that there was a moment, however brief, that my brother thought dying was better than living. It's just not the Gabe I knew. In a way, it feels like I'm grieving a stranger instead of the brother I knew."

After a long silence, Keenan said, "I think it's fair in some cases not to look for peace. The only way I found it was to finally admit that at least Annabel wasn't suffering anymore. Living was really painful for her. But I still look back and wish I'd taken her seriously when she said that person was lucky to be dead. I thought it was just a throwaway line but she actually meant it."

"You couldn't know that. People say shit like that all the time but they don't do it."

"But isn't it better just to take it seriously, like a cry for help? If you're wrong, so what? If you're right you might have time to save somebody's life." She turned in Gianna's arms. "I'm not saying that about Gabe. It sounds like he took everyone by surprise."

Gianna nodded grimly. "I wish I could have been there to see how he was acting, what he was saying. If I'd seen it for myself…nah, I'd have nightmares about it. It's probably good I wasn't there."

"If I had it to do over again, I'd have taken Annabel's advice to call 911 and go out to the front porch to wait. Instead, I thought there might be a chance to save her. Now I have that visual imprinted on my brain forever. And the smell."

"I'm so sorry." She cradled Keenan's head against her shoulder. "Of course you had to try. I can't imagine you just giving up."

"It's interesting what you said about Gabe's spirit. I kind of felt that way when I pried the door open on the shed, like all of Annabel's pain rushed out through that little sliver and hit me all at once. In a way it might have helped in the long run because it was never worse than that moment. And every day that passes it hurts a little less."

"I don't try to feel Gabe anymore, our twin connection. I used to sit out here and try to connect with him but now I think about connecting with you. It's not the same, but it feels stronger because you're real. Does that make sense?"

"Perfectly. I probably shouldn't admit this but I think about you about a million times a day. If I weren't so busy at work, I'd blow up your phone."

"I know that feeling." She hugged Keenan tightly, twisting gently side to side. "I'm so lucky I found you."

Keenan took her face in both hands and said, "I'm happy to just hold you tonight, but if you're going to say things like that you have to let me kiss you."

CHAPTER SEVENTEEN

Eight more minutes and Gianna would be out the door for the weekend. Any guilt she felt for blowing off work at four o'clock on a Friday was canceled out by all the days she'd watched the men loading up their golf clubs, knowing they wouldn't return for the day. She took perverse comfort in knowing Stefan hated golf.

A short rap on her office door and two of the golfers materialized: Uncle Jack with Stefan in tow. "Hey, Gianna, got a minute?"

"One minute, that's it. I'm on my way out the door. I already cleared it with Dad."

"Is there a party somewhere we don't know about? I'll get my coat."

Her uncle's joking manner was in sharp contrast to his hostile attitude the last time he'd darkened her door, causing her to wonder if Stefan knew of their confrontation. Determined not to be held up, she shut down her computer and straightened her desk to leave. "I'm heading out of town for the weekend."

"With Jaz?"

"No, why?"

Stefan stepped forward. "She never showed up for work today. She blocked off till nine o'clock for her...whatever, that thing she has to go to."

"Her check-in with her probation officer," Uncle Jack said, his voice matter-of-fact. "Last Friday of the month. We've always made an accommodation, her working extra hours during the week...which she did on Monday. But she never asked for the whole day off, and she's not answering her phone."

"Can't help you," Gianna said tersely. Unable to resist a chance to chide them both for forgetting, she added, "I saw her last night though. She got a bunch of our friends together at Mike's Beer Bar so we could raise a glass to Gabe. He died a year ago yesterday...not that anyone here noticed."

Uncle Jack held out his arms. "Aw, sweetheart, I'm sorry. I've been so preoccupied with all these invoicing glitches, I swear it never even crossed my mind. You should have said something."

She allowed herself to be hugged, though she didn't return it. "It's all right. We all move on at our own pace."

"That's no excuse. I should have remembered. Hell, your father should have reminded us."

Gianna scoffed. "Like that's ever going to happen. Sometimes I think he's forgotten he even had a son."

"Your dad, he's never been good with his emotions, Gianna. It's not his fault really. Him being the oldest, your granddad was always trying to toughen him up. I got to goof off and have fun."

"I wonder sometimes if Gabe felt that way too. About Dad toughening him up, I mean. Like he was trying to hide his weaknesses. Maybe that's why we didn't see his emotions until they erupted."

"That would make some sense." As Uncle Jack nodded pensively, so did Stefan, creating an almost comical effect of bobblehead dolls.

Itching to get out the door, Gianna said, "I'll give Jaz a call from the car, tell her she needs to touch base. Sorry, that's the best I can do."

Stefan caught her arm. "Can I fire her over this, Gianna?"

Before she could answer, Uncle Jack nudged him out the door. "Hold off on that. Until I say otherwise, anything having to do with warehouse personnel comes through me."

Interesting. Uncle Jack had taken back control of staffing in the warehouse. Could it be he was finally noticing the cracks in Prince Stefan's armor?

* * *

If northbound traffic on Highway 28 along the river was any indication, lots of others had the same idea to start their weekend early. Keenan wasn't bothered by the slog as long as Gianna was along for the ride.

"Still no answer," Gianna said, sliding her phone in her pocket.

"Are you getting worried?"

"Nah, her sister said she came home last night. She's probably off sulking about seeing us together at the party. I just hope she didn't blow off her probation officer this morning. If she did, she's screwed herself."

Keenan couldn't help feeling sorry for Jaz. Regardless of all the ways she'd lashed out, the pain in her eyes as she'd watched their friends celebrate Gianna's introduction of her as her new girlfriend had been heartbreaking to see. "You know, I'd be up for getting together sometime, the three of us. A movie, bowling, something fun."

"Excuse me, bowling? That would be a clown show." Gianna laughed. "This is our exit."

Gianna still hadn't told her where they were going. The ramp took them past a row of chain restaurants and hotels servicing the Pennsylvania Turnpike, which was visible ahead where it crossed the river. Keenan followed Gianna's turn-by-turn directions to a bait and tackle shop and parked in a space marked for "Rental Guest." With only backpacks and a cooler, which they carried together, they started down a steep staircase to a dock.

"Are you kidding me?" Keenan exclaimed. "You rented a houseboat?"

Gianna grinned with obvious pride as they stepped aboard the back of the *Ogajano'so*. "The blurb says it's Seneca for 'bringing dreams.' I guess we'll find out." She entered a code on a keypad and opened the door to the cabin.

"Gianna, this is amazing." They stepped first into a tidy room with a queen-sized platform bed and a two-person table that could easily be carried out to the deck. One step up took them through a narrow galley, past a shower and head, to a living area with a futon sofa, leather captain's chair and a fairly large TV. "Separate bedrooms. Nice touch."

"Not on your life."

Keenan spun around and took in the peaceful ambience of the river through windows that surrounded most of the cabin. "The one-upmanship stops right now. If I'm to top this, it'll have to be a pied-à-terre in Paris, and then you'll have to book something on the space station. It's not sustainable."

Gianna wrapped her in a hug from behind. "I'm glad you like it. It's ours till noon on Sunday."

"That long, huh? How ever will we pass the time?" She turned in Gianna's arms and drew her into a slow kiss that was interrupted by lively rocking caused by the wake of a large pleasure craft speeding past. "Think we'll need our lifejackets in bed?"

"What we need right now is a pinot grigio. Head up top and I'll pass you some snacks."

Keenan climbed the ladder outside to a topside deck furnished with a cushioned loveseat in faux wicker and matching coffee table. A pair of crew teams rowed past, alternately inching in front of each other. "This is so cool!"

Through a window from the living area, Gianna passed the wine first, followed by a cheese tray with bread and olives. When she climbed up to join her, she laid her phone on the coffee table.

"Still nothing from Jaz?"

"Nada. Doesn't matter now, the warehouse is closed and everyone's gone home. They'll deal with her on Monday morning. So glad that's not my headache anymore." She poured the wine and raised her glass for a toast. "To unsustainable one-upmanship."

"Pfft! To finding a houseboat on the river."

As the sun began to set, a steady stream of kayakers made its way back to the rental stand at the bait and tackle shop.

"Do you like to kayak?" Gianna asked. "We can rent a couple of those tomorrow if you like."

"Mom and I used to do it when we'd go camping. Dad's idea of a good time was lying around the RV with a book."

"Whereas mine's lying around with a naked lady."

"I might just ask you to prove that." Seeing Gianna's playful smile, hearing her flirt, knowing how proud she was to have found such a romantic getaway—it all added up to a thrill Keenan was only now giving herself permission to feel. "I guess I should warn you that I'm falling in love with you."

For an excruciating two or three seconds Gianna's look of surprise bordered on alarm, and Keenan's mind raced for how she could take the fear out of what she'd said. Backpedal? Make a joke?

"Sorry...please don't go jumping overboard." An awful choice of words, she realized with horror, though Gianna didn't react.

Gianna set down her drink as her lips turned upward in a tight smile she clearly was trying to control. "The only thing jumping right now is my heart rate."

"Should I take it back? Save it for later?"

"No! I planned to tell you that this weekend. You beat me to it." She fanned herself with her hands. "I wasn't sure if you were ready, on account of Annabel. I was afraid you might...I don't know, feel disloyal or something."

Keenan had thought about this and decided that Annabel's suicide freed her from any duty to their bond. "This might sound callous, but I don't feel I owe her anything. Annabel chose to leave me. She doesn't get to cast a shadow over us."

Gianna nodded. "And Jaz? Is she a shadow? I know she tries to be."

Keenan shook her head. "No, you'd have to let her come between us, and I don't see you doing that. Do you think she's a shadow?"

"I think she's…sad. I feel sorry for her but I can't help her anymore." Her seriousness gave way to a grin. "Tell me more about this falling in love business. How do you know it's love and not just sexy naked lady talk?"

"Part of it actually is the naked lady stuff. When you want me that way—and when you let me touch you—it makes me feel sexy."

"Because you *are* sexy. Sexy as hell."

Keenan didn't want to crack open all her old issues about body image, how it had taken her years to accept that her body would never have the curves and swells of a classically beautiful woman—certainly not like Gianna, whose shapely figure was enhanced by the muscle tone she got from rollerblading. "You make me feel good about myself in other ways too. I like that you respect what I do with Bennie. And we seem to share the same values, being kind to other people. You're serious about your job but it doesn't control your life."

"You're a lot closer to your family than I am," Gianna said wistfully.

"You were close to Gabe, so I know family's important to you. You'll get there with the others."

"I'm glad someone thinks so."

Keenan scooted closer and tucked herself under Gianna's shoulder. "This feels like it has promise, Gianna. You and me. But you can always pump the brakes if you think we're moving too fast. After nine years with Annabel, I may be a little more domestically inclined than you are."

"Don't bet on it. I'm the one who plunges into relationships. Shanice once told me to stop looking to others for validation, said I needed to spend some time alone and learn to like myself."

"Was she right?"

Gianna shrugged. "I grew up jealous of my own brother, how they laid the world at his feet. Sometimes I wonder if I went into those relationships so I could be somebody's center of attention."

"Please tell me you don't really believe that about yourself."

"I'm thirty-four years old and you'd be my fourth serious relationship. What does that sound like to you?"

"That you're not self-centered." She straightened so she could look Gianna in the eye. "Besides, the best part of being in a relationship isn't getting attention. It's giving it. Right?"

"Of course. I wasn't saying—" Gianna's phone chimed with a new message and she gave it a glance before picking it up. "It's from Jaz...a video."

They watched together. It was a selfie from what appeared to be a rooftop somewhere downtown. *I know why Gabe jumped, Gianna. Because he couldn't stand how much it hurt.*

"What the fuck? That's sick," Gianna said, playing it again.

"Where is she?"

"Oh my God! She's on the roof of the Bancroft. See, there's my building behind her."

Keenan leapt to her feet and began to pace the small deck. "Is she actually threatening to jump?"

"No way. She's just trying to get my attention."

"She certainly has mine. You need to call her."

Keenan's heart raced as she fought memories of those frantic moments as she'd searched the house for Annabel. The desperation she'd felt to find her before it was too late.

"I've called her three times already. I've texted, I've left a voice mail. If she wants to talk to me, she's had plenty of opportunities."

"Gianna, listen to me." She gripped both her arms hard. "You can't just ignore this. She's on Gabe's roof saying she understands why he jumped. It's a cry for help and that's a fucking emergency. You need to call her and keep her on the phone while I call 911."

Gianna groaned. "We can't do that. The police will arrest her for trespassing or something and she'll end up going to jail for violating her probation."

"She's better off in jail than dead."

"I know Jaz. She's not going to kill herself."

"You thought you knew Gabe too. How did that work out?" As soon as the words left her lips, she knew she'd cut Gianna to the bone. "I'm sorry. I shouldn't have said that. I'm scared is all."

Gianna shrugged out of her grasp and swung herself over the ladder to the deck below. Moments later she was inside the cabin speaking to someone over the phone, but Keenan couldn't make out what she was saying. When she finally made it down with the remnants of their wine and cheese, Gianna emerged and announced, "Okay, we need to go."

"Did you talk with her?"

Gianna ignored her question and began gathering her belongings.

"Gianna, please. I'm worried about her. Just tell me."

"I said I'd meet her there. I need you to drop me off."

Just knowing Gianna would soon be there to talk Jaz down from her impulsive threat flooded her with relief. She didn't care that their weekend was ruined, or even that she'd hurt Gianna with her rash remark. The only thing that mattered was stopping the irreversible act of a desperate woman.

* * *

It was nearly dark when Keenan pulled in front of the Bancroft. "Are you sure you don't want me to wait?" She'd apologized several times over the last forty minutes.

"Nope." Gianna had been in no mood to talk. It hurt her feelings that she'd shared something about Gabe in a vulnerable moment and Keenan had thrown it in her face. Even more, she'd weaponized it in order to manipulate Gianna into doing something. That was the kind of stunt Jaz would pull.

"Please call me later, Gianna. I know you're upset with me but I promise I'll make this right. Please don't let this ruin us."

With one foot out the door, Gianna turned back. "I need to go deal with Jaz. I'll call once I've had time to think about stuff. It's too much to process right now."

She didn't want to lose Keenan, but she'd just seen a side of her she didn't like. At the moment, her resentment was too strong to simply sweep away.

Inside the Bancroft lobby, she immediately recognized longtime security guard Alphonso and waved. He should have stopped her, but her familiar face probably convinced him she belonged there. That likely was how Jaz had gained entrance as well.

She took the elevator to the ninth floor and was glad to see they'd changed their décor from blue-green hues to muted taupe and gray. It felt different, though her stomach still clenched as she walked past Gabe's old apartment to the fire escape at the end of the hall. The staircase to the roof was cordoned off with a chain that she stepped over easily, and the door at the top was propped open with a block of wood.

"I was starting to wonder if you were coming," Jaz shouted from the walled edge, where she was sitting with a bottle of what appeared to be Baileys Irish Cream. Behind her, the lights of downtown were twinkling.

"I told you I was in Oakmont. It took a while to get here."

"In Oakmont with your girlfriend," Jaz said snippily. "I bet she's pissed. I hope so."

With her hands on her hips, Gianna took note of their surroundings. Two giant AC units, several vent fans, a utility room. There was nothing up here for tenants. She couldn't fathom why they'd leave the access door open.

"What's this about, Jaz? You trying to hurt me? Well you did, dragging me up here so I'd have to walk right past the door where my brother killed himself. Thanks for the memories."

"Good! I *wanted* it to hurt. Did you ever think about that?" Jaz was obviously drunk. "No, 'cause all you ever think about is yourself. You have the great job, the cool apartment. Now you have yourself the perfect little girlfriend who thinks she's hot shit. What do I have? Huh? Tell me, Gianna. Tell me why I shouldn't just take a flying leap off this roof."

Jaz stumbled to her feet and leaned over the wall, which was high enough to keep her from accidentally falling but easily surmountable if she really wanted to jump.

Gianna began to wish she'd called the cops after all. Jaz was hard enough to reason with when she was sober.

"What's with the Baileys, Jaz? You know you're not supposed to have any alcohol. You want to go to jail?"

"Like you care. You gonna turn me in?"

"I could, you know."

Jaz threw her head back and scoffed. "They can't lock up a dead person, Gianna. How long would you cry over me? A day maybe, that'd be my guess. Then off you'd go with your little girlfriend…and her stupid dog."

"This is getting old, Jaz. You're thirty-five years old. It's time to grow up. Figure out what you want out of life and stop throwing tantrums like a two-year-old."

"I want *you*, goddamnit! I don't give a shit about anything else." She raised a knee to the top of the wall. "If I can't have that, then I ain't got nothing else to live for."

"Take your fucking leg off that wall!" Gianna barked. She never really thought Jaz would do something so drastic, at least not if she was sober. All bets were off after half a bottle of Baileys. "Jesus Christ. How many times do I have to tell you how much you mean to me? I dropped everything and got here as fast as I could. Does that not tell you I care about you?"

Jaz turned and slumped against the wall, sliding down until she was a pile of drunken limbs. With her eyes closed, she screamed to the sky, "I can't *stand* you being with her!"

Gianna let her sob, only moving to snatch the bottle away as Jaz raised it to her lips. "You've had enough. Let me take you home."

"I don't want to go home. Take me to your place. I need to be with you. Just one more night, Gi. That's all, one last time. I promise I won't ever ask again."

That was never going to happen in a million years, at least not the way Jaz wanted it. However, Gianna saw some wisdom in taking Jaz back to her place to sober up. It was the only way she could be certain Jaz wouldn't try to drive in her condition. The trick was how to do it without letting Jaz think it was a button she could push whenever she wanted.

"I'll make you a deal, Jaz. I'll take you back to my place but we will not *be* together—not tonight, not ever again. And when you're sober, we're going to talk this out once and for all because I'm getting tired of all your drama. We need to come to a permanent understanding."

"I need you. That's all."

Of course. The one thing she couldn't have.

"Come on, let's get out of here."

She helped Jaz to her feet and led her down the stairs to Gabe's floor, past his apartment without a word. Jaz had been sober enough to grasp the significance of this place when she came up, but she seemed oblivious to it now. "Wait here," she said once they reached the lobby, where she raced over to Alphonso and told him not to let Jaz back in the building.

Once outside, Jaz forced her to reach into her pocket for her car keys, laughing and saying it made her hot. The irony wasn't lost on Gianna when they reached her apartment building and she had to use her phone to open the garage gate because Jaz's keycard had been disabled.

As they entered her apartment, Jaz drunkenly exclaimed, "Fuck, Stefan's gonna fire my ass. I didn't call in all day."

"I'll get them to give you one last chance," she said, already aware that, for whatever reason, Uncle Jack had ruled out firing her. "They'll probably dock your pay though."

"Whatever. Stefan's such a pussy, running to Jack about every little thing. He lets Rudy push him around too, like he needs Rudy's permission to take a shit. You should come down sometime and see who's really running the warehouse. 'Cause it ain't Stefan."

She handed Jaz some Tylenol and a glass of water. "Take this and go to bed. We'll talk tomorrow."

Jaz shuffled into the bedroom without picking up her feet. "I wasn't gonna jump, you know. I just wanted to scare you. I knew you'd come."

And she had, Gianna thought dismally. "Next time I'm calling the cops."

CHAPTER EIGHTEEN

The last time Gianna had been called to a closed-door meeting in her father's office, they promoted her from regional manager to VP for customer relations. Her actual job hadn't changed after that—she still shared managerial duties with Trish—but she'd appreciated the new title as recognition of her hard work. Two days later they'd named Stefan VP for distribution after only three months in a job she'd held for six years. It was hard not to be cynical about whatever news her dad had in store today.

He greeted her with a smile, gesturing to one of the chairs in front of his desk. "We have great news for the company, Gianna. I wanted to share it with you before we go public with an announcement."

She could only hope the great news for the company was also great news for her.

"Your uncle and I have been working with the bank to position TriState for our next growth phase. First we looked into new product lines we could service with our existing customers, like pharmaceuticals. We also considered adding warehouses in Altoona and Akron so we could compete for new customers in a larger territory. Unfortunately, both of those avenues are difficult to leverage for a company our size."

"In other words, we're too small to get bigger." Which left them with few options other than to sell to a larger company that would gobble up their territory and service it out of their own regional warehouses. In the back of her mind, she'd been expecting news like that for years.

"Precisely. Which led us to consider ways we might enter the market for the one sector that's actually growing."

The only sector still growing steadily was… "Home health care."

He smiled. "I knew you'd see the wisdom in this, Gianna. Bryson's encroaching on our hospitals but I can't see them going after home health. It's too fragmented."

"We're already servicing home health agencies, five of them at least."

"Yes, the agencies. But what about the thousands more potential customers who pay premium prices for supplies from Walgreens and Target? If we enroll them in a product plan and consolidate them under a home health umbrella, we'd be able to insulate ourselves against losses in the hospital sector. We can service that best if we merge with a company that's already off the ground, one that's expanding here in the tristate area."

A wave of nausea struck her and she began shaking her head. "As long as it's not WestPa."

"Gianna…" He rose and came around his desk to take the chair beside her. "I know this potentially carries some difficult personal issues, but sometimes we have to separate business from personal."

"Are you serious? You want to merge our company with the woman responsible for killing your son? That's not a personal issue, Dad. It's an atrocity." If she never crossed paths with Amy Tyler again, it would be too soon. "Don't you feel anything about Gabe's death? Or have you just forgotten it? It was a year ago last week and you didn't even acknowledge it."

Clearly taken aback, he sat motionless for half a minute pinching the bridge of his nose. "Your brother's death affected me deeply, Gianna. It still does. But your mother…it's as if grief is the only emotion she's able to feel. And no one else—not me, not you—is allowed to express it because ours somehow isn't deep enough. So I've learned to keep mine inside."

"Funny, I talked to Mom on the anniversary. We cried about it together over the phone and she told me she was glad to know there was someone else who remembered."

"Of course I remembered. I'm sorry if it seems like I haven't been there for you, sweetheart. I've never been one to show my feelings, but I promise you I feel Gabe's loss as deeply as anyone. But I should have realized you needed to hear it from me."

"It really would have helped." She leaned closer and grasped his hand. "It helps a lot to know how you really feel, Dad."

"Throwing myself into work was the only way I knew to get through it. I truly am sorry." He drew his hand away and returned to his stony expression. "Now about the merger…I get why you'd have qualms about WestPa, but they're the biggest—"

"Come on, how can you even think about merging this company with Amy Tyler?"

"Gianna, we have no choice if we want to continue to exist. The big fish are spreading out, putting warehouses in Youngstown, Wheeling. We can't compete with them on price once they decide they want this territory. They'll take all our hospitals and leave us scrambling for clinics and doctors' offices. If we don't get into the home health market, we won't have a business left in five years."

She couldn't argue with the business plan. If they were going to merge, there was no better partner than the biggest home health supplier in the region. "Fine, but what does this mean about Amy? She'll keep her headquarters in McKees Rocks, right?"

The look on his face said it all.

"You can't be serious. We have to work in the same building with her?"

"After the merger, she'll be named Vice President of Home Health. We'll probably give her Trish's office and move Trish down to the second floor."

"Sounds like a done deal." Gianna had heard enough. She rose and stalked to the door, where she turned and said, "If you're going to move Trish, you can move me down there too."

Shaken by the betrayal, she returned to her office and managed to close her door without slamming it. But she couldn't stop her fist from pounding the door jamb hard enough to cause her knuckles to throb.

She accepted the need to treat all their clients with respect, even the jagoffs, but how they could look past Amy's pivotal role in Gabe's suicide was utterly incomprehensible. Even more infuriating was the possibility of Amy usurping her on the ladder of succession. With those dismal facts piling up, it was becoming clear to Gianna that she no longer had a place at TriState.

Her mind raced as she began to filter what that meant. It could drive a permanent wedge between her and her father. She'd have to start a job search. Résumés, interviews, all in secret. Would she go to work for a competitor? What if they wanted her to move?

That thought sent her into a panic because it would mean leaving Keenan. Keenan, whom she hadn't spoken to since last weekend. Who had been helping her heal, who made her feel fantastic. Who was in love with her. All week she'd been thinking about how Keenan had triggered her fury. Only recently had she begun to forgive herself for not recognizing Gabe's sensitive state, and hearing Keenan's vicious reminder that she'd been wrong about him was devastating. Now she had to decide if she was going to let that destroy them.

* * *

Every time Keenan joined her parents for dinner on their back deck, she wondered why they didn't take all their meals there. Even with fall temperatures dropping, there was something idyllic about crickets chirping and white lights twinkling from the trellis.

"I can't believe Dad volunteered to do the dishes. Wonder what he wants."

Her mother laughed. "He wants me to go with him to Irwin this weekend to look at RVs. I guess he figures a few dirty dishes is worth getting me to agree to drop a hundred thousand dollars on a motor home."

"Already? I thought the plan was to wait till yinz retired."

"Covid's changed everything, hon. Your dad's getting tired of all the aggravation. I swear, if we get another big wave of some variant through here, I think he'll throw off his loupe and walk out for good."

It was true Covid had taken its toll on all of them. Many of the area dentists had dropped precautions, but Keenan was glad her parents continued to gear up in PPE to keep themselves safe. It was taxing though, and she feared it might be the norm for their practice indefinitely.

"I'm with Dad on this. There's no law that says you have to work till you're sixty-five. Yinz should think seriously about retiring a few years early. You're both healthy, you have plenty of money. If you really think you'd be happy traveling the country in an RV, why not go for it?"

"We've been talking about it. Your dad said the other day that you seemed a lot happier these days, like you might be back on your feet after Annabel. I told him that might have something to do with your girlfriend. He wondered if maybe you were ready to start thinking about settling down. We don't want to rush you into anything though. Your dad said he'd keep working till you were ready to take it over."

She'd told her mom about Jaz disrupting their weekend but not about the tiff with Gianna. With luck that would fix itself before she had to explain why they weren't seeing each other this week. So far though, Gianna's only communication had been a single text saying Jaz was off the roof and that she'd be in touch. Her texts and voice mails had gone unanswered for a full five days.

"About that...you know how much I enjoy working with you and Dad. I loved growing up here in Westwood." How to say this without hurting feelings? "I'm just not sure I want to spend my whole career here."

"By here, do you mean the clinic…or Pittsburgh, or…?"

It was hard to explain her new infatuation with the vibrancy of city living, which she'd glimpsed only recently through Gianna. Why that felt so much more authentic to her sense of self than these suburbs was a mystery even to her.

"I don't know, Mom. What I *do* know is I want you and Dad to get top dollar for the clinic when you sell it so you can spend it on whatever makes you happy. That's all the more important if you're thinking about retiring early. I honestly don't know if I'd want to invest as much as the practice is worth, and I'd feel terrible if you sold it to me at a discount and I decided down the road that I didn't want to stay here."

During the long stretch of quiet that followed, Keenan was consumed with guilt, figuring her mom saw this as a rejection of their life's work. Bennie seemed to pick up on her angst, launching himself into her lap.

"All I'm saying is I may be ready for something new."

"Something new with Gianna?"

She snorted. "I have no idea what's happening with her right now. We're taking a break…or rather, she's taking a break." She held up a hand to stop the inevitable barrage of questions. "It's my fault. I said something insensitive, a heat-of-the-moment mistake. A year from now it would only be a ten-minute spat, but right now I guess she's having to ask herself if she wants a relationship with an asshole."

"Oh, honey." As with every boo-boo Keenan could remember in her life, her mom's lower lip poked out in a pout of sympathy. "Can't yinz talk it over and work things out? You apologized, right?"

"Of course I did."

"Well, wha"—she sputtered—"send her some flowers or something. Let her know how you feel."

That actually wasn't a bad idea, Keenan thought. It would show Gianna she viewed her mistake as serious and very much wanted their relationship to work. "I might do that."

Hearing the optimism in her voice, Bennie thumped his tail and gave her hand a lick.

"This little guy is so intuitive. I took him to that story time thing at the library yesterday, and whenever I'd put him down with one of the kids he'd get up and come back to my lap. It's as if he knows this thing with Gianna has me upset."

"He'd rather do his therapy work for you than anyone."

"I know. I've been thinking it's time to cut back to just taking him to the clinic. Going out to all those places was good for me, I'll admit. It got my mind off Annabel, gave me something concrete to feel good about. But I'm starting to feel more selfish with my time. It's time I quit paying penance for not being able to stop her, and got on with my life."

Her mom rose to hug her. "Honey, I'm so glad to hear you say that. You've poured so much of yourself into helping other people, but every time you do it, it's like you're taking their pain on as your own. It's time for you to step out from under all that, find something to celebrate."

Keenan nudged Bennie from her lap so she could stand and stretch. "Thanks for hearing me out, Mom. I have decisions to make about what I'm going to do with myself, but you've definitely helped me with a big one."

Together they said, "The flowers."

* * *

Gianna took her mug of camomile tea to the balcony hoping the sounds of the night would help her relax. Wine might have served her better but she likely would have finished the bottle and given herself the mother of all hangovers on a day she wanted to be sharp. Tomorrow she would begin her job search.

It was surreal to think of leaving her family's company after almost twenty years, but the idea of having to face Amy Tyler every day was more than she could stand. Even worse was the possibility that someday the woman responsible for her brother's death would be her boss.

She wanted badly to talk to Keenan, whose steady, mature guidance would keep her from making an impulsive mistake. But after dismissing her apologies and blowing off her texts all week, it would be the epitome of selfishness to call her now for friendly advice.

Scrolling through her phone, she read their texts of the past few days. There were several imploring her for updates on Jaz, to which she'd finally replied curtly that the situation was in hand. Another was a clipped *it's fine*, and she'd answered Keenan's tenth apology with *no big deal* and nothing else. All of it passive-aggressive as hell, showing no concern that Keenan was so obviously upset.

What made it worse was that her tantrum had come on the heels of Keenan describing all the reasons she was falling in love. Now it was as if their deep, revealing confession hadn't happened at all.

"You stupid…" she mumbled, angry at herself. Why would Keenan want to be in a relationship with someone who'd punish her with the silent treatment? She probably was sitting at home thinking she'd dodged a bullet by escaping an immature hothead.

She typed out a text. *I'm sorry. Let's talk soon.* Her finger hovered over the send button for a few seconds before she deleted it. A text wouldn't do. She should go online right now and order flowers to be sent to Keenan's office tomorrow with a card saying she was sorry, and also an idiot, and would Keenan please still be her girlfriend.

It took three tries to find a florist who could guarantee delivery tomorrow, daffodils because the ad said they signified a new beginning.

Next she tapped the icon for the suicide survivor forum on the off chance Keenan had posted a photo of Bennie now that he was back at work. To her surprise, the top post was from Keenan with the subject line "Graduation Day!"

WINGÈD SERAPH: *From the moment I joined this forum over two years ago, I've looked forward to the day when I could write this post. It isn't the day I stop grieving, nor the day I pronounce myself free of needing the support of friends, but it's the day I can say I'm ready to restart my life with a new focus. All of you have helped make today possible for me and I thank you from the bottom of my heart.*

I considered fading away quietly as so many before me have done. But for those who've joined the forum recently, I want you to see that it's possible to rise from the worst day of your life to a place where you can know happiness again. I've been lucky enough to experience that recently and it's amazing!

I appreciate all the kind words you've shared for Bennie, who's been a key part of my revival. As a therapy dog he gave me purpose, a way to help change pain to comfort. He put himself between me and the rest of the world, starting the conversations and making sure we left everyone with a smile, even on those days when I didn't feel like smiling. We may do a few more visits here and there, but I'm considering granting him early retirement so I can repay the favor and lavish him with all the attention he deserves.

I thank you all again, and I wish you the very best for your journey ahead. Peace, out.

Below was a photo of Bennie relaxing in her lap. Already, the post had received over forty replies, which was over half of the active membership as far as Gianna could tell. Some congratulated and wished her well, others implored her to stay, and a few celebrated the idea that someday they too might "graduate" from needing support just to get through the day. Each post was marked with a heart emoji from Keenan signifying her appreciation.

One reply, however, was jolting for its rudeness.

AQUARIAN SOUL: *It's cool your happy and all but honestly I'm kinda tired of all the dog pictures. I joined to talk about a friend who killed himself, not a dog.*

It took Gianna two seconds to put together the fact that Jaz's birthday was February third, which made her an Aquarius. That's why she'd been scrolling frantically through her phone that night—she'd joined the forum after Gianna said she'd met a woman there, and she'd been looking up which forum member had a dog.

Unbelievable. Gianna couldn't delete the comment from the thread, but she hid it from her own view. She was done with Jaz's negativity.

Then she read Keenan's post twice more, paying special notice to her saying she'd experienced happiness recently. Was it too much to hope that was a reference to their relationship? She couldn't resist a reply if only to know Keenan would see it.

HALF-A-SET: *I'm so happy for you, Wingèd Seraph! You and sweet Bennie have brought comfort to all of us, and I'm delighted to know he'll be living his best life in the lap of luxury.*

Coincidentally, I too have experienced a great deal of happiness recently, and I'm very hopeful it signals the beginning of a new direction in my life. All the best.

She finished it with a pair of heart emojis—one for each of them.

CHAPTER NINETEEN

Sitting at her desk, Gianna couldn't stop smiling over how much better she felt today than she had all week. If she had it to do over, she'd have called Keenan at seven this morning before work. They could have talked directly. Instead, she'd waited long enough for a busy receptionist to tell her that Keenan had her hands in someone's mouth and couldn't come to the phone. The only reason she'd waited in the first place was hoping the flowers would be delivered first. She wanted Keenan to know she'd arrived at her apology on her own, not because she'd been prompted by her graduation post on the forum.

At least they'd "connected," if one could call it that. She'd waited anxiously for over an hour the night before until Keenan mercifully blessed her reply with a heart. Saw it, liked it. Then she tortured herself to sleep with doubts over why it had taken her so long to react. Was she withholding her approval or simply away from her computer? By morning, she'd received an actual reply to her post.

WINGÈD SERAPH: *New paths are sometimes challenging, but I firmly believe the rewards of persevering can be magnificent. I hope yours leads to a life where happiness abounds.*

It might have been ambiguous, a "Have a nice life!" kiss-off, if not for the emojis she appended: the same two hearts but with a puppy in the middle. Gianna's heart nearly burst with joy. Why hadn't she just picked up the phone right last night? Now she was frozen out at the mercy of a florist website, which she refreshed every two minutes to see if her daffodils had been delivered.

"Knock, knock." It was Carol Ann, her father's administrative assistant. "You wanted me to let you know when Trish was out of her meeting."

"Yes, thank you." Moments later she slithered into Trish's office and whispered loudly, "Please tell me you still have that headhunter's number."

"Whoa! Get in here and shut the door."

Gianna related the news of Amy Tyler's imminent arrival at their company.

Trish frowned as she leaned back and tapped her pen. "So that's what our meeting was really about. I've just spent an hour going over Jack's route changes that made absolutely no sense. Like why we're putting shipments to Butler and McKees Rocks on the same truck."

"They're in opposite directions!"

"But WestPa has its warehouse in McKees Rocks," Trish said. "Bet you anything we'll be shifting inventory over there."

Gianna snorted. "That's just plain dumb. I thought the whole idea of mergers was to combine operations."

"You'd think."

"Oh, there's one more tidbit you're going to love…but you didn't hear it from me." She shared her father's plan to move Trish down to the sales department on the second floor.

"She's getting *my* office? Oh hell no, I've been here since they built this place. If they think I'm just going to pack up and head down to a cubicle with a smile on my face, I've got news for them." She'd fished a scrap of paper from her desk drawer. "I was going to give you this headhunter's number but I may need it for myself."

"You'd seriously leave the company over this?"

"Damn right I would. Look, I told you I made peace a long time ago with the fact that I'd never get promoted above regional manager. I've always liked my job here. I felt respected." She gestured to her surroundings, which she'd personalized with a rug and chair coverings featuring the logo of the Duquesne Dukes. "I made this space mine so I'd like coming to work every day."

"For what it's worth, I told Dad if he put Amy on this floor, I'd be the one moving downstairs."

"That's the other thing. I like working with *you*, Gianna. If you're not here, that's one more thing not to like. Who'd want to work for a family that would sell out one of its own?"

Gianna rubbed her hands together. "All right then, who's hiring?"

"Let's find out." Looking through glasses on the end of her nose, Trish punched in a few keystrokes. "There are literally dozens of jobs in medical supply chain management. Where do you want to live?"

The question jolted her. "Is there anything...local?"

Trish peered across the desk. "Is this about your new girlfriend?"

"Maybe. I haven't talked to her yet. We've been taking a little break."

"You've been seeing her for what, a month? And you're taking a break already?" She shook her head. "I hate to be the one to tell you this..."

"It's not like that. Trust me, we're working through it. I think we both want this. It's just hard when you're used to old ways and you have to get used to new ones."

"I'm sure Jaz isn't helping."

"She's been the ex from hell but I'm done with her shit. She's on a very short leash right now and she knows it." Before sending Jaz home the morning after her escapade on the roof, Gianna told her she wanted no contact with her for thirty days and was blocking her phone, email and social media accounts. If Jaz couldn't respect that, she was prepared to make it permanent.

Somewhat surprisingly, Jaz had complied. So far, at least.

Trish glanced at the wall clock and stood. "I have a call with Youngstown Medical in four minutes and I have to pee. If you're really serious about all this, drop me an email and we'll get the ball rolling. Oh, and use my AOL address. Best to keep this off the company servers."

It felt serious, but she couldn't make a decision about leaving Pittsburgh without knowing where things stood with Keenan. Why did everything have to happen all at once?

She passed Uncle Jack in the hallway and he shook a thumb toward her office with a grin. "Can't wait to hear about that, Gianna."

That?

Her face fell. Keenan had refused her flowers. Rubbing salt in the wound, she'd even had them returned to—

"Hold on," she said aloud. The bouquet on her desk held lilies, not daffodils. And the card had her name on it.

I'm so sorry. The person I want to be would never hurt you. Please forgive me. K

* * *

Gianna raced to answer the knock on the door and laughed to discover that Keenan had raised her lips to the peephole in a playful kiss.

"Thought you'd never get here," Gianna said as she swept her inside with a hug that lifted her off her feet. Wearing slacks and a blazer, Keenan obviously had come directly from work. "I was so happy to hear from you today. I don't know what I'd have done if I hadn't."

"The flowers were Mom's idea," Keenan said. "Mine was crawling over broken glass."

"You mean these beautiful flowers?" Gianna led her to the arrangement on the granite bar, a dozen red, orange, and yellow lilies.

"Oh wow! They're gorgeous. I left yours at the clinic so I could look at them all day tomorrow, but I'll bring them home for the weekend."

"I brought mine home because I didn't want anyone else at TriState to enjoy them," Gianna growled. "Sorry, I had a shitty day at work. I don't want to think about that right now. I want to think about you."

Keenan stepped again into her open arms. "I'm so, so sorry, Gianna. What I said to you on the boat was mean and thoughtless and…"

"Forget it, I overreacted. I'm so used to Jaz agreeing with me on every little thing, I guess I convinced myself I was infallible. I like that you're not afraid to challenge me. And you were right, I needed to go get her. She was pretty drunk when I got there. She might have done something stupid."

"Then I'm very relieved you went." She visibly shuddered. "Think she'll try it again? You said she'd do it for attention."

Gianna explained where she'd left it with Jaz. "Those are the rules. If she breaks them, it's no contact forever. I refuse to be her hostage. She doesn't get to come between us anymore."

"I have something I need to say, Gianna. First of all, this." Keenan pulled her into a kiss, a whirlpool of warm, dizzying sweetness. When it ended, her eyes remained closed and she murmured, "I love you."

"Oh, wow." Butterflies swarmed her stomach. "I may have just swooned. I'm not sure though…I've never swooned before."

"If that's all it takes to make you swoon, you're going to be swooning a lot. I…*love* you. I was so scared I'd ruined everything."

Keenan loved her! This wonderful woman in her arms actually loved her. "It's taking every ounce of my self-control not to go out on my balcony and scream to everyone what you just said."

The look of joy on Keenan's face had to be a reflection of her own. "I won't stop you."

"I love you too. I'm not just saying it back to you, I promise. I was ready to tell you on the boat. I haven't felt this way about anyone…ever."

"Tell me."

"I want all of you. When we had this fight I realized, 'God, I have to fix this.' I kept thinking how awful it would be to lose you."

"You aren't going to lose me. I was already thinking what it would be like to grow old with you. We have so much to build on, Gianna. I'm willing to work for this."

"I am too." She drew Keenan to her chest and hugged her tightly. One of them would be testing that promise soon. How far would Keenan go to support her changing jobs? Or should she suck it up and stay at TriState?

Keenan grasped her hand and took a step toward the bedroom. "Come, let me show you how I feel."

Gianna knew already this time would be different.

* * *

"I've discovered I'm an ass woman," Keenan said, "and yours is amazing." She cupped each cheek, then lightly trailed her fingers through the crevice to the triangle at the top, where she dropped a dainty kiss. "No offense to your other body parts but this spot right here is my absolute favorite."

Gianna squirmed as if ticklish. "My clit says you're lying."

"I'll discuss that with your clit later. Right now I'm going into the kitchen to raid your fridge." It was after eight o'clock and her stomach was beginning to protest.

"I have cheese and crackers...and olives. Some frozen dinners maybe."

"Got any cereal?"

"That's my go-to. If I didn't love you before, I do now."

When Gianna went to the kitchen, Keenan rummaged in the dresser drawer for the T-shirt and shorts she'd worn the day they got caught in the rain. The room had space for another bureau, she noted, and the closet potentially could hold another rack. Still, it would be tight quarters should they decide to live together.

She joined Gianna at the counter. "When's your lease up?"

"End of December. I have to give them a thirty-day notice whether I stay or go." Gianna was sitting at the bar with cereal and milk. "If you want to live together, this building has larger units."

"Are you saying you don't want to share my parents' basement?" Keenan laughed and gave her a quick kiss. "What do you think? Are we rushing the U-Haul?"

"It doesn't feel that way to me but there's something else we need to talk about before we decide. It's kind of a big deal." That was underscored by her suddenly serious tone. "I found out today that TriState's merging with Amy Tyler's home health company. She was Gabe's girlfriend, the bitch who cheated on him and caused him to kill himself."

Her jaw dropped and her eyes went wide. "Gianna, that's obscene. What the hell are they thinking?"

"Apparently that it's all water under the bridge if it's good for business," she said, her voice heavy with sarcasm. "And they want to move Trish down to a cubicle on the second floor so Amy can have her office. I said fuck that, move me. I don't want to have to look at that woman's face every day."

Keenan was appalled. That would be like her parents going into business with someone from Annabel's family. "Have you sat down with your father—privately, one-on-one—and told him how this makes you feel? Surely he can find a better business partner than the person responsible for Gabe's death."

"That's another thing. I almost get the feeling Uncle Jack's running the company now. He sure seems to be calling the shots, like Stefan being groomed for CEO and Jack running the warehouse like it's his personal fiefdom. Now this. Dad's just rolling over like his lapdog."

"You think Jack's got something on him?"

"I can't imagine what it would be. Dad's not like that." She described the inevitable fate of losing their lucrative hospital accounts to one of the bigger supply companies. "On paper, this move makes sense because home health is a growth segment and the bigger companies aren't ready to get granular. But TriState can't afford a straight-up acquisition so they have to merge with an established company. That means taking on at least some of their executives—in this case, Amy—which will knock me even further down the ladder to be CEO. So not only do I have to work with her, she'll probably be my boss one day and I'll be stuck in the same job for the next thirty years. Just like Trish."

"That's a recipe for misery, Gianna. You have to get out of there."

"Thank you, Lord." Gianna raised her eyes and genuflected. "That's exactly how I feel but I didn't want you thinking, 'There she goes, flying off the handle, being impulsive again.' I swear it's not that. I've had this on my mind ever since I found out about Stefan."

"It's not impulsive. It's your gut warning you."

She sighed deeply as her shoulders sank. "My gut's also saying if I leave I'd be giving up my claim to ownership of TriState. What if two years from now a company like Bryson or Pfizer buys us out? I'd have nothing to show for eighteen years working there."

Keenan swiveled Gianna's stool and stepped between her thighs. "You'd have your mental health, plus eighteen years' experience to take somewhere else. And you'd have a future, Gianna. If you believe in yourself, this is an opportunity."

"Okay, so…what happens to us if I can't find a good job in Pittsburgh?"

She grasped Gianna's hands. "Have you already forgotten what I said? You aren't going to lose me. We'll do this together. You find a job that'll make you happy, and I'll check to see if the people there have teeth."

Gianna laughed heartily, expelling the tension of the last few moments.

"I want to make a life with you, Gianna. If you want that too, where we are doesn't matter."

"God, I love you."

"Then for gosh sakes, pass me the milk."

CHAPTER TWENTY

Keenan's fingers drummed the car's console as they neared Bloomfield, an upscale neighborhood with a high concentration of Italian families.

A case of nerves, Gianna thought. And who wouldn't be nervous, considering she'd painted her parents as ogres?

"Do your parents go to Mass on Sundays?"

"They stopped when Gabe died. Mom couldn't deal with people always asking how she was."

Keenan groaned. "It'll be a miracle if I don't say the wrong thing."

"Don't worry, just think of this as a Bennie visit." She'd shared only the basics about Keenan with her parents, that she was dentist and had a therapy dog. "I told them we were serious about each other. Was that okay?"

Hearing his name, Bennie whimpered from his travel crate in the back seat.

"Let's hope it's still true when this is over."

Gianna laughed, then took her hand and kissed it. "Nick called this morning, said they had Jaz over for dinner last night. He thought I should know that Jaz went to Night Moves on Friday. That's the club where her old coke buddies hang out."

"Uh-oh, you think that means she's using again?"

"She's definitely playing with fire. I told Nick she was on her own." She parked on the tree-lined street in front of the house where she'd grown up, a two-story brick foursquare with a wide porch and craftsman trim. "I'm not picking her up again."

Gianna opened the front door and announced their arrival. The dining table was already set with fine china, with the aroma of garlic and parmesan wafting from the kitchen.

Her father emerged from his study, dressed casually in jeans and a long-sleeved polo shirt. "Paul Del Vecchio," he said, extending his hand with what looked like an enthusiastic grin. Clearly he approved of Keenan on sight.

And no wonder, since she was dressed similarly in jeans and a blazer, the opposite of Jaz's flamboyant tight skirts and dramatic makeup. "Pleased to meet you, and this is Bennie."

He kneeled down to give Bennie a scratch. "Hello there, little fellow."

In her whole life, Gianna had never seen her father interact with an animal. This was a very good sign.

"You must be Keenan." Gianna's mother appeared from the kitchen wearing a crisp navy shirtwaist dress with a braided belt. Her smile was pleasant enough, though hardly vivacious. Still going through the motions but it was better than hiding in her room. "Call me Donna."

The four of them made small talk in the living room, mostly about Bennie, who pranced from one to the other each time he heard his name.

Keenan had calmed considerably, Gianna noted, now that she'd established a semblance of rapport with her mom. They were right to treat this visit like a therapy appointment at a nursing home or hospital. It remained to be seen if her mom would embrace Bennie the way those residents did.

"He sure knows how to work a room," Gianna said. She raised her eyebrows at Keenan, who returned a slight nod, a signal they'd arranged earlier. "Dad, can I speak to you a moment in the study?"

"What's on your mind, sweetheart?" he asked as she closed the door.

"That conversation we had in your office—Amy Tyler and WestPa—I've had some time to think about it, and it's just not a tenable situation for me. I've started looking for another job. I'm being held back, and it's not because I'm not the best at what I do. But for some reason, it always seems to be someone else's turn. Gabe, then Stefan. Considering all the years I've worked at TriState, it's unfair, and I think you know it. I want to work someplace where I can reach my full potential and be rewarded for it."

He pushed his hands in his pockets and walked to the window, which looked out into the backyard. "This is a tough business, Gianna. We can't always choose what makes us happy."

"It's not about making anyone happy, Dad. Unless you're talking about Uncle Jack, because he's pretty pleased with himself. His incompetent son is set to take over the company. How is that good for business?"

"He's not—" he stammered. "I told you, it's just a name on a bank form. Everyone knows Stefan isn't ready to be CEO. If your uncle and I stepped down today, I feel certain we'd name you CEO."

"You feel certain." Her tone was more combative than she'd wanted, but it pushed her buttons to hear his hypocritical reasoning. "And what about three years from now? Let's see, then I'd not only have Stefan in front of me, I'd have to go up against the woman who killed my brother. Who knows what sort of deal Uncle Jack's already made with her?"

"I'm just as skeptical about that as you are but Jack insists we have it wrong. He says Amy wasn't involved with that man, they were just friends. Gabe read it wrong and wouldn't listen to reason. She let us believe it all this time because we were grieving and needed someone to blame."

She gaped at him. "And you just took their word for it? Gabe would never have thrown himself off a ninth-floor balcony because he *suspected* something." But then she couldn't imagine him killing himself for any reason. "You know what? It doesn't matter. I don't want to work with her. Since we're being honest here, I don't like the direction TriState's taking with our customers. Uncle Jack seems to care more about playing golf and doing favors for his friends than servicing our orders. Did he tell you he banned me from the warehouse?"

He looked genuinely concerned as she told of having to deliver three orders in her SUV, only to have Uncle Jack rip her for interfering. "Jack did this? Why on earth would he get upset if all you were doing was taking care of your customers? Sounds like I need to have a talk with him."

"Don't bother on my account. I hope to be gone by the end of the year, but I'd appreciate it if you kept that between us until I'm ready to give my notice." She went on to promise she'd continue to work hard and take care of her customers regardless of Uncle Jack's edicts.

With his hands still in his pockets, he leaned against the desk and stared at the floor, like a schoolboy being scolded. "I think…" He sighed deeply before raising his eyes to look at her. "I think you're making a wise decision, Gianna."

It hit her like a punch to the gut, her own father not fighting to keep her.

"You didn't hear me say this, but I don't think the company will survive another three years. Bryson wants this territory, and they'll peel it off us one piece at a time starting with our biggest hospitals. I presented your uncle with a plan to sell them the company while our debt's manageable and it still has value, and he answered with this plan to service home health care. You watch, it'll be twice the work for half the money."

"Then why are you letting him do it? Aren't you supposed to be the CEO?"

"I *was*." His grim expression foreshadowed serious news. "I took money out of the company last year to buy stock in CTrust, that start-up that was developing a testing strip for coronaviruses."

"Oh my God…the company that turned out to be a fraud." It wasn't like him to be so careless. "How much did we lose?"

"A hundred thousand. It was right after Gabe died. I didn't have my head on straight. Jack was in Italy. I couldn't get in touch with him to talk about it, and the price was going up every minute. So I did something reckless. He was furious when he found out, rightly so. As compensation, I agreed to hand him the reins of the company for two years."

So she'd been right about Uncle Jack pulling the strings. Suddenly it all made sense. She should have known her father would support her advancement, since he'd practically groomed her as his replacement. He never would have gone into business with Amy Tyler.

"Do it, Gianna. You have my blessing."

Her father's support meant the world to her, especially now that she knew she'd always had it. Her future success, however, would be bittersweet if TriState went down like the *Titanic*.

* * *

Keenan didn't know whether to be annoyed or impressed that Gianna, when they first met, had observed how much she'd leaned on Bennie to carry the conversation. She also was right in thinking Donna would do the same, focusing her attention on Bennie to deflect other conversation.

"Does he have a favorite place to visit?" Donna asked. She sat alone on the settee, which Keenan judged to be a faux antique. Ever the gentleman, Bennie lay at her feet.

"He likes coming to the dental clinic. I think that's because he gets to spend the whole day with me. He does fine with kids at the library too, but his very favorite is the nursing home, like Oakberry Court. I remember Gianna saying her great-gran was there. That's actually how we met."

"Really? That was several years ago. I didn't realize you'd known one another that long."

She and Gianna had discussed what to say if her parents asked how they'd met, with Gianna insisting it was an open door to talk about their respective losses. Keenan hadn't considered how she'd handle it if Gianna wasn't there.

"Oh, we didn't meet there, but I used to take Bennie for visits. One night I posted a photo to our online forum. He was lying alongside one of the residents, and Gianna noticed the blanket had the Oakberry Court logo."

Donna leaned down to pet Bennie. "What's the forum? I'd love to go look at some of his photos."

"It's, uh…it's a support group for people who've lost a loved one to suicide. I found it really helped to connect with people who'd been through the same kind of loss."

There was no mistaking the shift in Donna's posture, from relaxed to guarded. She never looked up, focusing instead on Bennie. In an uncanny display of empathy, Bennie went to her and stood on her knee, clearly asking to be picked up.

"He's offering to sit in your lap. If you tell him no, he'll lie back down."

To her surprise, Donna patted her lap and leaned back to give Bennie space to curl up. He showed his gratitude by licking her fingers, then rolling over to bare his belly.

"Wow, he really likes you." He warmed to most women, but especially those like Donna who were soft-spoken.

"You lost someone too?" Donna asked, not looking up.

"My partner, two and a half years ago. She'd battled mild depression for most of her adult life, probably the result of childhood trauma involving her family. We moved here to get away from them—Pittsburgh's home to me—but that triggered a different trauma, and in the end she just didn't see a way to make it stop."

After a long moment, Donna replied, "I'd give anything to know why my son did what he did. They say he was in a jealous rage, wanting to get back at his fiancée, but I can't believe that. Literally, I mean. I simply cannot bring myself to believe Gabe would do something so violent. There wasn't a harsh bone in his body."

"Have you told Gianna how you feel? Because I think you'll find she feels exactly the same way."

"I don't know that there's anything more to say. Gianna has always imagined having a sixth sense because they were twins, but surely that's a myth. We can't feel things as they happen to someone else, can we?"

"Probably not…but Bennie seemed to know what you were feeling when we first broached the topic, so there has to be *some* truth to it, don't you think? At least he likes to think so."

"He's very sweet. I'm sure he's a great comfort to people who need a friend. But there's only so much a dog can do when it's a person you're missing."

"Can't argue with you there," Keenan replied, knowing she had to walk a fine line with Donna's extraordinary grief. She described Bennie's rough start in the puppy mill, how he was confined to a small, filthy crate with his mother and the rest of the litter. "Some of the puppies died, but Bennie was a fighter. The first month I had him, I was up every night coaxing him to eat and making sure he stayed warm. After a while, he probably thought *I* was his mom. It felt so good to see him grow and start getting a personality. I took him to work in a crate so I could play with him in my office every chance I got. He made me happy when the rest of my life made me almost unbearably sad. Training him as a therapy dog helped turn my focus outward— off myself and my grief." Her voice cracked in anticipation of what she was about to say. "He kept me busy while time took away the shock of it all, but it'll always be a gaping wound, you know? Of course you do. No one gets over tragedies like ours. I'm just glad to have some bright spots in my life now—like Bennie and Gianna."

"Gianna seems very happy with you," she said, finally smiling as she stroked Bennie's belly. "You're welcome to come any time…and you can bring this little fellow if you like."

"He'll be happy about that." And Gianna would be ecstatic.

* * *

"My husband's in love with you," Chad said as he loaded leftover chicken piccata into a takeaway dish for Gianna. "He's so happy for Keenan. It's been a long hard road for her."

"I feel so lucky she was ready," Gianna said. "We had lunch at my parents' house today and they liked her a lot, which is remarkable for them. They've never liked anyone I've brought home."

"It's hard to imagine anyone's parents rejecting Keenan. Who doesn't want a dentist in the family?"

They walked out to the living room, where Keenan and Brady were saying goodbye at the door. Bennie was on his leash, but it didn't stop him from playing with their poodle, Princess.

"Do you think Bennie knows that's his mother?" Gianna asked.

"We told them," Keenan answered seriously. "Secrets like that always come out in the end."

"You're nuts." She turned back to Chad. "Thanks again for the marvelous dinner. Let me know next time yinz are downtown. I'll have you up for a drink."

As they got in the car, Keenan said, "It's been a perfect day. I hope you don't ruin it by dropping us off and going home."

"What, you expect me to sleep over in your parents' basement? How very…high school." She raised her eyebrows and flashed a lascivious grin.

"Oh, come on. You really ought to check it out before settling on some chic hipster pad downtown with all the amenities. It'll be fun, like spelunking."

"I'll show you spelunking. I never get tired of ravishing your body."

Keenan reached across the console into Gianna's crotch. "Oh yeah?"

"Oooh, don't do that while I'm driving. I won't know if I'm coming or going."

A call came through the car's speaker, Nick's name on the screen. Gianna declined it. "He's calling late for a Sunday night. Probably to tell me Jaz is out with her cokehead friends or some such thing. I told him I wasn't Jaz's keeper anymore. As if I ever was."

"Mmm…I think it's fair to say you were at one time. You kept her out of jail at least."

"I guess that's true. But I couldn't keep her out of trouble." She pulled to the side of the driveway behind Keenan's car. "I'll have to get out early so I can get home and change. Can't let anyone at work catch me acting like a short-timer."

"What about your friend Trish? Think she'll quit too?"

"She might, although if I'm gone she'll get to keep her office. She may decide to stick around."

"Are you going to tell her what your dad said about the business going down?"

"It's not a sure thing, but yeah, I guess I should. Trish has always looked out for me. She deserves the chance for a better job too, especially since she's almost fifty. If she's going to make a career move, she needs to do it now."

Inside the back gate, Keenan let Bennie off his leash to run and do his business. He hurried so he could follow them through the basement door.

"Want a glass of wine? A cup of tea? Ice cream?"

Gianna pulled Keenan into her arms and said, "I vote we skip the snacks and get straight to the spelunking."

Their kiss took them to Keenan's bedroom, where they made love slowly and with a new passion that felt more committed than ever. For Gianna, it had been a momentous day, not only for her decision to leave TriState, but for introducing Keenan to her family.

"I got a weird feeling today, both from my parents and your friends." She lay on her back, with Keenan's head on her shoulder. "Maybe it was my imagination but it felt to me like they thought we were practically engaged. Did you notice that?"

"I wouldn't say engaged exactly, but Brady knows how I feel about you. I need to sit down with Mom and Dad and tell them we might be moving."

Gianna's phone chimed from the bedside table, another call from Nick.

"Maybe you should get that. I hope nothing's happened."

She'd been so focused on Jaz, it hadn't occurred to her there might be another reason for the late call. "Nick, how ya doing? Is everything okay?"

"I'm good, Shanice is good. Jaz though…she ain't so good. Got herself pulled over leaving Belvedere's, they caught her with two grams of cocaine. She's back in jail."

"Jesus Christ! How can anyone be that stupid?" She covered the phone and told Keenan what Jaz had done.

"I know, girl. She asked me to give you a call. She wants to talk to you."

"I'm not bailing her out this time, Nick. I told her that already. Either she didn't believe me or she just refuses to learn."

"I get it, Gi, I do. But she said for me to tell you she's not asking you for anything—not bail, not a lawyer. She knows she fucked up this time. But she still wants to talk to you."

Gianna sighed. "I can't, Nick. I just don't have it in me to go through this again."

"All right then, I delivered my message. I'll leave you to it."

The clipped reply left her feeling guilty. "Come on, Nick. Please don't think I'm being a bitch about this. I've more than paid my dues. I deserve to be free from all her bullshit. You have no idea what she's done to Keenan and me since we started dating."

"Oh, honey, I *do* know. Busting Keenan's windshield, going up on Gabe's roof. Yeah, she told us all of it when she was here Friday night. I don't blame you for how you feel. Like I said, I'm just the messenger."

"Okay, thanks. Love you." She set her phone aside and said to Keenan, "She'll go to jail this time. There's nothing I can do about it, even if I wanted to."

Keenan retrieved her pajamas and a nightshirt for Gianna and returned to bed. "Can I help?"

"It almost feels like everything she does is a test for me to prove how much I care about her. I refuse to be manipulated this time."

"I could go talk to her, see what she wants. That way she's not jerking you around."

"I don't want her jerking you around either. Whatever happens this time, she has it coming."

With Keenan lightly rubbing her back, they sat quietly for several minutes. There was nothing more to say, even less to do as far as Gianna was concerned. The news had put a damper on their night.

"You know, I probably should get dressed and go home. I'm not going to be very good company tonight."

"Sweetheart, I love you no matter what kind of mood you're in. If you want to be alone right now, I understand. Just know that I'm here for all of it, good or bad."

She was at peace with her decision, so why had she suddenly felt compelled to leave? Going home to slam doors and drawers wasn't going to make her feel better. Besides, she'd promised herself not to let Jaz pull her strings anymore. The bed was soft and warm, and so was Keenan.

"You're right, I'd rather be here with you, especially now that we're unofficially engaged."

CHAPTER TWENTY-ONE

Wearing a sly smile, Trish sat at her desk with her arms folded. "I can't say I'm surprised. They expect us to work our tails off signing up home health while our hospitals are leaving us for Bryson. It's not anyone's fault, Gianna. We're all fish swimming along until a bigger fish swallows us. What does that tell you?"

"That you and I need to work for the biggest fish."

"I've already started a spreadsheet. Position, location, salary, qualifications. You should come for dinner one night this week. I'll message you after I talk to Greg."

Walking back to her office, Gianna checked her watch. Eleven minutes talking to Trish. She'd dock that from her lunch hour, since she didn't want to job hunt on TriState's time. Now certain she was leaving, she felt an obligation to go through her customer list one by one to see how she could help them before she left.

"Hey, Gianna," Uncle Jack said as he followed her into her office and closed the door. "Quick question. Jaz has gone off the grid again. Didn't come in, didn't call. Any idea where she is?"

"Sitting in jail. Apparently she got arrested last night with cocaine in her pocket."

He gaped at her, the shock evident on his face. "Are you fucking kidding me?"

"A friend of ours called me last night with the news."

He danced from one foot to the other, unusually anxious about Jaz's predicament. "But you're trying to get her out, right? Does she have a lawyer? Did they set bail?"

Surprised by his concern, she played back his questions in her mind. "No I'm not, I have no idea and who cares? Jaz has used up all her goodwill with me. She's on her own."

"Aw, you can't do that, Gianna. Come on, she's been your friend for what, twenty years? You can't leave her hanging out to dry after all that."

It was bizarre that he was standing up for Jaz again. Those two couldn't stand each other.

"I'm done with her, Uncle Jack. She's made my life one big headache. All this time I've saved her from the consequences of her own actions. Catching her with drugs again was the absolute dealbreaker and she knew it. I'm not cleaning up after any more of her mistakes."

The phone on her desk buzzed, a call from her administrative assistant. She ignored it and made a mental note to check her messages later.

"Fine, you don't have to clean up anything. Just let her know we've got her back, and she still has a job here. That'll play to her advantage with a judge. I can pay for her lawyer if she needs one."

"What the hell? You despise Jaz. All those times you and Stefan wanted to fire her, but you didn't because of me. You should be celebrating getting rid of her once and for all."

Clearly agitated, he ran his hands through his thinning hair and began to pace. "That's just a personality clash, Gianna. Both of us are strong-willed and stubborn. You know that. The thing is, I *need* Jaz in the warehouse. She might be a pain in the ass but she's damn good at her job. I know Stefan isn't up to running things down there. Without Jaz he'll fuck the place up, and his whole future will be shot."

With her rising anger bordering on fury, all the complaints about Stefan she'd swallowed for the last year came spilling out. "You want me to stick my neck out for Stefan? Who sits in his office watching porn? Who can't do his own job but is somehow next in line to be CEO? The guy whose father won't even let me go down there to fix the orders he's fucked up? I'm not saving his ass either, Uncle Jack. It's time we all took responsibility for ourselves."

A purple blood vessel on his forehead pulsed as if it were ready to burst. He jabbed a finger into her shoulder. "There she is, daddy's little diva. Had us all fooled for years thinking you were the perfect prodigy. Then we find out you were the one buying blow and letting your girlfriend take the rap. You're the lowest of the low, Gianna. Prancing around like your shit don't stink."

"I made a mistake when I was fifteen years old," she snarled through gritted teeth. "Then I did everything I could to make up for it. If you think that disqualifies me from life, so be it. I'm not exactly clamoring for your approval anymore, Uncle Jack."

He flung her door open so hard it banged the bookcase and bounced back to hit him as he stormed out. A couple of weeks ago, their vicious fight had torn her to pieces inside. Now she harbored no more loyalty to him or the family business. Leaving TriState was a no-brainer. Leaving Pittsburgh was becoming more attractive by the day.

* * *

The McEvoys were gathered around a small table in the break room where they shared a coffeecake for breakfast. Keenan had just broken the news that she planned to move with Gianna if she found a new job elsewhere.

"It's not a done deal, is it?" her father asked, clearly upset. "You say she's looking here in Pittsburgh too."

"She is, but her expertise is health care supplies and TriState has most of the market here, at least for now. But she can't work for her family anymore." She detailed the major issues, a glass ceiling and the horror of having to work with the woman who caused Gabe to jump. "She's already at an executive level. You've seen how hard she works. She's ready for a job with more responsibility where she has a chance to move up."

He slumped in his chair, his face fallen. "I remember when you called to tell us you and Annabel were moving to Pittsburgh, that was one of the happiest days of my life. I always wanted you to be part of this practice."

They paused their conversation when Cassidy came in to warm a sausage biscuit in the microwave. The odor overpowered the maple in their coffeecake, spoiling Keenan's appetite.

"Dad, I've loved working with you and Mom. You guys are my heroes. I'm so glad you raised me to be a hero too. I actually feel like one every time we go out to do a rural clinic…which I hope we can still do no matter where I am."

"Honey, we couldn't be prouder of you than we already are. But this family clinic, it's our life's work. Ever since you came back, I've dreamed of handing it over to you."

"I know, Dad," she said solemnly, glancing at her mom for support. "You know what my dream is? That someone comes along and hands you a big pot of money, and you buy a big RV so yinz can head off and see the country."

Her mom rested a comforting hand on his forearm. "I've talked it over with her, Bruce. It doesn't have anything to do with us. She liked where she worked in Columbus, the public clinic with the low-income patients."

"I want you to get top dollar for this practice, Dad. I don't have that kind of money, and I'd rather not go into a lot of debt." He started to speak but she held up her hand. "I definitely don't want you cutting me a sweetheart deal. This is your nest egg. You earned it."

"Think of it this way, Bruce," her mom said as she took his hand. "We got a lot of what we hoped for with Keenan. She followed in your footsteps. Even went to Ohio State like you did. At least she's worked here for a while, and we'll keep seeing her when we go to the rural clinics. That's a lot of your dream right there."

He nodded his agreement, though his sad eyes told another story. "I'm being selfish, I know. What I want more than anything is for you to be happy, Keenan. We like Gianna a lot. If you like her enough to set up house, it could be my happiest day is yet to come."

"We love each other, Dad. I know how it's supposed to feel, and this is the real deal."

After heartfelt hugs, she returned to her office and closed the door, where she slid down to the floor to make a lap for Bennie. Her dad's disappointment made her want to cry, even more after his magnanimous wish for her happiness with Gianna. "You still love me, don't you, Bennie?" A quick text to Gianna to let her know the deed was done.

Just had the talk with Mom & Dad. It went okay. Dad's sad I might be leaving but he's happy for us. They really like you. So do I. She added a rainbow of heart emojis.

After a minute without a reply, she got ready for her workday, brushing her teeth and gargling with mint mouthwash. It was good to have fresh breath when it was trapped behind a face screen.

She'd seen her first patient and was finishing with a second when her phone, which was on the counter, chimed with a text from Gianna. Even without opening it, she could see part of its message.

Jaz's public defen

The rest was truncated but she was already filling in the blanks, probably that Jaz's public defender was relaying yet another message for Gianna to come see her in jail. No doubt the rest of the text was Gianna raging about it, but she'd have to wait to read what it was.

"All right, I think we're done," she said to Mr. Romano, who rubbed his numb jaw. "Cassidy will schedule you to come back in two weeks so we can seat that crown."

After seeing him out to reception, she retreated to her office to check her phone. A long text awaited.

Jaz's public defender called me a few minutes ago and said she wasn't going to fight the charges. She knows she screwed up and she's ready to go to jail this time if it comes to that. Then he said she had info that I needed to hear. URGENT. I have no idea what she's up to but I feel like I have to go see what info they're talking about. Can you come to my place when you get off work?

Keenan had to hand it to Jaz. The woman sure knew which buttons to push to make Gianna come running.

* * *

Brian Skodak was an earnest young man, only two years out of law school, he'd said. The court had assigned him to Jaz's case last night before she was interrogated by police.

Following his lead, Gianna placed her wallet and keys on a conveyer to go through security. She'd already made up her mind not to get drawn into Jaz's drama. What better way to draw a line under their time together than for her to leave town for another job while Jaz went to prison for a couple of years?

A guard ushered them into a small room with a table and four chairs.

"There's no recording of this so Jaz can say whatever she wants and it won't be held against her. The bottom line is she's cutting a deal with the DA for information on a drug ring."

"Good for her, but what's it got to do with me?"

Before he could answer, the door opened to Jaz, who was dressed in a red jumpsuit with white socks and slip-on canvas sneakers. Her guard marched her to the opposite side of the table and attached her handcuffs to a ring on the table.

"It's standard procedure," Skodak explained. "You could be in here for jaywalking and they'd do the same thing."

Seeing Jaz so humbled stirred a surprising wave of compassion. "Hey, Jaz. You okay in here?"

She managed a weak smile and said, "The food's for shit and the bed's worse, but other than that…yeah, I'm okay."

Gianna smiled back, even as her eyes watered with tears. Years of bad decisions had finally caught up with Jazmine Sadowski.

Brian cleared his throat, ending their moment of familiarity. "As I was saying, Jaz shared some knowledge with our DA that he found useful. If it pans out, she likely won't be charged for this offense. But her information involves…I'll let her tell you. She wanted you to hear it from her before you found out from someone else."

Her chin quivering, Jaz picked at her fingernails, unwilling to meet Gianna's pitying gaze. "Yeah, see…there's this thing…I didn't want to hurt you, Gianna. But Brian here said he might could get me off if I told them what I know."

"Wha…?" Surely she wasn't going back twenty years to report Gianna for buying coke. Her compassion waning, she said brusquely, "Come on, Jaz. Out with it."

"Jack's running drugs out of the warehouse," she blurted. "That's it. That's the big secret. Not our drugs though, we're just the delivery guys. That's why the trucks get called back, 'cause they send stuff out and then they find out whoever's supposed to receive them isn't working that day."

Gianna was so stunned, she said the only thing that made sense. "You're lying."

"They've been doing it for years, Gi. The reason I know is because I used to schedule the loads. I quit after Gabe died though. I didn't want to be messed up in it anymore." She scoffed. "All this time Stefan thought you were the one protecting my job. It was Jack. He was afraid if I got fired, I'd talk. He's right, I probably would've."

"And Stefan?"

"Stefan doesn't know shit—about *anything*, for that matter."

"Whose drugs are they?"

"Some guy he plays golf with."

Gianna didn't want it to be true, her own uncle dealing drugs. Still, it explained all the turmoil in the warehouse, and why Uncle Jack had shut her out. "Who all's involved in this?"

"Rudy took my place running things from the warehouse. That's why I called you that day he was going through the truck. I was hoping you'd catch him red-handed."

It made sense. He'd been searching through bins looking for his product.

"There's at least two drivers that I know of who pick up stuff, Derek and Eddie. But once it comes into the warehouse and Rudy packs it in the bins, it don't matter who the driver is 'cause they don't even know it's on the truck. They're delivering all kinds of shit. Coke, pills, heroin. Those bins of yours they pulled off the truck, I heard Derek say he had to pick up a package and get it to Wheeling before his contact there went off shift. Rudy called Jack and he told them to skip your deliveries."

Gianna's fists had balled so tightly they were turning white. "Can you prove any of this?"

"She won't have to," Skodak said. "The police got a warrant last night. All the TriState trucks are under surveillance right now. Deliveries will be monitored and searched after they've identified the recipient." He picked up his notes. "Right about now, police are arresting Gianetto Del Vecchio—that's Jack, right?—Gordon Rudolph—"

"That's Rudy," Jaz interjected.

"And Amy Tyler."

Startled, Gianna looked to Jaz for explanation.

"Her and Jack. It's always been her and Jack running the show. And"—she looked down, her brow furrowed—"in the warehouse it was me...and Gabe."

"No fucking way!" she yelled, pounding the table. "Gabe would never have gotten involved in drugs. Never!"

"Amy roped him in, Gianna. He did it to keep her from getting caught. Then they fucked up one of the orders and almost got caught anyway. It freaked him out and before you guys went to that conference he told Jack he couldn't do it anymore. That's when it all blew up and that shit happened with her ex-boyfriend. Some fancy-assed rich guy."

"A...Richard Kaminski," Skodak said as he fingered his notes again. "He's being picked up too."

With bile rising in the back of her throat, Gianna lunged for the wastebasket and threw up. How had her sweet, gentle brother allowed himself to get drawn into a massive drug ring? And right under her nose.

Jaz went on, "I think that's why Gabe killed himself, Gianna. He hated what he was doing, then he found out Amy was still with Richard and they were just using him."

The horror of it all. How humiliated must he have been to—

A savage thought struck her, one that better fit the brother she knew and loved. Gabe had found Amy and Richard together and became enraged. Uncle Jack was called to calm him down. They'd have argued, with Gabe threatening to expose everyone.

What if he hadn't killed himself?

* * *

Keenan tossed her jacket over Gianna's barstool and hurried to the couch, her arms wide for Gianna. "Tell me everything! Don't leave out a word."

"Well, I already told you about seeing Jaz. When I got back to work, there must have been ten cop cars in the lot. Sheriff, state police, DEA. They were going through the warehouse with dogs."

"Must have been a big shitshow."

"Uncle Jack and one of our warehouse workers were already sitting in the back of trooper cars. Everything was locked down. They sent us all home and told us not to talk to each other. I'm not even allowed to call Dad."

Keenan brushed Gianna's hair from her face and kissed her forehead. "What's going to happen to Jaz?"

"Not sure, but there's a pretty good chance she could walk. She told them how it all worked and she named names."

"It's got to be worth a lot to take out a whole network."

"It explains so many things I always wondered about. Why Gabe and Amy never set the date for their wedding. Bitch never intended to marry him. It was all a lie to keep him quiet."

"Despicable."

"I always thought it was strange that Uncle Jack would come back to the office after playing golf, no matter what time it was. Turns out he was picking up drugs from his golf buddy. I bet if I look back, those will be the nights Rudy was working even though he'd clocked out. He was slipping drugs into the next day's bins."

Gianna seemed awfully calm for someone whose family was crumbling around her. "How are you feeling about your uncle? Must be devastating."

"More like infuriating. Dad got a fair offer for TriState a few months ago but Jack blocked it so he and Amy could move their drugs through home health. He was making more money off drugs than the business. Didn't care that he was screwing the rest of us. Now the company's probably going to be worth half what it was."

"What a lowlife. I can't believe he'd do that to his own family."

"It's not just the family. There's my friend Trish. Almost forty years at the company and she's out of a job if it goes under."

Keenan stopped herself from pointing out how hard it might be to get hired elsewhere once employers learned they were part of a company that was running drugs. Given her surname, Gianna especially could have trouble.

"Our customers got screwed too. They didn't get their orders today, probably won't get them tomorrow either. And the hourly staff! Those guys got sent home today. Most of them can't afford to miss a paycheck."

Keenan was touched by Gianna's thoughtfulness, and mystified as to why she'd so far ignored the elephant in the room. "Did Jaz say anything else about Gabe?"

Gianna's breath hitched and her lips tightened. "I don't know if I want to hear the truth or not. Which is worse, having your brother kill himself or finding out your uncle killed him?"

She folded Gianna into her arms and held her. "You have to want the truth, Gianna. You can't heal without it."

CHAPTER TWENTY-TWO

Two Months Later

In a conference room at Pittsburgh's Wyndham Hotel, Gianna sat with her father opposite Kimberly Farmer, vice president at Bryson Solutions, and attorneys representing both companies. They'd announced the tentative sale of TriState Healthcare Supplies less than a week after the drug bust so Bryson could retain their customer network. Their teams had been in and out of town for the past seven weeks, inventorying stock and infrastructure, auditing the books and interviewing staff. The sale was now signed and sealed by all parties, the deal including the warehouse and its contents and the fleet; but not the office building. That was sold to a real estate management company.

Gianna caught her father checking his watch for the third time since the meeting started. Her phone was in her lap, set to vibrate should she get a text from the courthouse, where Jack, and Amy Tyler were set to enter pleas in the case involving Gabe's death, now ruled a homicide. She and her dad would have been there in person had Kimberly not specifically requested their presence at this closing meeting.

Many of TriState's employees had accepted a buyout but several had applied for work with Bryson, including Gianna. What an irony if she landed the top post, regional manager in charge of all area accounts, with oversight of the warehouse. She'd assumed she didn't have a chance in hell of getting it, as the Del Vecchio name was now mud in the tristate region, but the invitation to this meeting had gotten her hopes up.

Farmer was in her mid-fifties, Gianna guessed, smartly dressed in a gray wool suit with knee-high calfskin boots. Her Tumi carry-on stood by the door, ready for her snowy flight back to Chicago. Gianna wanted to work for a company that promoted women to positions of authority. Maybe she could be Kimberly someday.

Once the paperwork was complete, Farmer addressed Gianna and her father, "Our human resources department regrets that we weren't able to retain all of your warehouse staff. As you know, there were problems with some of the polygraphs, and we thought it best not to take any risks, especially since we're launching our pharmaceutical division next year."

Gianna smiled to herself as she imagined what Jaz would have said under her breath: *But we're highly experienced moving pharmaceuticals and other drugs.* In a deal with the DA, Jaz had promised testimony against all those implicated in the drug network in exchange for dropping the possession charges. She'd recently found work pulling orders at a fulfillment center in Mt. Lebanon, a job that paid far less than TriState, likely dooming her to living with her mother for years to come. Gianna had learned this from Brian Skodak, since Jaz was forbidden from contacting anyone at TriState until the criminal trials were over.

Courtroom just opened for spectators. I'm in.

Gianna nudged her father and showed him the text. Since they couldn't be at the hearing, Keenan had taken off work this afternoon to sit in on the proceedings at the courthouse and text them the highlights. They'd been advised by their family attorney what would take place and weren't expecting any surprises. All Gianna cared about was getting confirmation it was over.

"About staffing," Farmer said, likely aware their attention was divided. "We're retaining four of your office staff, including Trish Cantor, who's accepted our offer to be regional manager."

Though she'd known it was a long shot, Gianna's heart sank. It meant she'd almost certainly have to leave Pittsburgh if she wanted to land a decent job. So far her résumé had garnered only a few nibbles, all of them at a lower level than her experience and capabilities warranted. She hated the thought of starting over as an account representative, but she might have to if she wanted to get on with a good company and have a chance for advancement.

Despite her disappointment, she was genuinely glad for Trish, and not a bit surprised. Trish had worked there longer than she had and didn't come with Del Vecchio baggage. "I'm happy for Trish," she told Farmer. "She'll do a fantastic job."

Her phone vibrated and she looked down, surreptitiously reading Keenan's text.

Jack and Amy brought in.

She briefly met her father's eye and gave him a slight nod.

The remainder of the meeting covered terms of the handover, which didn't concern Gianna. She hadn't been allowed to enter the warehouse or communicate with customers since the acquisition was announced. Trish had served as de facto CEO while Gianna and her father worked behind the scenes to facilitate the sale.

Stefan also had been removed from his position—for being a Del Vecchio—but he had very little to offer the transition team. He'd hoped to return to teaching tennis in the Poconos, but Paige was now pregnant and they couldn't live on an assistant pro's salary. He'd recently started as a manager trainee at a sporting goods store, a job he probably enjoyed far more than running a warehouse. Last Gianna had heard, he hadn't spoken to his father since his arrest, when he'd learned he was being groomed for the drug trade. It turned out the man he and his father played golf with was none other than Richard Kaminski, Amy Tyler's ex-boyfriend and the head of their drug network.

Then there was Jack. She was making a conscious effort to disassociate him from the family. In her mind, he wasn't her uncle anymore, nor even her father's brother. He was a ruthless bastard who'd betrayed them in unforgivable ways, the *least* of which was turning TriState into an arm of a drug empire.

Farmer's voice interrupted her thoughts. "If there's no more, I think we're finished. Thank you, Paul. I know this has been a difficult time for you and your family, but I do hope you feel that you've been treated fairly throughout this process."

"We're very grateful Bryson Solutions was willing to sit down with us. Our customers couldn't be in better hands. Don't you agree, Gianna?"

Judge making statement. Asking attys questions.

She looked up from her phone. "Very much so. It's been a pleasure working with you and your team."

Papers rustled as everyone began to gather their belongings, and Gianna's father grasped her arm and whispered, "Any more from Keenan?"

She showed him the most recent text. "That's all I know. I'll forward all her texts so you can keep up."

Gianna tied off her scarf and shrugged into her wool coat. It was threatening snow, but she had only a two-block walk to her apartment, where she might as well start packing. Her lease was up on New Year's Eve, two weeks from now. She and Keenan had been hoping to move to a larger apartment in the same building, but only if Gianna had gotten the job. Their backup plan was for her to move to Keenan's "spelunking" apartment while she continued her job hunt.

"Gianna, do you have a moment?" Farmer asked, leading her toward a corner where they could speak privately. "I wanted to let you know that your experience in both the warehouse and client services made you the ideal candidate for the regional manager position. Rob and I personally recommended you for it, but Anthony was concerned it would pose a public relations issue."

"I understand," she replied. That made twice she'd been overlooked for the top job because of Jack Del Vecchio, but she was gratified at least to have someone finally validate her qualifications. "Trish Cantor will do a wonderful job for you."

"Anthony was quite impressed by your résumé though, and he wanted me to ask if you'd consider a similar position elsewhere. At the moment, we have another opening for regional manager, but you'd have to be willing to relocate."

Her heart began to pound. She was willing to go absolutely anywhere—but only if Keenan was.

* * *

Keenan entered the apartment, immediately greeted by Bennie, who'd spent the afternoon in his crate while Gianna was at her meeting. They'd been staying here since the drug bust, since Gianna had complained of feeling all alone.

"Is anyone home?" she called.

Gianna emerged from the bathroom and met her with a hug. She wore a strange smile for someone who'd lost out on a job she'd desperately wanted.

"Something's up with you."

"You first. Tell me how he looked in his red jumpsuit."

"Like a worm in handcuffs. Amy too."

"God, I bet that was a beautiful sight," Gianna said cynically. "Any issue with the plea?"

"Third degree murder, done and dusted. I was sitting next to a reporter for Channel Five who covers trials. She knows this judge. She thinks they'll get at least fifteen years. And if they're also convicted on the drug charges, their sentences could be consecutive because they'll consider that a separate offense."

"Which means Jack could die in prison."

Keenan nodded. She hated to think of anyone rotting away like that but it gave Gianna and her family a measure of peace to have someone pay for Gabe's death.

Jack and Amy had provided corroborating testimony that Richard Kaminski, angry at Gabe for threatening to expose their operation, had attacked and pushed him off the balcony. To avoid the risk of a death sentence, Kaminski had pleaded guilty to second-degree murder, a mandatory life sentence without parole.

"They'll be sentenced March first, after which you get to close the book forever on Jack and Amy."

"There's still the drug charges."

"Yeah, but those aren't really about you. What counts is you got justice for Gabe. It proves you were right about him all along, that he never would have killed himself."

"It never sat right with me." She smiled ruefully. "I should remind Mom about that, since she doesn't believe in twin telepathy."

"How is your mom? It has to be hard on her, going through Gabe's death again. We should take Bennie over there this weekend." They'd visited the Del Vecchios at home several times, each one warmer than the last. Donna had grown extremely fond of Bennie.

"That's a good idea." Gianna grasped her arm and tugged her to a barstool. "Now it's my turn to tell you stuff."

"I'm so sorry about the job. I know how much you wanted it."

"Can't say that I was surprised," she replied, though her face didn't show the expected disappointment. "They were right though. It would have been a heavy lift to overcome all the damage Jack did. I don't doubt some people out there will always wonder if I was involved and managed not to get caught."

"You said that might happen."

"But it wouldn't be a problem if they hired me to manage somewhere else."

So *that* was the reason for her sly smile. Keenan was overjoyed to hear the confidence in Gianna's voice as she shared what the higher-ups had said about her résumé. "They have an opening right now, but the woman didn't say where. I'm flying to Chicago tomorrow to interview with a guy named Anthony. A formality, he says. Then all I have to do is decide if we want it."

"We want it, Gianna. I don't care where it is." This was what they'd agreed to, to start a new life together. The only question was where.

CHAPTER TWENTY-THREE

Despite the snow and cold, the excitement was palpable as they climbed the stairs to the porch at the Del Vecchio home. Keenan had barely dried her tears from saying goodbye to her parents. Now to repeat that with the Del Vecchios. "How do you think your mom's going to react?"

"Not a clue. If she decides she doesn't want him, at least we won't be around to hear about it."

"Don't kid yourself. Buffalo's not that far away. Three hours and change. She could show up at our door tomorrow and give him back."

After acing her interview in Chicago, Gianna had been offered the regional manager post in Riverside County, California, or Buffalo, New York. They'd briefly considered the adventure of moving to the West Coast before choosing Buffalo, a blue collar city much like Pittsburgh. She'd spent two weeks training in Chicago at Bryson's headquarters and another two in Raleigh, where she shadowed the regional manager. She now was ready to take charge of her own region.

Keenan had interviewed at a handful of practices before accepting a job at a public clinic like the one she'd worked at in Columbus, where the primary clientele was low income patients.

After struggling to find a rental apartment with all the features they wanted, they took the leap and bought a sixth-floor condominium overlooking the marina. The small balcony off the living room sealed the deal.

"We're here!" Gianna announced from the foyer.

Keenan stooped down to unclip Bennie's leash. "Where's Donna? Go find Donna."

He whimpered, looking anxiously at Gianna. "Go on, little man. It'll be okay."

Donna answered from the back of the house and Bennie took off.

"Sounds like they're in the den," Gianna said. "I guess it's showtime."

They walked back to find Donna down on all fours greeting Bennie, who was just as taken with her as she was with him. Keenan had noticed a tremendous change in her demeanor since they first met, from sullen to bright. Like Gianna, she seemed lightened, relieved to know Gabe hadn't taken his own life. More importantly, she and Gianna had drawn closer since their revealing talk, and Keenan felt accepted into the family. And she *loved* Bennie.

"How's my sweet boy?" She nuzzled him until he rolled over for belly rubs.

Paul watched the feistiness from a recliner. Retired from business, he'd already found his bliss teaching classes in supply chain logistics at a community college in nearby Westmoreland County. "Are you two all packed? It's an ugly day for driving."

Keenan said, "We checked with the highway department a little while ago. The interstates are clear."

Donna looked up. "Are you hungry? I have some coffeecake."

"No thanks, Mom. We had breakfast with the McEvoys. Besides, we have to hit the road. The moving truck is supposed to be there at three o'clock."

She lumbered to her feet and took Gianna in her arms. "We're going to miss you, darling. You too, Keenan," she added, holding out a hand.

"Who do you think you're kidding, Donna? We know who you're going to miss most."

"My sweet little Bennie," she exclaimed in a baby-talk voice.

"Mom, Keenan and I were talking and…we know how much you love Bennie, how much you'd miss him if we took him away."

Keenan added, "He's been such a good companion to me, Donna. I don't know how I ever would have healed after Annabel if he hadn't been there with me. He needed me and I needed him." She gestured toward the kitchen and Gianna left to retrieve the special gift they'd brought. "When I saw how much you liked him, I asked my vet to keep an eye out for another little fellow like him who needed rescuing."

Gianna returned holding a tiny longhaired chihuahua, golden with a white chest and feet. "His name's Fabio, but you can change it if you want."

"Oh, my goodness!" Donna's hands went to her cheeks.

"He's six months old. A family got him for their mother but she turned out to be allergic." She handed the quivering pup to her mom, who instantly cradled him to her chest.

"Hello, little Fabio."

"I hope you want him, but if not, Bennie will be happy to take him back."

"Of course I want him."

Keenan caught Paul's eye with a questioning look.

"Looks like we have a new family member," he said, grinning in concession.

After watching the dogs play together for a few minutes, Gianna suggested it was time to hit the road. "I'll tell yinz what Keenan told her parents. We're just up the road, so we'll be back to visit."

Keenan added, "And we'll bring Bennie so he can play with his little brother."

"Mom, Dad…I know it's not the way any of us wanted this to happen, but I feel closer to you both than I have in a long time. I'm proud of us, the way we came through this horrible mess. I really love being part of this family."

They traded long hugs on the porch, and it was Gianna's turn to cry.

For a time, Keenan drove in silence, snaking through the city they'd called home until they picked up the highway toward Erie, where they'd parallel the lake all the way to Buffalo. She expected they'd get to know this road well, running back and forth for holidays and special occasions.

She brought Gianna's hand to her chest. "How are you feeling, sweetheart?"

"Happy…sad. Excited, anxious."

She was all those things too, especially excited. "You're going to do great, Gianna. And we're going to *love* our new place." She'd left most of what she'd acquired with Annabel behind in the basement. They planned to start with the sparse furnishings from Gianna's apartment and collect the rest over time.

"Did I tell you I wrote to Jaz? An actual letter mailed to her house. I told her about us moving to Buffalo, how I'd gotten a new job. I thanked her for finally telling me the truth."

"That's magnanimous considering she knew Jack was destroying the company from the inside out and didn't tell you."

"Yeah, I thought about that but I understand why she didn't say anything. When Gabe died, there wasn't anyone there for me. She stepped up to fill the gap. I'd broken up with her the year before and was hardly speaking to her, but she came around and offered to listen and be my friend when I really needed one. She had the old me back…at least in her mind. She thought she might have another chance and she wasn't going to say anything that might cause me to turn on her again."

"I don't care, it was selfish."

"I know," she said, looking out at the bare trees as they flashed past the window. "I forgave her. I also sent her a check for all the money she paid me through the court. I didn't owe it to her…it was just part of forgiving her. Then I wished her a happy life."

Every time she thought she knew Gianna, she learned something that made her love her even more. So generous and compassionate. She deserved all the love and loyalty Keenan could give.

She raised Gianna's hand to her lips and kissed it. "I am so in love with you. It's like a miracle. After Annabel, I never dreamed I'd find this kind of love again. And here you are."

"I never dreamed I'd find it at all, Keenan. I didn't even know this kind of love existed. But now I know how it feels to love someone completely. I'm never going to let it go."

"And I'm never letting *you* go."

About The Author

Though she'd always dreamed of becoming an astronaut, KG MacGregor earned her PhD in journalism and went to work as a political pollster and media researcher. In 2002, she began writing fanfiction for the *Xena: Warrior Princess* fandom and discovered her bliss. Since then, she has authored over two dozen novels, collecting a Lammy and nine Golden Crown Awards. KG is past-president of the Board of Trustees of the Lambda Literary Foundation. A native of the North Carolina mountains, she now makes her home in Nashville, TN with her partner, Jenny, and two raucous felines, Rozzie and Agnes.

Bella Books, Inc.

Women. Books. Even Better Together.

P.O. Box 10543
Tallahassee, FL 32302

Phone: 800-729-4992
www.bellabooks.com